HOLD TIGHT

Felicity Fair Thompson

Cover photographs
Shutterstock

Cover design
Alexandra Thompson

HOLD TIGHT

Felicity Fair Thompson

WIGHT DIAMOND PRESS

HOLD TIGHT
Copyright © Felicity Fair Thompson 2015
Published by Wight Diamond Press 2015
39 Ranelagh Road
Sandown IW PO36 8NT

Distributed worldwide by Lightning Source

ISBN 978-0-9535123-3-1

Typeset by Amolibros
Printed by Lightning Source

*To all those professionals
who try their hardest to protect children*

My thanks to Hampshire Constabulary who gave me time with a WPC involved with Child Protection to help me find correct terms and procedures to bring realism to this fictional story.

CHAPTER ONE

WEDNESDAY

This stretch of the motorway was always ghastly, even at the best of times. Today it was worse. The sun, low and brilliant out to the west, sent glaring shafts of white light across the freezing drizzle, cutting visibility and creating almost surreal conditions. Lunar grey, and mist. Where the water caught the light, it made weird cool colour spectrums, but on the autumn auburn of Jane Velalley's hair, it burned bright.

She was silently thanking God as she drove along she wasn't one of the lads in TRAFFIC Division. The surface of the road was greasy, slippery with the rain. Tyres hissed past. Sometimes she thought the choir of screaming engines, though muffled by her closed car windows, sounded like hurricane force winds, unstoppable, wild, and dangerous.

In front of her a supermarket lorry pulled out without signalling, throwing up a sheet of blinding spray. She braked sharply to keep her distance and squinted at the lorry's number plate. She gave up. No point trying to remember the registration number. Far too dangerous.

Better to concentrate on her own driving. A removal van careered by, then a school bus passed, the children inside drawing in the windows' condensation. More little faces pressed against the back window, smiling, laughing.

The case file on the passenger seat beside her slid onto the floor which made her think about the child she'd just been to see – the glazed look in the small boy's eyes outside the court when she'd asked him: 'Who hugs you when you feel sad?' Depressing just how often in her working week she saw that same defiant and lost expression.

Water gushed back from the wide rear wheels of the school bus. The slipstream forced Valalley to grip her steering wheel more firmly. Typical – the motorway system in all its glory.

Merging with the coastal M27 she travelled east along the leafier edges of the sprawling city of Southampton. It was an improvement on the old route and the former rush hour problems, but she was thankful to see the dividing signs looming out of the mist up ahead. Eastleigh, Heydon, Junction 6, 1 mile.

Only about ten minutes now to West Heydon Police Station. A couple of hours slog on paperwork till 5 p.m. and then she could get home. She was longing to see what Suzie had been up to all day. Even a few hours out working and it was surprising how much she missed her little niece. She began to plan what they could do together when she got home. Even for Suzie, she thought determinedly, three has to be an age of discovery and fun.

She indicated and slowed, waiting to move into the slip lane, following behind the school bus and the van. In the other lanes the through traffic hurtled on.

The slip road began to drop down into deeper mist and shadow. On the rim of the high embankment ahead to her right in a sudden shaft of sunlight, something caught her eye. A figure. A familiar sort of shape. Hooded. Flowing black robe like something learned in childhood brushes with Sunday School. Biblical.

She focussed on the road then glanced up again. Nothing. Imagination, of course. A trick of the weird light, probably. In her head she began sorting out dinner. There was Ocean pie in the freezer; that with some fresh vegetables…

But there was something up on the embankment.

There. There it was again. A large white dog bounding along. A dog! What she had seen the first time presumably, only optical illusion must have made it seem shadowy, black against the odd light. How stupid letting a pet loose out here, in this weather, beside the motorway, near the slip road. Crazy. The oblique yellow lines on the road indicating the roundabout ahead were dazzling her in spite of the gloom. She applied gentle pressure on the brakes, keeping her distance from the bus in front. Then she saw it again suddenly – the dog, running down the embankment, leaping down towards the traffic ahead of her.

'Shit!'

In an instant it had vanished. The brake lights on the school bus flashed. Velalley pumped her own brakes violently. The van ahead of the bus swerved out, careering sideways across the slippery surface into the right side barrier, and the bus, unable to avoid it, caught the protruding rear corner of the van in a dreadful splintering crunch. As it began to spin back towards her, brakes screeching, there was a brief glimpse of the driver, horror on his face, fear in his eyes.

She clutched her own steering wheel in terror. Awful memories flashed across her mind. Her sister's mangled car. The beautiful red hair brushed out so formally over the satin pillow. Suzie's face. Suzie, little Suzie, now. Just when she'd settled in, just when she'd begun to forget the loss of her mother and father in that fearful road pile-up. Oh God, Suzie, it's happening again. You're going to lose me the same way... the very same way. Her tyres were sliding. The brakes weren't acting fast enough. She'd never stop in time. She braced herself for impact. 'Suzie! Erik, take care of her,' she screamed.

Suddenly between the bus and the left hand barrier a narrow space opened up. A chance. An outside chance. She measured it instinctively. Could she get through there fast before the bus would spin too far? Fast enough? She rammed her foot down. The barrier rushed towards her left. The bus loomed in on her right, sliding, sliding ever closer. The space was narrowing. She crunched down harder on the accelerator. And suddenly, the bus was whizzing by her, the barrier too. She was through. Inches behind her in the rear view mirror, she saw the space close up and the bus complete its full circle before it caught a second glancing blow on the van, shuddered, and rolled over. She pulled up on the hard shoulder, totally unable for a moment to take her shaking hands off the steering wheel, unable to believe she had survived.

But she must move. She must! She steeled herself and grabbed her radio. 'WPC Velalley to Control.' The radio crackled. 'Answer me!'

'Go ahead, Velalley.'

The carnage behind her was almost impossible to describe. She gave her location and told them hurry, for God's sake. Then grabbing the torch from the glove box she leapt out of her car and raced back. Fumes of petrol stung her eyes and throat. There were muffled screams coming from inside the bus, blood on the windows, and a small hand clawing at the glass. She bit her lip hard and forced herself away and into a run.

The van driver was slumped forward in his cab. A car behind, crushed in at the front, steam rising, hissing into the cold air, and shocked faces, staring eyes behind the windscreen. Beyond that, two more vehicles locked and twisted together, and the smell of scorched rubber. Past them, only mist and weird glare.

'God,' she whispered, running harder now as the incline increased. Ahead of her a man climbed out of the furthest car. There was no leaking fuel up here.

'Are your lights still working?' she shouted breathlessly to him.

He looked dazed for a moment. Maybe he hadn't heard her. 'Turn on your hazard lights. Quick!' He went to reach back into his car. Suddenly behind him, there were more headlights. 'Look out!' she screamed.

Just in time he leapt away. There was a screech of brakes and an awful crunch of metal on metal as another car ploughed into his, shunting it forward. Velalley kept on running towards him, the mist and rain stinging her face and the cold dank air biting deep into her lungs. 'Come on,' she cried, as she reached him and sped on past to the car behind. She sniffed the air as she ran. Still no obvious smell of fuel. 'Quick, hazard lights!' she ordered that driver as she passed him.

'Won't work,' he shouted, urgently flicking the switches.

Now her flashlight was on, shining out through the grey drizzle – but would anyone see it in this strange glare? She could hear something else approaching, the groan of shifting gears, dim headlights of another vehicle. She stopped, waving her flashlight frantically. Behind her running footsteps closed in. There was the sound of heavy breath, like her own.

'Here, I've got one.'

Together they signalled out into the gloom. There was the hiss of wet tyres skidding, but the car stopped just in time, inches from disaster. The window wound down urgently. 'What the bloody hell!'

'Accident,' she cried, 'put on your hazard lights!'

'What?'

'Police,' she raised her voice, 'hazard lights on. Now!'

'How do I know this isn't a bloody carjack?'

'WPC Velalley, West Heydon. I'll charge you if you don't.'

The man behind her grabbed her arm. 'Look!'

More headlights. More. 'Hazard lights! Now!' she ordered.

The flashing orange lights lit up the fog - and were answered by a single blue light above two flashing white headlamps, and away in the distance, the sound of wailing sirens speeding towards them.

The first squad car pulled up and Detective Sergeant Blake leapt out. 'Bloody hell! Back up, beam on, Gibbeson, so they can see our lights,' he ordered the driver. He and Velalley began to sprint back down the hill together.

'There's a school bus turned over at the front.'

'Ambulances on the way,' he puffed, having trouble keeping up with her. 'You all right?'

'Yes.' She wanted to tell him how she'd got through between the bus and the barrier, tell him about the gap closing so fast, how she'd managed in the face of disaster to accelerate to safety, but suddenly it seemed so unimportant, just something any reasonably competent driver could do. Instead it was their shoes hitting the sloping wet tarmac that mattered, and the moaning, and the screaming ahead of them, and now the stench of leaking fuel, and the strange white light contrasting the grey shadows. And when they reached the school bus, the sight of a young boy, his skull shattered by a broken rear window, and his blood dripping onto the road, lying dark red there for an instant before it was diffused by the rain.

'Jesus wept,' Blake panted, hesitating. 'Where the hell do we start!' Then his experience took over. 'Over there!'

There was movement from one of the centre windows of the bus and Velalley rushed towards it.

'Help me, help, please.'

Velalley clambered up, reached into the tangled metal.

'I bumped my head.' The little girl's voice trembled, 'and my knee's bleeding.'

'Let's try and get you out. Here, take my hand.' She pulled the child slowly, carefully, clear. 'You're safe, you're safe,' she urged, putting her arms round her, trying to calm her distress. But there were more cries, more, though now, thank God, she could hear ambulances arriving, fire engines, and the sudden fizzing of flame retardant foam. People shouting. Running. Sirens. 'Over here,' she called, 'over here.'

'Here!' Blake was shouting further down too, as medics moved in to take over from her, wrapping the first child gently in a blanket, and reaching past her, down again through the broken window into the twisted frame of the bus.

She climbed down and stood back, and her hands and clothes were wet with blood. Then she saw the mangled body of the dog. Its head was almost severed from its body, its tongue lolling into its own blood. She drew back, suddenly feeling physically sick.

'Velalley?' Detective Inspector Kendrick's authoritative voice boomed through the havoc.

She swallowed, and took a long, deep calming breath and began to walk briskly up the road.

'What the hell happened?' he asked, when she reached him.

'A dog,' she said, pointing, but deliberately avoiding looking back. 'A dog ran down the embankment and out onto the road. The van swerved to avoid it, and the bus hit the van.'

'Hazard lights your idea?'

She felt a surge of excitement, that her instincts had been right. 'Yes, sir –'

'You little fool! Didn't you realise one spark could have sent this whole lot up?'

Velalley clenched her fists tight in righteous indignation. 'But –' There were more sirens up on the motorway.

Kendrick turned angrily away from her and bellowed

to Toms. 'Take a couple of men with you up there. We'll have to divert away from this chaos.'

Sergeant Blake came over. He looked shocked, his greying hair emphasizing how pale he was. 'Just hauled out that kid at the back. There was a girl underneath him. She was dead too.'

Velalley shuddered. Thankfully Blake, if he saw it, ignored it. To anybody else it might show feminine weakness, but she knew she could trust him at least not to think that.

Kendrick was shouting across to PC Gibbeson. 'And do we know how many children were on the bus?'

PC Warren is checking now,' Gibbeson called. Poor man. His voice was shaking.

'Okay, Blake, take Gibbeson and do what you can to help. We need details. And Velalley, you'd better start making some pretty good notes. I want your report on my desk by tonight!'

In a constant scream of sirens the casualties were slowly released from the wreckage and stretchered to ambulances. Velalley looked up at the embankment and then back at the wrecked bus, and wiped the rain off her face with the back of her hand. Everyone else seemed to have been given tasks, but Kendrick was ignoring her and she felt useless in the face of so much activity. The petrol had been drained away, and firemen had sprayed foam to make the area safe so that rescuers could use an acetylene torch to free a severely injured child trapped under the body of the bus driver. The scene must have been like this the night Beth died. Another motorway pile-up.

In the centre of the road six black body-bags were lined up. But five of these seemed so oversized. The bodies inside were pathetically small. What if one day it was Suzie in a school bus like that? Suffer the little children... Sunday school again. The strange religious image of the figure flashed back into her mind. She dismissed it immediately. It was down to the dog of course. Beside the other five, the sixth black bag contained the body from the van, and one more bag was spread out near the front of the bus waiting for the driver. The sight of that one made Velalley shiver – it might have been for her.

The emergency helicopter lifted away with a sudden roar and a splutter of greasy spray.

'That's all the children accounted for,' shouted Gibbeson to her, over the whirring. 'The adults in the cars came off lightly.'

'Have we been in touch with the school? How do we know those children we talked to could remember all their friends? They were in deep shock.'

'Warren has spoken direct to the Headmistress,' Gibbeson said. 'Twenty-two, she told him, and that's what we've got. Fucking dog.' He glanced down the road towards it.

'I'll go and make a note of any skid marks,' she said. An accident investigation team would be here any minute to do it more thoroughly, but she had to write her own report and immediate observations might help.

She skirted round the emergency teams trying not to get in their way. So many children dead and injured because of an animal. The bus driver. The van driver too. Some child's father, some poor woman's husband. And how many

16

more, she thought furiously, if she hadn't signalled into the gloom? People like her sister and brother-in-law? And there hadn't been any petrol up there. There hadn't been.

Still, what if Kendrick had been right? She tried to put that thought aside. Besides, real policing was about caring, doing the best you could. She was grateful though to be feeling angry. It would be an odious task examining the area and the decapitated creature itself. She wrote the date, the twenty-eighth, in her notebook and made general notes about the marks on the road surface and then turned her attention to the bedraggled body of the dog. It took time to establish among the throat innards without touching it that there was a collar. It was no longer intact. In fact the metal disc had been ripped off and had rolled a few feet away towards the edge of the road. When she found it, it was dented and covered in blood. As she leaned down to wipe it clean on the narrow grass verge, something caught her eye in the deep ditch beyond. Something dark, partly hidden by branches. She stood up. Now she couldn't see anything. She leaned back down, and saw the outline of whatever it was again.

Clutching the disc tightly, Velalley climbed down to investigate. Maybe something had fallen off the van, or it might be more wreckage from the bus. With stick she pulled back the branches. Another victim from the accident? A teacher? Was there a teacher? No. That woman had been accounted for.

Someone else?

She crouched down quickly and felt the neck where it was exposed for a pulse. There was none. The flesh was cold, stone cold, and on the air was a separate smell, a layer quite distinguishable from the petrol fumes and carbon monoxide. An unpleasant, rancid odour. The shapely body was draped in a swathe of black material and pulled down over the head was a kind of hood. She frowned and glanced momentarily up at the empty embankment above her.

The hood was encrusted, not with mud as she'd first thought, but with dried blood and she was convinced she could hear a strange humming, a primeval chant, almost a singing sound. With the stick she lifted the fabric up gingerly. Instantly a cloud of black flies burst out up into her face.

'Ahhh…'

She hit out into the air. When she could focus again, what she saw made her want to retch. More blood, pale though and surprisingly pink, partly obliterated the gaping mouth, and one glazed eye stared out from what was left of a human skull. She recoiled in horror.

After a moment she climbed back up to the road and walked unsteadily towards Detective Inspector Kendrick.

'What the hell's the matter now, Velalley?'

'She looks like she's seen a ghost.' There was concern in Sergeant Blake's voice.

'Perhaps I have, sir. I seem to have found a body.'

'Another one?' Kendrick turned to Blake. 'I thought you said –'

Velalley interrupted him. 'This one's different, sir.'

CHAPTER TWO

Usually Erik Velalley found it infinitely satisfying to lean on the smooth polished wood bar of the Ship Inn and gaze out across Southampton Water. After hours in his one room office, and calling on clients trying to explain the vagaries of tax to people who found figures incomprehensible, drinking a single beer here before going home to his wife was usually a moment to unwind, interesting and pleasant, a simple daily enjoyment to look forward to.

The inn, built in the 1700s, was the kind of pub locals loved and tourists flocked to for good beer, a wealth of dark oak beams, whitewashed walls, and a roaring log fire in a huge stone inglenook. Lunchtimes and evenings it was crowded out, but in the late afternoons Erik, along with Peter Miles whose flat and studio were next door to it, could practically guarantee to have the place to themselves. Pete would sit on a high bar stool in his long cashmere coat and expound on the ins and outs of the business of photography, and very occasionally he would ask Erik's advice on tax, though he never seemed remotely interested enough to listen to the answers. Erik knew that because the questions were so general, and nearly always the same. It was only done to humour him.

To anyone watching them, they must make an odd couple, Erik thought. Pete with his very black, black hair, Roman nose, and expressive hands which he used constantly to add extra breadth to his airy and florid descriptions of his fascinating life. And him, earthy Erik. True, he knew his shoulders were broad and he was tall, but with his earnest brown eyes and ruffled brown hair, his well cut brown business suit and brown laced shoes, standing drinking his one brown beer with his brown wool coat over his arm, he must look like a faithful hound listening to his master's voice. But Pete was always so fascinating to listen to. The Ship Inn was where they had met the year before and now they came here most days. Pete was fond of saying that he thought one of the joys of being self employed was being able to abandon work at half past four to drink a pint in such picturesque old world surroundings, and relax.

Erik wished his own days could be like that. But today had been hectic, and his secretary had been off sick, and he had still to go home to collect some papers for a promised evening house call to an elderly lady before he could finally relax. And through the leaded casement window there was no usual nostalgic view of the old three masted ship gently rising and falling on its ropes beside the Royal Pier. Instead there was the repetitive whine of a foghorn hidden somewhere out in the harbour and layer on layer of freezing winter fog. He stared out at it gloomily. The greyness seemed to represent everything he was feeling.

'Wish you had somewhere warm and comfortable close by to go to? I don't envy you driving home through that.'

'Mmm?'

'The fog,' Pete said cheerfully. 'Miles away, were you?'

Erik nodded, feeling for once rather irritated by the other man's presence.

'Did a shoot out in this today. Atmospheric stuff. First rain in ages. I bloody nearly drowned out there. Freezing too but the client wanted genuine winter landscape.'

'Oh?'

'Well, don't sound so interested.'

'Sorry.'

'You seem a bit down.'

'Am I? Sorry.'

'Sorry again? Things must be bad. At work? No, you usually enjoy that. Trouble with the 'little wife' again then?'

Erik took a steadying sip of his pint. 'If there is, I wouldn't know,' he said crossly.

'No?'

'I don't see much of her at present.'

Pete's eyes narrowed. Gossip appealed to him.

'Jane's having to do all the hours God sends,' Erik said, seeing he should explain his little outburst, but somehow angry with Jane for making it necessary. 'They're short staffed down at the Station and she's hardly ever at home – and when she is, she's caught up with her sister's child.'

'That's women for you. Always interested in someone else.' Pete took a large gulp of beer. 'How come you two ended up with that kid? I thought you were both heavily into your careers.'

'We are, or rather we were. We made this arrangement to leave having children to a few years. Then Beth and her husband were killed in a car crash and Jane was determined to step in.'

Pete picked at a fleck of dust on the smooth black cashmere of his coat. 'Must be impossible if she's legally required to do overtime.'

'Since we've taken Suzie on, it seems to be more often too.'

'What about the grandmother? Didn't you tell me she lives in Southampton? Can't she have the kid?'

'Jane worries about that. Laura has high blood pressure, and Jane thinks it would be too much for her. She's hardly over her other daughter's death.'

'So how do you cope?'

'Right now? The child minder's doing extra hours.'

'At least she doesn't expect you to do it.'

Erik ran his finger round in a circle on the highly polished surface of the bar. 'Actually I mightn't mind sometimes, if she needed me.'

'Leaves some useful free time, though, doesn't it, with her otherwise engaged?'

'Jane's got it all organised,' Erik said curtly, un-hunching his shoulders and straightening up. He knew exactly what Pete meant and he was anxious to avoid picking up on it if possible. 'As long as Suzie is settled and happy, that's all that matters, I suppose.'

'And what about Marilyn?'

The question was loaded. Erik took a quick sip of his beer as if he hadn't heard.

But Pete looked at him innocently. 'Seen her lately?'

He played for time. 'Who?'

'Who? Marilyn Farr of course!'

'Not for – for weeks.'

'Ah! I thought you saw her earlier this week.'

'If you don't mind I really don't want to discuss it.'

'Sure? I've known you long enough now to see when things are getting to you.'

'And a year gives you that distinction, does it?'

Pete's dark eyes flashed. 'Jesus.'

'It's over with her, Pete, all right? And it was never really on. I'd be grateful if you'd keep what you know to yourself.'

The barman looked up.

'Ssh!' Pete smiled at the barman who looked away again. 'Don't bite my head off! Oh, so it's all my fault for introducing you to my best model, right?' A dark curl fell across his forehead. He pushed it back with a long finger. 'I want her next week for the first studio shoot I've booked for ages, and I can't get hold of her. Maybe she's away on location. I thought she might have told you what she was doing.'

'I said, I haven't seen her.'

But Pete seemed determined to pursue it. 'I could use someone else, but that divine figure and – well, you know. Tell me it's none of business if you like, but she's pretty special to you, right?'

'You're right. It's none of your business. Look, I don't know if I can make it tomorrow. I'll ring you, okay?'

Pete tossed his head impatiently and returned to recounting his day. 'I can't stay long. Printing to do. Of course there was absolutely no point in shooting colour in this weather but I was in luck. I got some marvellous shots…'

Erik, concentrating on finishing what was left of his beer, gazed out at the grey fog again. It appeared to be lifting a little but it would still be miserable driving.

★

Halfway home the windscreen was clouding over faster then the de-mister could clear it. Erik switched it across to blow on full power.

Just ahead of him in the mist the traffic lights at the intersection were still green. He put his foot down slightly to beat them.

Green. Nearly there.

Green, amber. Maybe...

Red.

'Shit.' He pulled up and revved the engine, rubbing a hand fretfully across the cold condensation in front of him. He glanced back up at the lights. Still red.

In spite of the shroud of fog he knew this intersection well. Not once, day or night, did the volume of traffic crossing it ever seem to justify the length of time that was allocated to it.

And it was while waiting here, just like this, that he had seen Marilyn that evening. She was standing under the bus shelter on the opposite corner. Even though she was wrapped in a huge black cape, he recognised her immediately as the stunning young woman with the magnetic green eyes he had met briefly in the Ship Inn on the arm of Pete Miles.

Ordinarily he wouldn't have considered stopping but it was cold and getting dark. Along this route the buses were few and far between. When the lights changed he had crossed the intersection and pulled in. He pressed to lower the window, the high-pitched whirring responding to his fingertip control.

'Miss Farr?'

She looked surprised to hear her name. She leaned down to see who it was. Her eyes shone like bright emeralds.

'Oh! Peter's friend! Hello.' Her voice was low, succulent and fleshy, like overripe peaches. The front of her cape fell open and the neckline of her blouse was so low cut that he could see the curved lace of her bra. Raindrops glistened in her blonde hair. She smiled. Her teeth were even and white.

'I'm going across town,' he'd said. 'Can I drop you somewhere?'

A car horn behind him jerked him back to the present. He lifted his foot sharply off the clutch – and immediately stalled. The guy in the classy sports car behind honked again. Erik twisted the ignition key angrily. At the third try the engine started up and he pulled away fast, as green turned back to amber.

It gave him a moment of satisfaction glancing back in the rear view mirror to see the sports car still stranded at the lights.

Now. Home for the papers he needed, then he would make his call brief. Old Mrs Thornton was his nicest client. She would understand if he explained this was his wife's first evening off for ages, and how anxious he was to tell Jane he loved her.

CHAPTER THREE

'You're telling me WPC Velalley gets caught up in a major accident on that motorway exit with dead bodies strewn everywhere, and while she's there, she conveniently happens on a corpse?'

Superintendent Maitland of the West Heydon District of the Hampshire Constabulary was framed in the doorway of the DI's office.

Detective Sergeant Mick Blake smiled over at him wryly. 'It is rather macabre, sir.'

Sitting behind his desk, his keen eyes absorbing everything, Detective Inspector Kendrick, the third man in the room, smoothed a hand over his immaculately styled black hair. 'That young woman was nothing but trouble,' he said, sounding less than sympathetic.

'Rubbish!' said Blake.

Kendrick glared at him.

'She was very observant,' Blake said, defending her anyway. Ever since the DI's long time mistress had walked out on him, Kendrick was nothing but trouble himself. 'I'd even say she turned it into our lucky day.'

The Superintendent raised an eyebrow. 'Jesus, it's not mine. With a pile-up like that on our patch, a murder is all we need. I've got enough on my plate already.'

'The woman's body might have lain in the ditch undiscovered for months.'

'How long's she been dead?'

'A few days. More maybe.'

'And it *is* murder?'

Kendrick waived off the suggestion of anything else.

'Do we know the identity then?'

'Well, Sergeant?'

Blake sighed. What did Kendrick expect? Bloody miracles? He kept his voice calm. 'Not yet, sir. It's going to take time.'

'Well, get on with it.' Maitland turned on his heel. 'And you keep me informed, Kendrick.' Kendrick scowled after him.

'Right, Blake, what else?' he snapped.

'Probably in her twenties, sir. The skull is almost totally crushed and what's left of the facial skin and tissue is badly decomposed but the pathologist thinks death was caused by one original fatal blow.'

Kendrick smiled derisively. 'That's easy.'

Murder wasn't easy! Even to a hard man like Kendrick though, Blake hardly liked to repeat what the pathologist had suggested. 'The head was beaten in,' he said quietly, 'a day, maybe more, after death.'

Kendrick scowled and lit himself a cigarette. 'Afterwards,' he nodded, 'to hinder any investigation.'

'Or somebody really hated her.'

Kendrick turned away and stared through the window. Outside the mist was beginning to thin. Far out in the faded navy blue of the night, a procession of faint white headlights indicated that on the motorway the traffic was moving freely again.

There was a knock at the office door.

'That'll be Velalley,' Blake said. 'I told her to report up here before going home.'

It was unusual, Blake thought, as he listened to her answering the DI's questions clearly and briskly, for WPC Jane Velalley to look anything but well groomed. Tonight though, there was dried blood on her clothes and wisps of the auburn hair escaping from the clip that held it up and back from her face. The normally enthusiastic cornflower blue eyes looked tired. She seemed anxious to be gone. Not surprisingly. She'd put in a full day on her current case – and child protection was never easy. And on her way back from a court hearing over some impossible kid, she'd been involved in the district's worst accident ever, and then, then she'd discovered a horribly mutilated corpse in a ditch, and managed to keep her head and her stomach under control. Many of the young men in the squad would have suffered meltdown in similar circumstances. In spite of the delicate hands pressing together and the slender figure, this girl was certainly made of stern stuff. A few months ago when her appointment had been confirmed, Blake had been as pleased for her as if she had been his own daughter, and at twenty-three she was an intelligent and energetic addition to the Station. Ambitious too. There was just one problem. Now she had her sister's kid to think of. Even he knew that was bound to affect her concentration.

The DI leaned forward and steepled his hands on the desk in front of him, concentrating on her. 'Bloody miracle, wasn't it? Seeing it from the road?'

'It caught my eye, sir. I'd just found the dog's identity disc and –'

'I want that dog owner nicked.'

Blake shrugged. 'After the horse has bolted, if you ask me.'

'It belonged to a Juliet Frayne, sir.' Velalley glanced over at him, then back to Kendrick. 'It's all in the report on Sergeant Blake's desk.'

'Good. So you've realised how bloody foolish you were.'

'But –' she began.

'What?' Kendrick's voice was like thunder.

'My sister and her husband were killed, sir, in a similar accident simply because there was nothing to warn them of a pile-up ahead.'

'People drive too fast in bad weather,' Kendrick said, ignoring her now and opening a file.

Blake could see the colour rising up Velalley's neck. She looked as if she could cheerfully commit murder herself.

He took pity on her and checked his watch.

'It's late,' he said.

'Yes, sir.'

He looked at the DI. 'Nothing now that can't wait till tomorrow, is there?'

'You like policing?' Kendrick asked, looking up at Velalley.

She frowned. 'Of course, sir.'

'Get on all right with all the men here, do you?'

'Yes,' she said coldly. 'So, will that be all, sir?'

The DI lit another cigarette. For a moment he seemed reluctant to let her leave. He ran his eye slowly down over her figure. Then he nodded.

'Go on, then,' Blake told her. 'Home to your husband and that child.'

'Sexy little lady,' Kendrick murmured, when the door had closed. Then to Blake: 'Keep her in with us on this one.'

Blake frowned. 'She's got a load of work on already. And if you think...'

The DI swung his chair away dismissively and gazed out the window again, past the reflection of his office, into the black hole of the winter night.

Velalley's report lay on the desk in Blake's office. He picked it up and opened it. The first paragraph was written in her clear and concise manner, no wasted emotion or flowery language. Too much so. She was trying very hard to prove that in spite of the circumstances she could be objective. He went out into the corridor and collected a sweet black coffee from the machine. He sat back down at his desk, sipped the coffee, and read the whole report carefully. The first half related to the accident; the second, to her discovery of the dead woman.

When he'd finished he leaned back in his chair. The accident team would deal with the crash report but the Scenes of Crime boys would be back soon, too, from an initial fingertip search of the ditch. Considering the condition of the fabric it was wrapped in, Blake calculated the body had to have been dumped in the previous few hours – and well after the beating. It would have been too dangerous for the murderer to inflict injuries like that within sight of the busy roads. He took another comforting sip of coffee to remove the sour taste of disgust. When the hell kind of person could to that to a young women? To any human being? Even a dead one.

The phone on his desk buzzed. He picked it up.

'No,' he replied after a moment. 'There's no story. Where'd you get this anyway? I know you rang earlier. No, I didn't say you couldn't print it. The DI wants a blackout on it for a few hours until we piece together what we have...come on, give me a break. The accident investigation team have a job to do out there too, you know. No.' He frowned. 'Jesus. What you paid is your problem. What about the bus and all those dead kids? Haven't you got enough carnage for your fucking front page?'

CHAPTER FOUR

Only patches of powdery fog remained as Velalley drove through the dark streets towards home. Stretching away in the distance on the other side of the valley the lights of large Edwardian mansions glinted on the hill. In between, where she lived, lit by the orange glow of sodium street lighting, were post war pebble-dashed houses and some original narrow streets of Victorian terraces.

She was angry to have missed Suzie's bedtime. 'Is she all right?'

'She's asleep, Jane. I didn't know what time you'd be back,' Erik said accusingly. 'It was sheer chance when you phoned I was still here.'

She followed him through into the kitchen without taking off her coat. 'If you'd had the day I've had.'

'Well, mine hasn't been too clever actually. You didn't tell me Marietta wanted to go early. I had to cancel my last appointment.'

'I forgot, for Christ's sake.'

'I managed to re-make a time for next week.' He sounded angry.

'Did they mind?'

He didn't answer, just opened the fridge. His shoulders

were tense under the woolly pullover that he liked to change into in the evenings, and his hair was untidy. His face looked strained, its strong clarity marred by a frustrated frown. It was evident he'd had a tiring day himself. He pulled out a bottle of wine. 'Want a glass?'

'Please.' She pulled the clips from her hair and flopped down at the table.

'So did you see the news?' He dug the corkscrew in and twisted. 'There was some frightful pile up on the motorway. I was so grateful to think you weren't involved.' He turned in time to see her expression change. 'You were! Jane!'

'It wasn't so bad,' she said, playing it down.

'It looked horrendous! Sometimes it scares the shit out of me when I think what you get in to.'

She took the offered glass of wine and savoured its cold, clean, slate flavour. 'I was coming back from a court hearing. I told you I was going to Winchester.'

Erik began to pour wine for himself.

She leaned wearily on her hand. 'Will Suzie have a nice enough life with us? We're both involved in our work, and some of the kids out there...' The expression on the boy's face today crossed her mind again – such cocky defiance.

Erik was putting the wine back in the fridge. Perhaps he hadn't heard.

'Anyway,' she said, concentrating again, 'I was on my way back and this dog ran out into the traffic –' At last she could relax and talk about her narrow escape. Of feeling the tyres slipping, knowing she could not stop. How the space between the bus and the barrier opened up, and the chance was there. That she'd seen it and seized it. 'The van swerved and the bus hit it and –'

Erik had hesitated, his glass poised inches from his lips. There was apprehension in his eyes, horror at what she might be going to say. Then he caught sight of the blood on her skirt. If he heard more of the truth, the prospect of his imagining the worst every time anything happened would vastly increase. She brushed at the stain and tempered her words. 'I helped. It was just lucky I saw what happened.'

He relaxed a little, reached over and tilted her face up, smiling earnestly into her eyes. 'Thank God, darling, you weren't actually involved.'

She leaned her head appreciatively against his hand, and noticed one of Suzie's pictures lying next to the newspaper on the table. 'What's that?'

'That's your goodnight painting.'

She pulled it towards her. The colours were bright and bountiful – a generous, uninhibited world as only a three year old could see it. Two stick figures, one tall, one short. It made her smile to visualize Suzie doing it. Her little tongue would be pressed hard against her lip, and she would be leaning in close, deep in concentration, holding the coloured pen tightly. Probably a red gold wisp of fuzzy hair would be falling endearingly over her forehead.

'Fancy a take-away?'

'Hmm?'

'I could nip down to the Chinese. You don't want to start cooking now.'

She sighed with relief at the thought of staying exactly where she was. 'Nice.'

Erik poured more wine for her, and left her leaning her elbows on the table.

She concentrated on the picture's colours trying to make her mind drift away from the day's disasters. Two stick figures in triangular skirts. Mother and daughter, hand in hand. Both redheads. The scarlet felt tip colouring-in spilled haphazardly past the woolly outline that was the mother's hair.

Like blood seeping out across the face.

She pushed the picture away and pulled the evening newspaper over instead. On the front page was a picture of the crash. She gulped down her wine, and hurried upstairs to check on Suzie.

Erik leaned across on his elbow and kissed her shoulder. 'What time are you on duty tomorrow?'

She sighed and adjusted her pillow. 'Two p.m.'

'So you don't have to get up early.'

'You seem to forget small children don't understand shifts.'

'I'll get up and give her breakfast, and Marrietta will be here at nine.'

'I bet you Marrietta will be late.'

'What do we pay a home help for then?'

'She's young. You can't blame her wanting to go out. She likes a night life.'

'So do you, don't you?' Erik ran an exploring finger across her collar bone. 'Jane?'

Though his kiss was inviting and sweet, her mind was still wandering, unable to settle. To the murdered woman. To the DI's attitude. She tried to concentrate, but as Erik's hand travelled downwards, the overturning bus invaded her mind. Glass splintered, the tyres spun again, in hideous action replay. A child's fingers clawed against one of the windows; and for a moment she pictured herself lying amongst the injured children.

She pulled away from his caress. 'Not tonight, Erik. I –'

He withdrew his hand slightly.

'Would you mind if we didn't?' she said.

For a moment he looked concerned. 'Are you all right?'

'I just don't want to,' she snapped. Immediately she saw the hurt in his eyes and wished she'd had the kindness to lie.

'Then, yes, I do mind!' he said, and rolled back angrily to his own side of the bed. He switched off the lamp, and shifted about noisily, making a big production of getting comfortable.

Velalley turned over, tears welling up in her eyes. She wept silently in the darkness with frustration. Her carefully laid plans for herself for the future were disintegrating. She swallowed hard and buried her face in her pillow, hoping Erik would not hear her. Perhaps she shouldn't have taken Suzie on. Maybe it was a terrible mistake.

CHAPTER FIVE

Edged by the river and a narrow canal, which diverted water into a lake in the grounds of a nearby manor house, the small town of Heydon had once been far enough into the countryside to offer tranquillity. But the port and the coastal towns had long since reached back across the countryside towards the developing airport, and unlucky places like Heydon had lost out to progressive urbanisation. The view from the windows of the fifties style police station included a glimpse of the church spire but the rest of the early Norman building was hidden by the elevated section of the intervening motorway that had sliced right through the town. Beyond the road, council estates, recession hit warehouses and a swathe of waste land were out of sight and out of the mind of the older, and better-off half of the community – at their end of the paved-in High Street near the public buildings, were nicer shops and better housing, and Heydon's pride, the sparkling new shopping Mall with its smart frontage and cool interior.

Beyond the delivery yard behind it, crushed coke cans and plastic bags littered the grass bank where a path dropped down steeply into the old railway cutting. A young girl, dressed in school-navy windcheater and jeans, swore as the tapered heels on her shoes caught on protruding stones. She ignored the crying of the small child who was stumbling and dragging at her hand as they clambered down the path together.

Ahead of them some little way along, the motorway bridge crossed over the cutting. Breathlessly the girl hurried the child along under the concrete pylons and the roar of the lunchtime traffic. Then they joined the towpath beside the glinting canal. A butterfly caught in the slipstream, fluttered past them and away over the water towards the rear of the old disused warehousing with its grubby walls and broken windows.

Eventually the pair turned away from the canal and made their way across the huge stretch of wasteland, then up the side of a ridge, climbing slowly and painfully, for the child was tired now. At the top on the other side of the North West Road loomed a rectangular block of flats, deserted except for a few stray squatters, and one or two of the original inhabitants. None of them, the girl's father included, bothered to pay rent.

Once there had been a proper recreation area with a playground for the children living here. Now all that was left of the recreation area was ruptured tarmac and the burnt out skeleton of a car lying in the shadow of the building. Fearful of that, the little girl pulled back, but the older girl dragged her on. Drifts of litter lined the base of the walls which were themselves disfigured by the wild scrapings and scribblings of the young and disenchanted. The dark concrete stairwell, as the pair climbed up slowly to the fifth floor, smelled damp and sour.

No curtains twitched to see them as they passed a dozen doors, boarded up and kicked in. No one noticed that at the far end of the landing the girl opened the door to one of the few remaining habitable flats, and pushing the child ahead of her, disappeared inside.

On the other side of Heydon, Jane Velalley had buttoned up Suzie's coat and gratefully sent her out into the lunchtime sunshine with Marrietta.

Now ten minutes and two painkillers later, her headache was subsiding. Wrapped in her dressing gown and hunched over breakfast at the kitchen table, she listened vaguely to the news and weather forecast, realising she was already missing Suzie's company, the little songs, the constant chattering. Wondering how she could balance their new life with a child, she tried hard not to think about the boy at court, or the parents of those children in the wrecked bus.

An anticyclone moving in from the west will keep conditions cold and clear. Any leftover mist patches will give way to dry and sunny weather over the whole of the area…

Her husband rose angrily from his chair and helped himself to more coffee.

She glanced up. 'What?'

'You haven't heard a word I've said.'

'You don't understand,' she cried, 'I feel like I'm living under siege.'

'I couldn't agree with you more.' Erik peered into the refrigerator and rescued the last of the cheese.

'Make yourself another sandwich, for God's sake. I'll sort dinner out later.'

'And what's Suzie supposed to eat for her tea? Look, Jane, when do you get a day off? Read-my-lips. I want to see you. We need to talk.'

'Why aren't you working this morning?'

'Jane, I –'

'Tonight,' she said. 'I'm home tonight. There's her favourite baked beans in the cupboard, and some fruit. With the fresh bread they bring home –'

'Tonight?' He stopped buttering the bread and glanced across at her. 'Aren't you on duty then?'

'I told you I might not have to do the extra shift. But it depends what's happening, who's in. If the streets are quiet I'll be able to get away.'

'And you're the only one available, I suppose. What's the matter with those guys?' He looked at her more carefully. 'You look exhausted.'

'Complimentary, aren't you!' She stirred her coffee again. 'Once I'd got up to Suzie in the middle of the night I couldn't seem to get back to sleep. I started thinking about the accident again. Yesterday's,' she added quickly, 'and work in general.'

'Dedicated WPC Jane Velalley. Without people like you out there to enforce the rules, society will disintegrate. I've heard it all before, Jane. What criminal wouldn't give his right arm to see a pretty redhead like you racing to arrest him?'

'You think it's a joke, don't you? Upholding the law's one of the most demanding jobs around. If I was a nurse, or a fire fighter or a lifeboat man –'

'Oh, it's no joke, believe me. Listen, your energy is what I fell in love with, for Christ's sake, but now...'

'What?'

He cut the sandwich awkwardly and returned to the table. 'Now… well, now there's Suzie, and I've got work to do as well, Jane. When you're out so much Suzie misses you. She's only little, and she needs attention.'

'Hey, now that's not fair!' She raised her voice, as if shouting might make what he was saying less true. 'You know with the staff shortages just at present I can hardly say to Blake I can't do the overtime.'

'They're expecting too much of you lately.'

'Don't be ridiculous! Anyway I've got to show I can handle it.'

'For the sake of your career.'

'Yes!'

'Then we should never have taken Suzie.'

'Who else out there loves her, for God's sake?' She could hear herself screaming. 'Look,' she said, trying to sound more reasonable, 'the problem at work is temporary. I'll tell them I need proper time off. I'll sort it out.'

'It'd be nice to see you, to have you in cooking a meal sometime.'

'Oh, great! Last night's take-away was your suggestion.'

'Okay, okay.'

The telephone rang.

'I'll get that.' He leapt up and went out into the hall.

She looked at her watch and swallowed down the rest of her coffee. There was so much to organise here.

'For you,' he called.

'Don't worry,' she assured him, as she took the receiver, 'it'll all happen. Groceries will arrive this afternoon. Suzie has Marrietta to look after her and she's staying on into the evening if necessary. You can go and see all your precious clients, no bother. Yes?'

'Velalley?' The voice was urgent. 'A child has been abducted.'

'What?'

'Get down here right away. We need you on this one.'

Velalley hurried along the station corridor towards 'TRAUMA', her black shoes clicking on the polished vinyl. She tried to ignore a mental picture of tins of baked beans in the cupboard, and lamb chops still in the front of the plastic basket in the freezer, and yet another microwave-zapped meal tonight. She was due more time off and if she talked to him, Blake would understand that she couldn't do more than her share. But right now... Well, sorting that out would just have to wait a few more hours. But what did fresh, slowly cooked meat taste like, for God's sake? At the first opportunity she'd have to ring the house and if Erik was out, she'd just have to instruct Marrietta, tell her she'd be late and to take the meat out of the freezer, and just hope the girl might remember.

Reaching the door she hesitated, and took a moment to compose herself. Then she moistened her lips, smoothed her hair and prepared to do her job. C.U.P.I. Confidence, understanding, patience, information.

Her subject huddled in a corner chair jumped to her feet as she entered the room.

'Have you found her yet?'

Velalley wished she could say yes, allay this poor girl's worst fears. Instead she heard her trained, calm voice answering: 'Not yet, I'm afraid. It's only been two hours.'

The wide grey eyes clouded over, and Faye Simmons sank back down into her chair, her dark hair falling forward over her ashen face. Her hands pressed tightly together and her white trainers bore down hard into the floor.

Velalley cleared her throat. 'Faye, I'm WPC Jane Velalley. We need to talk. First, can I get you a cup of tea?'

The girl shook her head miserably.

'Sure? It might help.'

'No thanks.'

In spite of its careful relaxed set, the room felt agitated, the air spiked with imaginary needles. Velalley sat down on the edge of one of the chairs.

'We need to talk, Faye,' she repeated. The hands, the long sensitive fingers, writhed about in the other woman's blue-jeaned lap. She persevered. 'What's Angie like?'

'I told them. Don't they know?' There was such awful alarm, a thin high-pitched note of panic in the voice.

'We know her description, Faye, of course,' Velalley said quietly. 'She's four years old, fair hair. Tell me again what she was wearing?'

'A pale blue shell suit... um... a pink tee-shirt underneath... white socks, navy shoes – with a strap. They're a bit scuffed.'

'And what's she like? Can you tell me more about her?'

Like the things I notice about Suzie, she thought. The particular way she talks, what her laugh sounds like. Does she run ahead or walk alongside? Information that comes from the heart. Knowledge gleaned close in like this, one to one, could be vitally important, had proved to be so before, in all sorts of cases. Calming the subject down into ordinary conversation quickly filled in valuable details.

'Is she naughty, you mean, don't you?' Faye said accusingly. 'They said that at the supermarket. They said she was hiding. They spent so long looking, while all the time someone was taking my baby away.'

Velalley felt her stomach churn. She licked her lips nervously and continued. 'Did you see anybody? Was anyone following you?'

'No. I don't know. I told them already. I don't know.' A single sob escaped. 'There were just people.' She fished in her pocket, produced a crumpled tissue and blew her nose. She was making a huge effort to stay in control. 'Angie wouldn't just go off with a stranger,' she whispered.

The ring on her fourth finger was being twisted, round and round.

'Where can we contact your husband?'

'I'm not married.'

'The child's father, then?'

Round and round went the ring.

'No.' Her tone was determinedly uncooperative. 'No.'

'Does he live locally?'

'I don't know. He has nothing to do with it.'

'We must make certain, Faye.'

'I've no idea where he is.'

'Do your parents know what's happened yet?'

Faye turned her face away. 'All I want is Angie back.'

'I know. That's what we all want. But we need to talk to these people. And surely your mother and father...?'

'They're in Devon.'

'On holiday?'

'They live near Okehampton.'

The grandparents must be advised and soon. Any mention of the disappearance heard cold on the news would be appalling. 'Do you have the address? They'll want to know.'

Faye poked around in her bag, and producing an aging address book, reluctantly passed it over.

'Try if you want. Longman.'

Velalley flipped to 'L' and made a note. 'Can we keep this for a while? There may be some leads.'

Faye shrugged nervously.

There were not many names in it. Not many friends. 'Would Angie's father be listed in here?'

'No. No! I don't want him informed.'

'But he might be involved, Faye.'

'No, I said. Chris –'

The name.

Faye paused, obviously angry with herself for saying it, then: 'He's got nothing to do with it.' Her voice rose accusingly. 'God, why aren't you out there trying to find my Angie instead of asking all these questions?'

'There's at least six constables out on a house to house all round the area and we're organising search parties. But you're Angie's mother, Faye. You know more than anyone about her. Your information is vital. And we've got to consider – Chris, did you say his name was?'

'Consider him?'

Velalley persevered gently. 'How long since you last saw him?'

Faye hesitated, her eyes darting around the room. 'Um... um... four and a half years ago.' She bit her lip nervously. 'He doesn't know Angie exists.'

'Where does he live?'

'I've told you, I've no idea.'

'Do you have a boyfriend at the moment?'

'Stop it. Stop asking me things. No, I don't. There's no-one, I tell you.'

Velalley tried a kinder tack. 'Does Angie go to a play school?'

'None round where I live. Not free anyway. I can't afford the crèche.'

'Is she a confident child?'

'Sometimes. Sometimes she surprises me.'

'Where did you go just before the supermarket?'

'Nowhere. We went straight there.'

'On the bus?'

'Walking.'

'It's quite a distance.' She thought of Suzie's little legs. 'Angie doesn't mind that?'

'What else can I do?' Faye looked at her in despair. 'What kind of person would steal a child?'

Velalley shook her head. There was no safe answer. To consider for one moment the mental state of such an individual would threaten this woman's fragile hold on her own sanity.

'Have you got children?' There were dark circles under the enquiring grey eyes, the skin over the high delicate cheekbones was drained of all colour.

'One little girl.' There was no need to go into why.

'Like me.'

It moved them closer, Velalley thought.

'How old?'

'Three.'

Faye's lip quivered. 'I guess women like you have it worked out,' she said. 'This job and all. Does your husband look after her?'

'Part of the time. And I have a child minder.'

Faye stood up and walked to the window. 'Easy for you then.'

'Not always,' Velalley said quietly.

Faye seemed to consider carefully before she said: 'He left. Before Angie... before Angie was born. He doesn't know about her and... and I haven't seen him since.'

'You would be entitled to some financial support from him now, you know.'

'I wouldn't want it.'

'Yes, well.' A familiar battle, one Faye could be advised on later, for the moment better ignored. She had secretly been hoping if this man was not a suspect he might be of practical use now, and be able to offer some help. Comfort, if nothing else.

Faye turned to her imploringly. 'Please, I don't want him to find out about Angie. Or where I am.'

Velalley frowned, willing Faye to explain. Why might be vitally important. Faye remained silent. She tried to reassure her. 'It will be very hard to keep you out of it, but I promise we can investigate him discreetly. There would be no reason for him to know we were there. But we need to make absolutely certain. Unless he's involved he won't even notice us.'

'No?' Faye began to laugh, softly at first, then louder, faster, until the laugh became huge heaving sobs.

Velalley sat very still listening to the sound trembling on the air, imagining what it would be like to lose Suzie now...

She held herself back. She did not go to Faye. Even one slight crumb of comfort now would somehow remove from this poor woman part of her reserve of inner strength, and perhaps even diminish her own, and Velalley knew that over the next few hours, perhaps even days, she and Faye Simmons would badly need every bit of it.

CHAPTER SIX

'Stay with it, Velalley, we need that man's name, some lead on him. And anything else you can get. We've got nothing to go on.'

They were out on the landing beside the door to Faye's flat.

'Any leads on the murder?' Velalley asked, keeping her voice down.

'Not a damn thing on that either,' Blake said.

The flat on the west side of town was a first floor conversion, cold and cramped, no place for a child, yet standing in the living room once the DI and Sergeant Blake had gone, there was an air of homeliness Velalley felt, a genuinely caring atmosphere.

Still hugging her jacket around her, Faye Simmons sank nervously into one of the two chairs. 'Thanks for staying with me. I don't think –'

'I know. Let me light the gas fire. You're shivering.'

'I'm behind on the bills.'

'You need warmth right now,' Velalley said firmly. No ignition button. 'Matches?'

Sensibly kept high up. The gas fire popped and a blue flame rose up the white coral columns.

'I'll ring the help line when I go back to the station and

see if I can square it for now. They wouldn't want any bad publicity on this.'

'Are you going? Please don't leave me!'

Velalley replaced the fireguard and straightened up. 'I'll be with you most of the time now, Faye, until...' She steered off any conclusion, for herself too. Trying to keep things low key, she asked: 'Mind if I look around?'

'The place is a tip,' Faye said, eyeing her nervously as she moved about the room.

'Maybe there's something here to help us find Angie. Is that the bedroom?'

A small bedroom, two single beds, surprisingly neat. Beds made, nightgowns folded on the pillow, an endearingly battered teddy. On one wall, paintings, proudly pinned up – poster paint applied to cheap white butcher's paper, obviously Angie's creations, and refreshingly simple in bright uninhibited colours. Just like Susie's efforts, Velalley thought. On the worn out chest of drawers was a discarded airmail envelope and she made a note of the address written on the back. Beside that the image of a small slim child stared out at her with round, appealing blue eyes and very straight, shiny blonde hair – clearly a better photo than the one they had.

'Is this picture recent, Faye?'

'It's all I've got.' The voice trembled.

'We'll take special care of it,' she promised, coming back into the main room. 'It would really help.'

Faye didn't answer, just stared blindly at the photo in Velalley's hand. She felt impelled to put it down beside her, and she watched Faye touch it gently as if it wasn't real, as though right now it was intangible like the missing child.

'I told you they've contacted your mother and father, didn't I? They're on their way.'

'Are they?' Faye's chin lifted determinedly. 'They never knew Chris, and Angie won't remember them, it's so long since...'

'How did you meet him?'

'Art school,' she answered vaguely.

Art school. That narrowed it slightly. But where? Velalley opened her mouth to ask, but Faye had suddenly realised what she'd said. She stared sullenly into the fire.

'Please tell me Faye. It's terribly important. If we're to find Angie –'

'But he won't have anything to do with it.'

'Please, Faye. You must! It's your child's safety!'

But Faye turned her head away. It was obvious she wouldn't say anymore. Maybe it might be enough?

Velalley's radio phone crackled, the in-coming voice broken up into short staccato bursts. She tried to get through herself. No response. 'Listen, I need to check in. Is there a phone anywhere?'

'On the ground floor landing. If it still works.'

Instead she went right out into the street and called in on her radio phone again. 'That's not much to go on, Velalley.'

'It's all I can get so far. We need to set up a better link in her flat, sir.'

'I'm sending a mobile that'll work anywhere. And you're due a break.' The radio hissed for a moment then Blake came back on line. 'Okay, Colston's taken the mobile. She's on her way.'

'Cloggs Colston? Jesus, isn't there anyone else?'

'No, there isn't,' Blake said coldly.

Velalley tried to justify her outburst. 'Judith Colston might – um… this girl's on a short fuse, sir.'

'Colston's all I've got. Go home, Velalley, take a few hours. You'll be on this one till it breaks and you're on the extra shift tonight already.'

Velalley glanced at her watch and was shocked at the time. Marrietta would be waiting to leave. Would she have put Suzie to bed? What if Erik was late? 'How long till Colston's here?'

'About ten minutes.'

She shivered. It was getting dark and the air temperature was dropping fast. 'Any progress?'

'Not a sodding thing yet. We're doing house to house near you now – the whole west side.'

She read him the envelope address from her notes. 'And I've a recent photo of Angie to bring in. Sir, while I'm on the way, could someone possibly ring my child minder, and warn her I'm working late again?'

Velalley reversed into the tight residents-only parking space under the street lamp with a mounting sense of unease. Erik's car was gone and Marrietta's was nowhere to be seen either. She locked her own and sprinted up the narrow steps of the Victorian semi she and Erik had managed to buy four years before.

The front door opened and her mother, Laura Bennett, plump and red-faced, blocked her way accusingly.

'Mum!'

'Why didn't you warn me?' Laura demanded.

'I didn't know I'd be as late as this. Where's Erik?'

'I've no idea.'

'Did Marrietta call you then?'

'Yes. I've been here since teatime.'

'What?'

'She didn't know where to contact Erik, nor could she get through to you, so very sensibly she rang me. I sent her off to the doctor immediately. The girl's got chicken pox!'

'What? She never mentioned feeling sick!'

'Well, it's very infectious. Suzie'll be next no doubt.'

'God, I can't bear it! Where is she?'

'Watching TV. I keep telling you, Jane, living like this is no good for the child. If it's going to work out she needs you at home.'

'Don't start, Mother!'

'Could you put your career on hold until Suzie's settled, at least until she goes to school?'

'Things work as they are. And Suzie and I spend lots of time together on my days off.'

'I suppose I could have had her.'

'Mum, you couldn't, you know you couldn't! It wouldn't be fair. It's too big a job. Anyway you haven't got room.'

'It's fine when Erik's here, but if he's busy – one sneeze and the whole system collapses.'

'I'm sure he didn't say he'd be out.'

'Well, if it wasn't for me –'

'I know, Mum, and I'm grateful.'

'Jane?'

'Hello, darling!' Suzie ran to her and her narrow little body snuggled inside her arms, all energy and warmth. 'Who's Jane's best girl?'

'Mawietta's got spots!'

'I know. Let's see if you have,' she lifted Suzie's jumper and tickled into the round little belly. The skin was as downy and tender as a ripe peach. Suzie collapsed inwards convulsed with giggles then tugged urgently at her skirt wanting more as Velalley peeled off her coat wearily.

'I'll make us some dinner.'

Laura adjusted the front edges of her knitted jacket, one over another. 'There's a nice casserole in the oven,' she said.

There was till the fresh smell of bath time on Suzie's skin and Velalley lingered near her a moment savouring the sweetness. Then she kissed her gently on the forehead, switched on the night-light and turned out the main one.

'Sleep tight, darling.'

As she walked down the stairs there was a welcome aroma of fresh coffee.

'Sit down,' Laura called from the kitchen, 'you look tired out.'

'I'll ring you a cab to take you home. My treat.'

'All in good time.'

Velalley settled gratefully onto the sofa and kicked off her shoes.

Her mother bustled in with the mugs and a slice of home baked cake. 'Suzie helped me make this.'

'Look, thanks, Mum. But what about you? Are you all right?'

'Don't fuss,' said Laura, sitting down.

'Things are really difficult at work. I expect you've heard. A little girl was snatched today. From that big supermarket in the Eastern Mall.'

'No, Jane!'

'Mum, she's only a few months older than Suzie.'

'Haven't they found her yet?'

She shook her head. 'Worse, the longer it goes on too. That poor woman. It'd break your heart to see the little girl's nightie folded on her bed, and her teddy...'

'This police work, dear. I wish you wouldn't do it.'

'At least I feel I'm doing something worthwhile - I can help people. We'll find her.' She picked agitatedly at the slice of cake. 'That's if she's still alive.'

'Sometimes it's a mercy they kill them.'

'Every case is different,' Velalley said quietly.

'This town used to be such a nice place to live,' Laura said wistfully. 'These days... I don't know. A thing like that, here. It's just terrible.'

'Mmn.'

'Perhaps my generation has a lot to answer for. We gave up mothering for our independence. The hand that rocks the cradle... the mother used to be so protective and have such influence. Now the children run riot.'

'Well, the mother in this case stays at home.'

'It'd solve a lot of things though, if being a wife and mother really counted. I mean, counted. You know, you hear them on those game shows on the telly... "Oh, I'm only a housewife"... It's an art, running a household. Your sister knew that.'

Velalley winced at the veiled criticism, but there had been the faintest break in her mother's voice too. She thought of the crash and her mother's grief. To lose a daughter like that... A sister...

'Worse still, think of the men,' Laura continued, her voice rising bravely to cover any suggestion of distress.

'They have no direction now. They have no jobs. They can't look forward to the role of being father or husband – the women divorce them more often than not. It's the men who are out on the streets creating trouble! Women are a much calmer breed. And the stress!' She was over-excited now. 'The career woman works all day, comes home exhausted to housework and children. They all eat junk food to save time. There's no family life. They're too tired even for sex –' She faltered suddenly. 'I mean, a loving relationship.'

It would be amusing her mother could still get so keyed up, if it wasn't for her blood pressure, and how she must still be feeling. But it wasn't funny trying to juggle time for Suzie and have a career either – and now with Marrietta ill… 'You worked, Mum,' she countered with frustration.

'Only part time! And that was different. When your father left –'

'Look, I didn't expect to get Suzie. I'm trying so hard.'

'I don't mean you, dear.'

Velalley sighed, knowing she probably did.

But she was too tired and frustrated to argue the point – and she and Erik had things organised. It was just a matter of teamwork.

'Well,' she said, 'this young woman gave up her college course and found herself a flat. She wants to be at home with her child.'

'Don't you?'

'Mum! Please! I spend lots of time with Suzie, but I work too. I'm organising things as well as I can. Please don't start telling me –'

Mercifully her mother picked back up on her original theme. 'And so many girls opt for single parenthood now. I ask you, where's the father image, and the discipline?'

'You managed.'

'Maybe.'

'You can't dictate to people about how to live their lives. And this girl's a good mother, I'm sure of it. A little depressed but –'

'Too young.'

'Look Mum, you know nothing about it! She took her eyes off that child for one minute.'

'That's all it takes nowadays,' Laura said defensively. 'What kind of sick society do we live in when someone wants to steal a little child?'

They drank their coffee in silence.

After a while Velalley suggested they put on the news. The snatch was lead story, with the Chief Super making a statement, but there had been no developments. Local feelings were running high, the public wanted assurances.

There were media suggestions the mother might have killed the child, hidden the body.

'Oh God,' whispered Vellalley.

The Police were appealing for help.

Children who had escaped harm in the motorway pile-up the previous day were featured at their school's assembly saying prayers for their dead and injured class mates. That was followed by comment by various authorities on motorway safety. Velalley didn't have the heart to frighten her mother by mentioning her own involvement. The murder was reported briefly too.

Afterwards Laura said: 'It's all doom and gloom. Doesn't anything nice happen anymore?'

'It's late, Mum, I'll call that cab.'

'I miss Beth.'

'I know Mum. So do I.'

'What about tomorrow? Marietta's off for ten days.'

God, she thought. Ten days! 'Erik can re-organise his week, I expect.'

'He's very late.'

Velalley frowned and glanced uneasily at her watch.

'I think he said something about dinner with a client,' she lied, to avoid inviting more criticism. 'Anyhow, if necessary the agency will help.'

Laura sniffed. 'Agency?'

'Mum, I'm too tired –'

'I meant so last minute?'

'They understand when I'm on call.'

'Jane?' Suzie, in her little white cotton nightie, was standing on the stairs.

Velalley leapt to her feet and ran up to her. 'Darling! What's wrong?' She felt Suzie's forehead. Only slightly warm, no more, though her little face was flushed.

Suzie wriggled in her arms. 'I had a bad dweam.'

The telephone rang and Laura answered.

She held out the receiver.

'It's Erik.'

Velalley passed Suzie over to her mother and took the phone.

'Tonight? But Erik... no, you didn't tell me... Marrietta's ill and she can't... Couldn't you possibly... God, how am I supposed to ...?'

Laura began to climb the stairs with Suzie. 'Come on sweetie, back to bed.'

Velalley hung up, furious that Erik could let her down just when she needed him. She was sure he hadn't mentioned any conference.

The phone rang again immediately. She snatched it up. 'Erik?'

'Sergeant Blake here. I know you've only had a couple of hours, Velalley, but Faye Simmons is beside herself and she keeps asking for you.'

'I – um – I've got problems here, sir. Isn't Colston with her?'

'Yes, but you said yourself. Trouble with the kid?'

'Yes.' She had heard it suddenly in his voice too. He sounded just like the DI – you shouldn't be trying to have a career. This is not a job for women with children... 'Nothing I can't handle, sir.'

'Can you get back right away then?'

God, Suzie had to come first. 'I –' But she thought of the dread in Faye's frantic grey eyes... and a frightened little child somewhere out there in the night. And what would her sister have expected her to do? Not go?

'I'll have to be a little while. My child minder's sick.'

'Okay, okay.'

Her mother had reached to top of the stairs. Suzie was already fast asleep on her shoulder.

'Mum?'

CHAPTER SEVEN

Detective Inspector Kendrick leaned round Blake's door and pointed to his watch. 'Got time for one quick drink?'

'No,' said Blake wearily, but he got up from his chair and followed him out past the Incident Room and through the Control Room. The phones were running hot. The computers were buzzing.

'Nothing on the kid yet, then?' Kendrick said, as they emerged into the cold.

'No.' Blake sniffed the air appreciatively. There was a smell of cargo ships and sea salt drifting up the river with the tide. He and Kendrick crossed the road together and entered the Mayflower Inn. Kendrick winked at the barmaid and began to chat her up as he ordered the drinks. Blake headed over to the snug. The log fire was dying down but it would still be reasonably warm.

He sat sipping his scotch and listening to the DI's detailed and macabre update on the motorway murder investigation.

'I'm getting far too old for blood and guts,' he growled after a while.

'Damn awful case,' Kendrick observed. 'Brutal. We're

dealing with a total nutter. We've got our hands full, what with this missing kid and the accident investigation lot descending on me today with a brief from,' he smiled cynically, 'the very highest level.'

Blake nodded.

The DI took an enthusiastic gulp of his beer. 'So it's our ambitious young redhead sitting in with Simmons.'

'Velalley is in Child Protection.'

'I wanted her on this murder case. You're not keeping her away from me, are you?'

Blake took a steady sip of scotch to avoid replying.

Kendrick was miffed. He leaned back in his chair. 'Don't let anything get by us on it, Blake, just to prove a point. The Super would have my guts, and I'd relish having yours.'

'She's worked with me before. But she's busy enough on this abduction. You know her sister was killed in a road crash recently and she's taken on the child?'

Kendrick raised a disapproving eyebrow. 'So what if things go wrong at home? There'll be conflicting loyalties.'

'She hasn't asked for any favours, and she can stand the heat. Perhaps she'll notice things now someone else might not.'

'Never had anything like this in practice, though, has she?'

'She'll do.'

Kendrick finished off his beer. 'Well, be warned, if we don't get a result quickly, the press will move in on us and it will be very uncomfortable. People get worked up about missing kids.'

'The trouble is there's absolutely nothing to go on.'

'No theories?'

Blake shook his head.

'Could the child have wandered?'

'I don't see how. And we've been through that super-market with a fine toothcomb. Twice. No clues at all.'

'Faye Simmons is a single mother, isn't she? What about the father?'

'We haven't been able to trace him yet.'

'Hell! What's the matter with you?'

The barmaid was smiling across at them. 'Did you want another?' asked Kendrick, rising to his feet with his empty glass.

Blake shook his head. 'Velalley's had a couple of hours off and she'll be back at Simmons's flat shortly. I want to go over there and check on things.'

Kendrick smirked.

'Oh, for Christ's sake,' Blake said sharply, 'Judith Colston's been there in the meantime.'

While Kendrick was back at the bar, Blake gazed into the fire. 'It's an awful task, sitting waiting,' he said, when the DI returned. 'You need someone sympathetic.'

'Well,' said Kendrick, looking at his watch, 'I'm off.' He downed his drink and stood up.

Blake followed him back across the road to the car park at the rear of the police station and Kendrick drove away smartly. Blake took things more slowly. He used the radio to tell the Control Room where he was going, then he indicated and waited to pull out into the street. The moon was full and bright rising above the town as he turned west towards Faye Simmons's flat.

CHAPTER EIGHT

A wall of window high, high up. The child leaned against it watching the night closing in, several times huffing against the glass to mist it up and then pressing her hand into the condensation and watching the imprint slowly fade. First the moon rose, then little lights, street lamps, had appeared in the east on the hills, like early evening stars, sparks in the gathering darkness. Gradually long chains of sodium lights on the motorway laced the suburban streets in the distance into geometric shapes. Angie watched it all, hypnotised by the pretty patterns of light.

The girl who called herself Carrie was pacing about increasingly nervously, occasionally going into the kitchen to fetch herself a can of lager. She did not switch on the lighting in the flat and for this Angie was somehow thankful, instinctively feeling that without Mummy, the darkness offered her some refuge, some shadow to draw back into.

At one point Carrie disappeared into the bedroom. For a few minutes there was scuffling, and a rearranging of things, an opening and closing of cupboards. When she returned she moved about the room more easily, looking pleased with herself. When the moon was high overhead and there was only inky blackness outside the window and the lights all over the central area of the town sparked like bright clusters of diamonds and Angie was sinking into a kind of abstracted torpor, she snapped on the light.

Angie widened her eyes and blinked, adjusting to the sudden change. Carrie rubbed her nose and coughed a bit and covered her mouth with a tissue. Then there was a fizz as she opened another can of lager. Reaching into her pocket and squeaking the childproof lid off a small brown bottle, she swallowed a pill down with a gulp of liquid.

'Right, you.' She caught Angie's hand and hauled her away from the window and propelled her into the bedroom.

The little girl, frightened of disobeying, made no attempt to struggle, battling instead against her own increasing exhaustion. Her eyelids were lead heavy, her limbs weighed her down. Soon sleep would be irresistible. Standing next to the bed, imagining the warm blankets around her, the downy pillows under her head, she swayed slightly on her thin little legs as Carried turned down the cover.

She didn't protest though, when instead Carrie led her roughly over to a cupboard built into the side of the room and pushed her inside. A little floor space. A torn rug. A lumpy pillow. She was even pleased when Carrie shut her in. She sat down, the salty taste of her thumb comfortingly familiar. She was alone at last in total covering darkness.

CHAPTER NINE

Judith Colston, red faced and apologetic, was waiting at Faye's door when Velalley arrived back. 'All I said was how come it was so long before she noticed the kid was missing.'

Velalley winced. As usual Judith could be relied upon to put her size ten clogs firmly in when angels would be terrified.

'You didn't mean anything, I'm sure.' She handed Judith her coat. 'Go home. It's okay. Blake's downstairs, he'll give you a lift back.'

'But you've hardly had any kip.'

Velalley sighed. 'I've had a meal and I'm fine, don't worry.'

'Jane? Is that you?'

'Yes, I'm back, Faye. With you in a minute.'

Judith shot her a baleful glance and pulled on her coat. She seemed eager to escape.

'Hang on,' Velalley said, 'did she tell you anything useful?'

'Sat staring into space mostly. I was trying to get her talking.'

'Where's the new mobile?'

'In the kitchen.'

'Okay.'

'Night, then.'

Faye was huddled uncomfortably on the sofa. The fire was still on so the room was warm, but she was visibly trembling and she'd obviously been crying.

'You've been home?' she asked.

'Yes.'

'Your child okay?'

'She's with my mother.' Velalley felt almost guilty Suzie was safe – and then more that Suzie wasn't her child, as if she was lying to Faye to gain her friendship. 'I've just had a word with the Detective Sergeant, Faye. They've started a detailed search west of the shopping centre.'

'Round the old factories?' The grey eyes were wild with terror.

Velalley put her hand over Faye's to steady her. 'It would be good shelter.'

Faye pushed her hand away and leapt to her feet. 'I can't just sit here.'

'You should stay here. Wait here for any news.'

'What if Angie... What if she just wandered off and is waiting for me to come back for her?' She grabbed her coat and headed for the door.

'Wait!'

But Faye was already halfway down the stairs. Velalley grabbed the new mobile and Faye's flat keys and chased her out into the street. 'Where are you going? The supermarket will be closed.'

Tears were streaming down Faye's face. 'Take me there? Please?'

Her sanity seemed to depend on it.

'Okay. Get in the car.'

Once they were moving, Velalley radioed Blake.

'What!'

'It's important to her, sir.'

'All right, all right. Do what you have to do, but stay in contact.'

As they drove in and parked, the arc lighting in the car park gave the Eastern Shopping Mall a weird ghostly appearance, the illuminated parts of its pale exterior gleaming amongst the shadows. It was late. There was no one around. Faye leapt out of the car and made straight for the entrance, banging on each of the line of locked glass doors.

'Angie, Angie? What if she's trapped in there?'

She ran on, to the next entrance, and the next, hammering, calling out, begging for someone to let her in. Finally she broke down. 'Where is she?' she sobbed. 'Where's my baby?'

There was a sound above them and a security guard leaned out of an upstairs window. 'What's going on?' he shouted down.

'Thank God,' cried Faye. 'Let me in. My child's somewhere in there.'

'No-one in here, lady.'

'Let me in!' Faye screamed.

'I'm calling the police,' he threatened.

'No need, sir,' Velalley called up, producing her warrant card and holding it up as if he might see it. 'WPC Velalley, West Heydon. Everything's under control.'

'We've had your lot here all afternoon searching the place again. I know for a fact there's no child in here.'

'Please,' begged Faye.

'I can't let anyone in this time of night! It's more than my job's worth.'

He was too far away to start explaining. 'I understand,' Velalley called up. 'Don't worry, sir. Come on,' she said softly to Faye, leading her back to the car, 'they've searched there. Let's go home.'

They drove back through the dark streets and Velalley called in again on her radio. 'Anything?'

'Not yet. I've got every available man on it.'

She glanced across at Faye. 'We're going back to the flat now, sir. We'll be there if any news comes through.'

From the bedroom she fetched a duvet. Not from the child's bed – the nightie placed just so on the pillow, and the teddy, that needed preserving somehow. When she tucked the cover gently round Faye's legs, the young woman barely noticed. The kettle took an age to boil but the tea was hot and sweet, like Erik would make it. Medicinal. Reviving to Velalley herself even if most of Faye's remained in the mug.

'Why don't they ring?' Faye asked distractedly.

'As soon as they have anything, I'm sure –'

'It's my fault. If only I'd kept hold of her hand.'

'Faye, you mustn't think that. How can it be your fault? You can't hold a child's hand every minute. I know sometimes with Suzie –'

'Suzie,' she repeated softly. 'Is her hair red like yours?'

'More a sort of goldie red.' Exactly like Beth's had been. 'Like my sister's –'

Faye interrupted her. 'Angie's is fair.'

'Is her father blonde then?'

But Faye didn't reply. She sat staring into the flame of the gas fire.

Velalley waited but Faye said no more. After a while in the silence she wondered briefly how Erik's conference was going, and where he was staying. He'd mentioned some hotel.

The hands on the wall clock crept on relentlessly towards midnight. Its ticking was almost unbearable. The longer this goes on, Velalley thought, the worse…

'Oh God, if I'd kept hold of her.'

'You mustn't blame yourself, Faye. It could have happened to anyone. Just as easily to me.'

'But it didn't happen to you,' Faye said bitterly. 'How can you know what it feels like?'

There was no answer to that. Velalley could only thank God she didn't know. Suzie wasn't hers. It wouldn't be the same, would it? No. No, she must keep a tight grip on her own emotions. Suzie was perfectly safe with her grandmother, and while others could only sympathise and shake their heads, at least she herself could offer this poor woman something practical – she could sit here too. It was little enough comfort but at least Faye wouldn't have to wait alone.

'She's out there somewhere in the dark, my little baby.' Faye hid her face in despair.

'We'll find her.'

'Please God. Don't let them… hurt… her.'

Unspoken, another prayer began to whisper through Velalley's mind: Please God, don't let them kill her.

CHAPTER TEN

Erik Velalley lay on the hotel bed in the dark unable to sleep and feeling like death. The afternoon with clients had been long enough, without the added frustration of driving up to London, followed by dinner. He had decided at the last minute to stay over. Not just because he felt dog-tired and knew he shouldn't undertake driving back down the motorway in such a state, and not because now he knew of a perfectly nice little hotel overlooking the Thames. It was a way of saying by his actions what he couldn't bring himself to put into words.

It was useless trying to sleep. He got up and stood at the window and stared out at the river. A barge went by, the resonating sounds of its chugging, like the reflections of its lights on the water, rippling towards him through the darkness.

But what could he say?

Look, Jane, I don't want to be there when you're not, just because it's convenient? I can see how much Suzie means to you – but remember me? I'm your husband... But there was much more to it than that. Much more.

Somewhere in the dark room was a hospitality fridge. He felt for it and opened the half bottle of wine it contained and poured some into a glass from the bathroom. He returned to the window and sipped his drink slowly and went on watching the river.

He had been a fool of course, a fool ever to think that sleeping with Marilyn might help, that because a beautiful young woman had looked at him he would feel less left out. God, it was all going to end in disaster. Jane would never understand if he confessed, but he knew he could not live with his conscience if he didn't. And what if someone else told her first?

But how could he say it was because of Suzie? How could he blame her? Be jealous of a child? And that child particularly, that sweet innocent little kid who needed Jane so much?

And Marilyn wasn't even beautiful, not really, not now. Superficially maybe, all eyes, face, figure, but not achingly lovely like Jane could be, not gentle and friendly and caring. Marilyn would never have put her arms round him like Jane did and be all things to him, all at once – mother, sister, lover and friend.

But now... he wiped away a tear and took another gulp of wine to steady himself. Maybe the only way forward was to tell her and pray that she would understand. Maybe. Maybe...

Out on the River Thames the tide was running deep and fast, pulling the moonlight out and away in silver trails towards the sea.

In his office in Heydon's West Side Police Station, Detective Sergeant Mick Blake yawned and sat down. Tilting his chair back he stared anxiously up at the area plan on the wall. Out in those deserted, moonlit streets right now, the search was continuing. During the first few hours men had covered all the roads in close proximity to the shopping Mall, and started a second broader sweep, and a third, but so far the house to house had yielded nothing. No witnesses, no sightings, nothing. No ransom note had arrived either. As yet all they had to go on was the statement from one supermarket checkout girl, who thought she might have seen the child with a young woman. But she saw hundreds of people in the store every day of her working life. He wondered how much detail a person like that could be relied on to remember.

Nothing had come from the roadblocks set up to contain the area either, nor the town centre enquiries. Everyone wanted to help but no one it seemed knew anything. At least there was no lack of volunteers from the public to search – thank God, in view of the staff shortages at the moment. Kendrick, who knew a case to keep clear of when he saw one, was heavily involved instead in the murder enquiry, and stuck with the repercussions of the accident, and what with a couple of the constables off sick too... Blake himself was on an extra ten hour shift now like the rest, but at least an incident like this did bring out the best in the lads, as it did in the whole community – an innocent little kid, missing, injured, murdered, whatever. In spite of the society which allowed it to happen, things couldn't be too bad, if a kid out there in danger could touch so many hearts. Then he thought of the murdered woman. Maybe he was being over-optimistic.

'A needle in a bloody haystack,' he muttered, still staring intently at the map. His eyes fell on the canal where at daylight the divers would begin a laborious and depressing search that could take anything up to two days. Then there was the wide strip of wasteland to the north of it – a fingertip search of that was planned to start at first light. Then there were the old empty warehouses on the south side of that, the railway cutting, the busy roads, car parks. Everywhere there were hazards, and for a small child who could not possibly comprehend the dangers...

He stood up and walked purposefully out of his office and down the hall past the murder incident room which was quiet – just a radio operator and a couple of men working in there on the computers.

'Anything new?' he asked, leaning round into the Control Room.

The radio operator shook his head. 'Tweets of course. Rough, some of them.'

'Your wife phoned earlier, sir,' one of the computer guys said. 'Nothing important. And a call from a witness who says that on Wednesday morning he remembers seeing a driver changing a wheel on a small van on the Heydon slip road.'

'Give that to the DI as soon as he comes in. Heard from those two constables he sent down to the docks?'

'Phillips and Toms?'

'Mmm. The girls down there know anything about our murdered woman?'

'No joy so far, but the lads are still making enquiries.'

'Taking their time, aren't they?' He looked at his watch. 'What else?'

'Beattie and Jackson've caught a kid trying breaking and entering. They're bringing him in now.'

'Just up Jackson's street – preventative policing.'

'There was a scuffle down near the bus station a while ago, nothing serious, just good humoured leftovers from a stag party. Trying to put the bridegroom head first in a rubbish skip. You know the sort of thing.'

The radio hissed, and Jackson came on. 'We're on our way back with this fucking little bastard...'

'Remind Jacko when he comes in we could do with a little less language on the air waves.'

'Sir.'

'And give the kid's parents a wake-up call.'

'Yes, sir.'

Down at the incident desk they were dealing with the regulars, a couple of addicts, a drunk or two, a speeding motorist as well, by the sound of it. The shouts of protest were all too familiar, yet the Desk Sergeant there was managing to maintain a polite cordiality. Blake helped himself to a coffee out of the machine in the hall and returned to his office. He hated being confined to the station in the small hours. Under cover of darkness so much could happen out there and there was practically nothing you could do. The ordinary people of the district were at rest, investigations came to a halt, and this building itself took on a kind of harshness, an echoey, haunted quality.

He sat down at his desk and reached for the files again. He cast aside the drugs report the DI had given him earlier telling him to be sure to read, and pulled the one under it out again and opened it. The missing child's little face stared up at him.

'Where are you, Angie?' he whispered.

He glanced back up at the map and then at the clock on the wall above it. Three o'clock. A few hours more of darkness before they could return in earnest to the search. Tomorrow they would have to fan out further, and locally get closer in, begin retracing their steps, and see what they might have missed.

His head was pounding. He pulled a pack of pain killers from his desk drawer and swallowed a couple with the coffee. Another five hours on duty yet before the DI would be back and he could go home and get some rest.

CHAPTER ELEVEN

Picturing Suzie, Velalley thought how easily a trusting child abandons itself to sleep, arms flung wide, in total peace. But sleep did not come easily to Faye Simmons in the last hours of that night. Nor to Velalley herself.

Faye wasn't exactly asleep anyhow. She had sunk into a kind of unconsciousness, a weird level of half awake slumbering. She was fighting the effects of the sedative given to her earlier by her doctor, determined against all odds to stay alert in case. For Angie. Nevertheless the night hours and the tension had got the better of her, and she lay on the sofa with her eyes closed in a sort of trance-like immobility.

Velalley sat watching over her, much as she did with Suzie when she woke with her nightmares, and she listened for Faye's feverish breathing and an occasional anguished little moaning sound. The fire on low level gave the room a soft red glow creating long dark shadows.

She shifted uncomfortably in her chair. Sitting so still was making her cold. She did not dare to turn the heat too high for Faye's sake but so far she had resisted the thought of robbing Angie's carefully made little bed of its duvet for herself.

After a while though, she could bear the cold no longer. Perhaps there was a blanket. Something. She rose and moved quietly across the room into the bedroom. Inside the only cupboard were the child's clothes, heartbreakingly small. Two dresses and a playsuit properly pressed and hanging neatly on old wire coathangers. Little piles of knickers and vests, ironed and folded. For Faye herself no more than jeans, a shabby skirt and blouse, an anorak, a couple of jumpers, and a worn pair of black court shoes. No spare blankets.

Velalley glanced over at the child's bed, the folded white nightie, the elderly threadbare teddy, very likely into its second generation. Behind her in the other room Faye began her faint moaning again. She gathered up the duvet, and the bear.

Faye's forehead was creased in anguish, and the dark hair circling it was damp with sweat; it was a fragile face, with delicate features. Aside from the dark lines under her eyes, she might be quite beautiful. Velalley knelt down and tucked the old teddy in next to her. Disturbed but not actually alert, the young woman's body instinctively curled in around it and her cheek found the comfortable softness of its aging fur.

Another hour passed before Velalley herself began to doze. Thank God Suzie was in her mother's hands tonight of all nights. Beth's child... No. Her child now. Her child at least was safe from harm...

She woke up with a start and took a moment to register where she was. Over on the sofa Faye was still in her comatose state.

It was getting light. She looked at her watch: six a.m. Stretching away some of the stiffness, she eased her aching body forward out of the chair. It was colder. She turned up the fire and crept past Faye into the damp little bathroom.

On the way back she stopped at the window and looked out. Down below in the street there was a cluster of several cars, and a small crowd of people, and while she watched a police car pulled up. Her heart turned over. Something was happening. Closing the kitchen door quietly behind her, she reached for the mobile phone.

'Sergeant Blake? One of our cars just arrived.'

'Yeah, you've got a problem, Velalley. The press know where you are.'

'God, Simmons can't take that, sir. What'll we do?'

'Stay where you are. We've got people there. No one'll get up unauthorised. If you need anything, radio down. Anything at all.'

'There's static. The signal's still not good.'

'Ring me then.'

'Any progress?' she asked hopefully.

'Nothing yet.'

'When I saw the car I thought –'

'Yeah.' He sounded depressed. 'The grandparents will be there soon. When they come you can have a couple of hours, and Colston can be on hand.'

'I'm not sure. Do you really think...'

'Oh, and Velalley –'

'Hang on, sir, there's someone at the door.'

The bell had woken Faye. As Velalley hurried past to answer it she sat up staring. It was dreadful having to dash her hopes. 'Just one of our lot, I'm afraid.'

Velalley put her foot against the door and opened it just a crack in case. A tall handsome woman with a mane of black hair stood there, flanked by a shorter sour faced man of about fifty. 'Where is she then? Where's our daughter?'

'Mr and Mrs Longman?'

Behind them Judith Colston was hesitating nervously by the top of the stairs.

'We're here now,' said Ida Longman, pushing in past Velalley. 'She doesn't need you.'

CHAPTER TWELVE

FRIDAY

After a clear cold start, dry and sunny for most of the day, with some cloud developing towards evening. Wind from the north east, light to moderate...

Velalley switched off the car radio and turned left past the High Street to call in at the station on her way home.

Sergeant Blake's frustration was showing. His normal easy going humour was beginning to fray at the edges. 'Nothing yet. Not a sodding thing! No witnesses in the car park. Nothing! We reckon she was probably taken down the cutting that runs along the rear.'

'Where's that lead?'

'Straight to the canal. They're dragging it now.'

Velalley kept a grip on herself. 'Anything else?'

'This supermarket girl, the one who thought she saw the kid taken – she says the young woman can't have been more than fifteen as the outside, and quite possibly younger. It ties in. In her statement she mentions a navy blue anorak.'

'But Angie was in a pale blue shell suit, according to Faye.'

'Wake up, Velalley! The witness means the other girl. Sort of school look about her, she said. I've asked Colston to find out if Simmons remembers seeing anyone like that.'

'She has no real recollection, just a feeling of someone nearby. But that place is always so busy. Did you see my notes?'

Blake nodded curtly.

'Any progress on Angie's father?' she asked.

'No name on the birth certificate, but that address on the airmail envelope you found – a girlfriend in Australia. We've traced her – she says Faye would probably kill her for telling but there was a Chris 'Dowry', 'Dory', something like that. We're working on it.'

'What about the art school connection?'

'The grandparents say he went to a different college. According to them he was a bit of a thug.'

'Might explain why she's not anxious to see him,' Velalley suggested. 'Anyway she told me the parents never met him. She seems so certain he's not involved.'

'We can't be sure till we find him. There's nothing on the voting register. They're sorting through the records of art colleges down in the office. Three of the original four in the area have closed. It's going to take time. It'd help if you could get something on it from Simmons herself.'

'She clams up on it.'

'Doesn't she bloody realise?' He sighed. 'Okay, okay. Keep trying.'

'What about those reporters? How long can we keep them at bay?'

'There's plenty for them to get their teeth into now with the Marilyn Farr case. With a bit of luck they'll home in on her! Anyway they've got the kid's photo and we're keeping them informed on the search. The DI's left strict instructions they shouldn't have access to Simmons or her family. Don't want it turned into a media circus. There'll be someone on the door night and day.'

'I didn't like leaving her with them, sir.'

'Who? The Longmans? They're her parents, aren't they?'

'Yes, but –' She tried hard to stifle a sudden yawn. It had been a long night.

He looked at her sympathetically. 'Go on, get home for a couple of hours while your luck's in.'

She hesitated by the door and looked back at him. 'Who's Marilyn Farr?'

'Your motorway discovery.'

As she passed the switchboard, one of the telephone operators called to her: 'Velalley? Your Mum rang a few minutes ago. The kid's not well apparently but she says not to worry, she's there.'

Until she pulled into the busy car park, her head buzzing with awful thoughts of chicken pox symptoms and what Suzie might now need, Velalley had not realised quite where she was heading. Now the domed shape of the Eastern Shopping Mall loomed like the Taj Mahal ahead of her, the last place Angie had been seen.

The walls of the Broad Walk were decorated with a bright tiled frieze on a Sailor's Hornpipe theme. Jolly Jack Tar, yachts, ships – the kind of passenger liners nearby Southampton was famous for. Seagulls. Lurid blue ocean. The Broadwalk led through into the main circular hall and the supermarket's entrance. The centre was already packed with morning shoppers, but there were other people too, eating in the informal tables set out in the restaurants on the lower floor, or window shopping, or just leaning over the chrome railings. Kids too, hanging around. Half term, of course. In these milling crowds how easy it would be to disappear. Who would see you here, among so many others?

As she took a trolley and wheeled through gathering the shopping she needed, a small boy wandered past her and she was impelled to say: 'Where's your mother?'

The child stared at her vacantly. Then a woman ran up, grabbed him and glared at Velalley. As he was led away there was a resounding slap and a howl which made Velalley feel guilty. He hadn't actually done anything. Other shoppers looked at her, then averted their eyes.

She winced. It destroyed trust, and incident like this. People became suspicious of even the most ordinary reactions. But wasn't it all too easy to let children wander? I have to make Susie want to stay beside me, she thought, involve her, so that what I'm doing interests her. But she knew there were bound to be times when she'd look away, preoccupied with some case or other. Today was a good example she realised as she paid the cashier. She'd done all the shopping on remote control.

'Isn't Erik back yet?'

Her mother didn't seem perturbed. 'I'm sure my neighbour can be prevailed on to keep an eye on my flat.' The doctor was due to call later in the morning, merely a formality, Laura said, since it was almost certainly chicken pox, what with Marietta.

Suzie was tucked up in bed looking flushed and uncomfortable.

'Would you like anything, darling? Some orange juice maybe?'

'Granny Laura'll get it if I do.'

The remark stung Velalley like an arrow. She felt useless and accused, her new position as Suzie's protector challenged by her own mother. She bit her tongue and told herself not to be so stupidly ultra-sensitive. She managed to smile and say: 'It's nice having Granny around, isn't it?'

'Where's Ewik?'

'He'll be home very soon.' She took Suzie in her arms and gave her a cuddle.

When eventually she was downstairs again, Laura demanded: 'So who's going to look after the child?'

'Mum, I'll organise it.'

Her mother shrugged her shoulders. 'I can stay on.'

'I can't ask you.'

'And why not?' She sounded offended.

'It's not fair, Mum.'

'Look Jane, it's good for me. She's so like Beth. And anyway, if you can't be here, at least she can have her grandmother.'

'Mum –'

'Don't argue,' said Laura, taking over, 'how long have you got?'

'I'm back on duty at three. The woman's parents are with her now.'

'See?' Laura was triumphant. 'We grandparents are some use! A rest for you first then. I'm going to do that pile of ironing.'

'You mustn't! I just haven't had a chance –'

'I'm doing it, and I'll wake you before two. Then you can freshen up and have something to eat before you go back.'

As Velalley undressed she tidied the bedroom, vaguely hanging up a blouse from yesterday, gathering up small things for washing, putting away a pair of Erik's shoes. She was puzzled to see sand in them. Tipping it out into the washbasin she stared uncertainly at it. They hadn't been to the beach for ages.

She pulled the curtains across shutting out the brightness of the morning. It was always odd preparing to sleep when other people had begun the day. Disorientating. In the warmth and comfort of bed, she let her thoughts return to Faye. At least having her parents with her would be a help. It was such a relief to have her own mother here now, doing things for her, and to know that Suzie was in safe hands.

Was it this afternoon Erik said he would be home? She closed her eyes. In the summer they would take Suzie to the beach... they would lie together on the warm yellow sand, holding hands, and watch the child running in and out of the waves.

CHAPTER THIRTEEN

Angie put her hand out to the chair beside her and used it to lever herself even further back against the back of the chair. Under her fingers the stained stretch cover was stiff and matted and she picked at it nervously with her fingernail.

Outside the window white clouds were scudding across the early afternoon sky. Their shadows crossed the roofs of the houses and darted over the wasteland, then scooted up the hill leading out of the town and away over the green fields beyond. Straight down below on the North West Road, though it made Angie dizzy to watch for too long, cars waited at the traffic lights and then drove on. She thought how little and pretty they were, like the toy car at the supermarket Mummy let her ride sometimes.

But it was Carrie, not Mummy, who came into the room carrying a tray of food. There was a familiar hamburgery sort of smell. On the tray were two burgers in buns, clumsily made and drenched in tomato sauce, and a can of lager.

Carrie held out one of the plates.

'Come on.'

Angie shook her head. Her tummy felt taut and achey

but somehow she didn't want that to stop, not until Mummy came. She tucked both her hands behind her back and pressed harder against the back of the chair.

The older girl shrugged and put one hamburger at Angie's end of the low table and sat down on the couch to eat her own.

'Okay. You can do what you want.' She sounded cross again. For a while she sat, munching silently and watching.

Angie began picking nervously at the back of the stretch cover again, where Carrie couldn't see.

'On Christmas Eve,' Carrie said suddenly, 'when I was a little kid Mum left out cake for Father Christmas. And when I'd gone to bed and couldn't see, she said he ate it! Finished the lot.'

Crumbs on the plate, lovely shiny glitter – magic snow from his boots Mummy said. Excitement, warm hugs, the rustle of paper on little homemade presents. Angie looked across at the soggy hamburger and then back at Carrie. This didn't feel a bit like Christmas.

'Don't believe in him, eh? Sensible kid.' Carrie licked her fingers. 'Want to see what my mother bought me before she went away?'

She stood up and offered her hand.

Angie stayed where she was.

'Okay. I'll bring her in here.'

Her? For a moment while Carrie was out of the room Angie was elated at the thought of someone else being here. A mummy, a grown-up, anyone, then she wouldn't have to be so frightened anymore. She leaned eagerly round the chair, straining to hear a voice, some sound.

After a couple of minutes Carrie returned. In her arms

was a small figure dressed in a blue frock, with a head of shining yellow hair and bright staring eyes.

'Meet Madeline.'

She held the doll up close to Angie's face and the little girl felt the cold brush of the beautiful plastic lips on her cheek. She stretched out a hand.

'Don't touch,' screamed Carrie, and slapped her sharply on the arm.

The sting of it made Angie's eyes smart and she shrank back. Carrie grabbed her and pulled her roughly out of the chair and over to the couch. She struggled but the teenager was sturdily built and her grip was too strong.

'Now,' said Carrie forcefully, letting go suddenly and breathing fast as she concentrated on arranging the doll on the couch, 'you and Madeline can sit together like good girls. And if you don't I'll smack you. Very hard next time.'

Fearfully Angie obediently worked herself back into the seat and sat very still.

Carrie took another swig of lager to stop a sudden bout of coughing. Then she picked up the uneaten hamburger and put it on the couch between the doll and Angie.

'Maybe you're both mice,' she said softly, in complete change of mood, 'and come creeping, creeping, in my flat and you find a dinner on the chair.'

Angie turned her head away.

Outside the window the little white clouds were flying, flying away, and their shadows were running, running, running up the hill, back to their mummies.

CHAPTER FOURTEEN

To Velalley it seemed barely a few minutes since she'd closed her eyes when her mother woke her with a cup of tea.

'The doctor's been,' Laura said, pulling back the curtains, 'and I was right, of course. The spots are already beginning to show. He thinks it's a mild case, but he says call if we need him. Suzie's to stay in bed, or wrap up warm by the television. He's keen on that idea for later – it'll keep her mind off scratching. He thinks it's wonderful you've taken Suzie on. Oh, and he's very impressed you're comforting that poor mother.'

'How did he find out?'

Laura hesitated at the door.

'You didn't tell him!'

'Shall I make you bacon and eggs?'

'What I said to you was confidential Police business. Mum!'

'It was on the news,' Laura said defensively.

Velalley sighed heavily. 'What I'm doing wasn't.'

'Have a nice shower, dear, and come down. Oh, and Erik rang. He wants to talk to you. He left a number. I said you'd phone him back.'

Velalley swung herself out of bed. 'Why isn't he home?'

The hot shower and washing her hair brought her back to life. She dressed and went downstairs. There was a neat pile of ironing in the living room and a delicious smell of bacon frying in the kitchen.

'I'll make up the beds with fresh linen later,' Laura called. 'How many eggs? Two?'

A lilty voice answered the phone, maddeningly chummy and feminine. '…hs's Hotel?'

'Can I speak to Erik Velalley?'

'Who shall I say is calling?'

'His wife,' Velalley said coldly.

'Just one moment.'

Erik came on the line. 'Jane.'

'Where the hell are you?'

'London'

'I realise that!'

'Listen, when are you off duty?'

'Never,' she said. 'Things are desperate.'

'Come on, I need to talk to you.'

'You're talking to me.'

'I can't say this on the phone.' His voice was different somehow.

She paused, her fingers slipped a little on the receiver. 'What do you mean?'

'Why didn't you let me know Suzie was ill?'

'It's only chicken pox. Most children get it.'

'You taking time off to take care of her?' The usual criticism.

'Are you?'

His silence was only to be expected. 'Anyway Suzie's fine. Mum's staying.'

'As always, the career girl.'

'God, I don't need this.'

'All right, all right.'

'I didn't know you had a conference.'

'I told you, Jane, but you weren't listening. So when have you got time off?'

'I'm caught up on a case.'

'What's new?'

'That missing child.'

'Oh.'

'Tomorrow afternoon? I'm not due in to work until five. When are you back?'

'Okay, tomorrow. I'll be back then.'

'What do you mean, you need to talk to me?'

But Erik had hung up. She replaced the receiver thoughtfully. She was sure he hadn't mentioned any conference.

Three police cars and a street fracas greeted Velalley on her return to duty.

'What's happening?' she gasped to the rookie officer on the door when she'd skirted her way through it.

'Bloody press,' he said, 'they're fighting for the story.'

'Can't we fend them off?'

'They've had word from Simmons apparently. It's out to the highest bidder.'

'You're kidding!'

Colston was inside, in the hall. 'I'm due off,' she said, looking at her watch.

'What? Couldn't you stay a few minutes?'

'I've got a dental appointment.'

'Okay, okay.'

Velalley bounded up the stairs.

Inside the flat Faye was sitting wide-eyed, as if she might be on the verge of complete hysteria. She was hardly in a fit state to be giving interviews.

Ida Longman looked at Velalley implacably. 'You don't seem to understand. It's worth a lot of money – money she could well do with to help her get a proper place, be independent. Tell her, George.'

'Are you insinuating we don't know what's best for our own daughter?' demanded George Longman.

Velalley turned to Faye. 'The DI's instruction to me is no press access. I'd have to clear it with him first. And you don't have to do this.'

'It'll raise public awareness,' George Longman pointed out.

'This is madness, Faye. I don't think you understand what you'd be taking on. The flat would be full of reporters and photographers all firing questions at you.'

'Surely it would be worth it,' Ida insisted.

Velalley kept her eyes on Faye who shrank away from them all, as if she was being physically squeezed into the corner of the chair.

'Angie's photograph is already in all the papers today, and on every TV news nationwide, Faye. There's huge public sympathy. We don't know where Angie's being held. We don't want to… we can't jeopardise her chances. Honestly it's really not worth it.'

'But what about Angie's future?' demanded the child's

grandmother. 'Doesn't she have a right to be financially secure?'

'Mrs Longman, what Angie has a right to,' Velalley faced her, phrasing her words very carefully, 'is for us to find her just as quickly as we can. There's loads of helpful press coverage without doing this. Controlled information is what we need. What if the person who took Angie reads something we say?' She glanced over at Faye knowing she must realise the implications. 'Talking directly to the press may not be in the child's best interests right now.'

Ida Longman retreated to the window and stood looking down on the commotion in the street below.

Velalley turned back to Faye. 'If you really want to do this, it'll be possible later. When Angie's... back. And you said –'

Faye buried her head in her hands.

'You could make an appeal on television now to the public if you feel up to it. If that's what you want. And everyone, everyone, Faye, will see it.' She paused letting those words sink in. 'But the Chief Superintendent has already been doing that at every opportunity. People don't expect you to appear – they understand how distraught you must feel.'

Faye shook her head suddenly as if she'd suddenly come to her senses. 'No, not TV. I don't want my picture taken.'

'If you invite them up here you won't be able to avoid it. Even if not TV, you will be on the front page of every national newspaper. So what do you want to do?'

Faye looked ruefully across at her mother and then back at her. 'How do we put a stop to it?'

Velalley breathed a sigh of relief. 'I'll see how the DI wants to handle it.'

In the relative privacy of the kitchen she rang in and spoke to Kendrick.

'Christ, I'm up to my neck. Okay, Velalley. You're on your own. Go down there, put it nicely, but get rid of them. And don't screw up!'

She descended the stairs trying to work out what on earth she was going to say. Mrs Simmons has no comment... No. Mrs Simmons apologises....

She took a deep breath and stepped out onto the doorstep beside the other PC into a barrage of reporters. Flashlights popped and made her blink even though it was still bright daylight. She cleared her throat. There was expectant silence. 'I'm sure...'

'Speak up!'

She swallowed nervously and spoke up, 'I'm sure you will all understand how... how distraught Mrs Simmons is over the disappearance of her daughter. What she needs most at this moment is privacy. She is unable to make any statement... personally... but she has asked me to say that... she is very grateful for your sympathetic coverage. And she thanks you for continuing to do your utmost to help the authorities find little Angie... for her.'

The faces were all staring up at her, wanting more. She stepped back, looked down at her shoes, then turned to go inside.

'Is that it?'

'How's she coping?'

'Did she do it?'

'What's it like, waiting?'

Velalley stepped back into the hall.

'Well done,' whispered the PC, as he shut the door firmly between them.

Back upstairs Velalley made some tea and then arranged with Sergeant Blake for temporary accommodation in the area to be found for Mr and Mrs Longman.

'Ring in again when they want transporting. I hear it's rough down there.'

'It's okay, sir, we're coping.'

'Tell the parents they are not to speak to the press. We're into Angie's second day. It's moving into a more dangerous phase.'

'Yes,' Velalley said quietly. Suddenly she wished Erik would come home.

'Are you still there?'

'Yes, sir.'

'It's been a bad day here so far too. A couple of burglaries, a hit and run. It goes on.'

'Does it ever stop?'

CHAPTER FIFTEEN

Detective Sergeant Blake hung up his coat and took off his uniform jacket wearily. It was 7 p.m. and his wife was out, gone to her meditation evening or some such, but there was a note on the kitchen table. He picked it up.

'Three minutes on full power.'

He opened the microwave. Shepherd's pie and peas. He poured a scotch while he waited for the ping. Then he seated himself at the kitchen table and ate, grateful for the undemanding isolation. In the fridge he found a strawberry yoghurt for dessert. Then he washed up the cutlery and plates and put them away, made some coffee, and sat himself down in a comfortable chair with the missing child's file.

He studied again the photograph Velalley had brought in: Angie hugging a scuffed yellow teddy. The blue eyes caught looking up in a moment of fun. A pretty little kid, he thought, slowly tracing the shape of her face with his finger.

So where do you start looking when a child disappears?

He began turning over what little information there was in the file. When he came to the end he was no wiser. Thirty-three hours had passed and still there was practically nothing to go on, no clues to piece together, and no witnesses. But like discovering the identity of the murdered woman, somebody somewhere knew. The dog belonging to that girl who'd worked with Marilyn had been the clue there. And someone must know something in this instance too, or seen something. There was that girl at the supermarket – perhaps if they talked to her again.

This case was getting to him like nothing else ever had before. It was frustrating and humiliating to feel so bloody helpless.

'I'm quite sure it must be a sin to be so proud,' his mother whispered to him, the day years ago when his appointment was confirmed in the county's police force. 'My only son, standing up for law and order.'

Policing isn't what it was though, he thought, not the comfortable bobby-on-the-beat image it used to be. It had changed with the years like he had. Once he had enjoyed it, felt he was getting somewhere, that he stood for something, but all the technology and innovative detective work in the world and the mountains of paperwork all meant nothing if in the end the criminals had nothing to fear from the law. It was a battle against the courts now. A youth who knifes a man is set free, a rapist is given a suspended sentence, a convicted murderer is given the day off from jail to murder again. Could you take pride in the job when there was no proper justice?

He took a comforting sip of coffee and leaned back in the chair. No wonder ordinary people resorted to violence easily; the simple protest marches of his youth seemed polite affairs compared to ugly inner city riots, or internet crime. Now turning over the stone exposed a kind of criminal he could never have imagined once. Society seemed to have lost its way and it was becoming more and more difficult to keep control. Nevertheless he was entrenched. The Force was his life and he couldn't visualize any other. Thank goodness, though, his mother wasn't around to see the goings-on now. As for the idea of someone in this town snatching a young child...

'Whoever your are,' he whispered, 'I'll –'

The phone ringing made him jump.

He picked it up urgently. 'Blake?... oh, it's you, Denholm.'

'Any news?'

'Not a sodding thing.'

'I see the press and TV boys have been bugging the mother. Who's the WPC?'

'Jane Velalley. It's a good thing, I think, to have a woman in there on this one.'

'I'll be picking up the pieces with the victims when she's through.'

'I'll let you know when we get to the counselling stage.'

'Hope you find the child.'

'Christ, so do I. I'm getting too old for this game.'

'You?'

'Me.'

'You haven't got much longer to go – three years, is it? It'll fly past.'

'But in the meantime it's a nasty world out there,' Blake said, bending the blind at the window beside him and thinking how cold and crisp and dark it was outside.

'You don't see the half of it,' Denholm said. 'I get the

victims, those poor sods who have to work out how to survive afterwards.'

They hung up.

Three more years.

A vague, meaningless retirement wasn't something Blake had ever looked forward to before. Sometimes he even resented the younger men at the Station with all that interesting work stretching out ahead of them.

But not tonight. Not tonight.

'The world's changed, Mum,' he sighed, as he felt in his trouser pocket for the car keys.

He looked at his watch, finished his coffee and forced himself wearily back into the jacket of his uniform and his topcoat.

CHAPTER SIXTEEN

Ida Longman paced up and down the small living room of Faye's flat, wringing her hands. 'What can the police be doing?'

'As soon as there's anything, they'll contact us,' Velalley said.

'I told you, Faye, didn't I? I told here living here was a mistake.'

'A financial disaster,' George chipped in.

'But oh, no. She won't take our advice. Independent to a fault, our daughter – ever since she met that man.'

'Do you by any chance remember which art college he went to, Mrs Longman?'

'I don't know. Can't she tell you?'

Velalley glanced quickly over at Faye.

'There seems to be some confusion,' she said protectively.

'She packed it all in,' George said, 'just when things were going well. All that expense. A year into the course and all the work. Turned round and told us she had packed it in. Didn't see her for months.'

'Then,' said Ida, 'out of the blue, there's Angie.'

'She never confided in us, never asked our opinion.

And he didn't stay around, did he? Left her in the lurch, young devil.'

'He should be contributing to the child's keep. It's the law, isn't it?'

'Faye doesn't know where he is,' said Velalley carefully. Her support at this moment might pay off.

'Is that what she told you?'

'She protects him,' George said, 'and why should we help? Our savings don't stretch to it.'

'I've never asked you to,' Faye burst out.

Velalley went to her side. 'I don't think this is really the time for recriminations.'

'What kind of life is this?' Ida muttered, moving round the room picking up small items, inspecting them and putting them down again. She came to a tiny drawing of Angie. 'Faye did this. See? A child, I ask you, in a place like this.'

'Put that down,' Faye cried hysterically.

Ida stared at her daughter, then obeyed, carefully balancing the picture back on the shelf.

Velalley leaned down, speaking privately to Faye. 'Do you want them to go?'

Faye sighed. 'It's late. They need a good night's sleep,' she said generously.

'They weren't always so bad,' she said, when they'd driven off to their temporary lodgings, and Velalley had made her some tea. 'I've disappointed them. I'm not the daughter they remember. I've changed.'

'This Chris,' Velalley began, 'we're still trying to trace him –'

Faye turned on her, eyes blazing. 'Leave it alone, can't you?' She drew back into her chair and stared fixedly into the orange and blue glow of the gas fire.

Velalley sat in shocked silence for a while, watching her, unsure what to say or do for the best.

When Faye spoke again her voice was calmer. 'I might as well tell you, so you'll understand.'

Velalley remained silent, receptive.

'My parents scraped together enough for me to go to Art College – and I loved it. It was the best year of my life, the work, making new friends. And maybe I'd have got somewhere with it.'

She hesitated, as if she might not continue. She edged even further back into the chair pulling her bare feet up and hugging her knees defensively. 'Anyhow, one night there was an inter-college party. It was fun. We all had a few drinks. There were drugs there of course, but that wasn't my scene. Quite late in the evening I met Chris and we started talking. He was nice enough, very interested in painting. We seemed to have a lot in common. He asked me where I lived and offered to take me home, and I though why not? He was nice looking, polite. He opened the car door for me, we chatted. It took me several minutes to realise we weren't on the right road – we were heading out of town. I thought maybe he'd missed the turning and I said, Chris, this isn't the right way, but he took no notice. I said, Turn round, please. He just kept on driving. No answer. Nothing. I pleaded with him to take me home but he didn't.

'Eventually he stopped the car out in the middle of a dark field, not a light or a house in sight. And he started to ... touch me and...' Her chin began to quiver and she fought to control it. 'I panicked. I got out of the car – stupid, I know, but I thought I might make a run for it... and then he began hitting me...' her face contorted as she confronted the memory. 'I really thought he was going to kill me... I think he would have... only then I made up my mind.'

She glanced across at Velalley.

'I let him rape me... I made out I liked it. I told him how wonderful he was... and afterwards... afterwards he actually drove me home, just as if it had been some ordinary date! I made myself kiss him goodnight and promise to go out with him, and I waved to him as he drove away. It was the most awful, terrifying night of my life... but I'd survived – and there was a kind of victory in that for me. Do you see?'

Velalley nodded.

'And the next day I went to the Master of the college and told him what had happened.'

'That took courage.'

Faye laughed bitterly. 'Well, he didn't believe me – in spite of the bruises! He told me I must be imagining it, that it was obvious I'd consented. Much later I realised he was probably more concerned about the College's reputation than one student's problems. They were after a huge grant at the time. But I left that day. I was really scared I'd see Chris again. I mean, he'd driven me home to my flat – he knew exactly where I lived. I packed up and moved in with a girlfriend. Then a few weeks later I discovered I was pregnant. I was so stupid I hadn't even thought about the morning after pill.

'Well, the Master hadn't believed what had happened so why should anyone else? Anyway by then it was sort of too late. I just wanted to forget, find some new direction for myself and to get over that dreadful feeling of being used – of being responsible.'

'But you weren't!'

'Oh, I know that now. Anyhow I didn't have an abortion. That would've compounded the problem for me – and added to the awful irrational feelings of guilt. It was bad enough. So I changed my name and moved here. And Angie was born. Her little life seemed to make everything right, something beautiful and pure out of an ugly and terrifying moment.'

Velalley stared at Faye, realising she was actually envious of her, of her astonishing strength of character, but even as she watched, the fissures began to show in Faye's composure, the cracks began to open up again, and widen.

'Now if it came to sex I couldn't let go, I know. Taking what he wanted from me in that few seconds of satisfaction for him, Chris robbed me of wanting any physical pleasure with anyone. Now I would just want it to be over. Some victory, eh?'

'You survived, Faye.'

'And for what?' she said, her voice breaking. 'So that Angie could be stolen from me?'

It was 10 p.m. and Colston was due back shortly. The glow of the fire was all that lit the room, and there was still no news of Angie. Faye was curled up on the couch in her restless comatose state again, and Velalley sat leaning forward onto her knees, staring into the flame.

She thought about Erik, and the four years they had been together. To start with wonderful. Even now she could remember every detail of the first time they'd made love, the magic of it, the fierceness of it, and the gentle sweetness. At the beginning she counted the hours until she got home to him, and she loved taking care of him, doing things for him, spoiling him. And he would find little gifts for her: sometimes something to remind her of a walk, a seagull's feather, a polished brown chestnut, a smooth pebble from the beach, or a golden leaf. And they would leave little notes for each other.

It was hard to tell where, with his work and hers, time seemed to have overtaken them, gradually limiting their intimacy and closeness. Somehow there didn't seem to be time to write messages, nor the same opportunities for walks by the river, or days at the beach. No occasional evenings out, not even at the local pub, no quiet moments alone together, and very few late night conversations leading delightfully on into lovemaking. And now in the few weeks since Suzie's arrival into the household, everything seemed to be falling completely to pieces. So determined to prove she could easily be both working woman, wife, and now mother, she knew she had suddenly become angry and sensitive and over defensive.

Surely though, Erik of all people would see she needed time to adjust to her new role.

As soon as this case was over she really must try to organise things better, and make certain to arrange an evening out. And time. Time to make love. Time to just sit and talk.

That's what he wants to do tomorrow, she thought,

cheered now at the prospect of his return. I must tell him how much I care about him. How much I appreciate that he's accepted the idea of Suzie so easily. What if, like Faye, I was on my own?

Without Erik's love and affection it would be impossible to cope – it was as if she drew her strength and confidence from him. Knowing she could rely on him made her feel safe. If she didn't have him…

For a second time she realised she admired Faye. Her courage to survive on her own with her child was extraordinary. But if Angie wasn't found alive, what then? She seriously doubted Faye's capacity to stretch her strength much further. This waiting was unbearable, but what if…

Velalley, though she hadn't been to church for years, found herself praying. Dear God, Angie's just a child like Suzie, a little phoenix risen from the ashes of her mother's dreams. Keep her safe, God, keep her safe for Faye.

CHAPTER SEVENTEEN

Detective Inspector Kendrick was back and wanting a complete update from Blake while he waited by the doors for his transport home. He was in full evening dress and smelt heavily of cigar smoke and Scotch whisky.

'Good do, was it?'

'Bloody awful. A load of political dicks sounding off about accountability. They piss me off. What do they know about policing the streets?'

Blake raised an eyebrow, and immediately wished he hadn't.

'So, just how bloody far have you got?'

'Colston's taken over for the night with Simmons, otherwise there's nothing new on it. Velalley did manage to convince Simmons to give us the boyfriend's name.'

'That's what I want,' he muttered, 'the boyfriend's name.'

'Sorry?'

'There are a couple of photos of our Marilyn in the incident room now,' Kendrick said. 'Take a look at them.' He glanced down at his watch. 'And we ought to do that woman for wasting police time.'

'Simmons? She was afraid –'

'It is him then!'

'No, I don't think so. We have him under surveillance right now but there's nothing suspicious so far. She didn't want him involved because Angie's the result of an alleged rape. According to her, Drury has no idea he has a daughter.'

'Any record of it?'

'She didn't report it. Not officially. Nor did the College.'

Kendrick loosened his bow tie. 'Can't have been much if she didn't pursue it,' he said.

Typical of the man, Blake thought, to see it in that light. 'No other leads?'

'Not a sodding thing.'

A car drew up beside the front doors.

'Right, stay on it. See you in the morning.'

Blake sighed and went back inside. He stopped off to look at the photographs as Kendrick had suggested. One was a black and white portrait. Clearly Marilyn Farr had been a stunningly beautiful woman. The clarity and detail of her injuries in the other print made him feel quite sick.

He headed for Control.

'So what's Drury up to?'

'Nothing, sir. Gone to bed by the looks.'

'Where the rest of us ought to be if we had any sense. I'll be in my office.'

On the way to the Incident Room he stopped at the coffee machine in the corridor and pressed for black and sweet to settle his stomach and keep him awake.

'Sergeant Blake?' Barry called urgently after him down the hall. 'An alarm's gone off, sir, near the Lamb's Head in

Royston Road, round the back of the estate. Phillips says it looks suspicious.'

'Who's he with?'

'Johnson.'

'Tell them to take a look, and for God's sake stick together. I don't want any heroics up at Quale tonight.'

CHAPTER EIGHTEEN

'Mumm-ee!'

It was just after midnight. Jane Velalley rolled dutifully out of bed and padded along the hall towards the soft sheen night-light of the end bedroom.

Suzie was sitting up, wide-eyed and confused, surrounded by a tangle of bedclothes.

'Ssh, darling.' She hugged her tight, whispering, gently rocking back and forth, and slowly Suzie began a garbled attempt to find words to recount her fright. She spoke abstractedly. Velalley repeated what she said. Suzie echoed it back again. It made no sense, but it was understandable that there should be a huge sense of grief even though Suzie was so young. The loss she was feeling would be very deep. Gradually though, with tender coaxing and reassurance, the little girl's fear unravelled into the more mundane childish matters of teddy, and pillows, and the prospect of snuggling down again under the warm bedclothes.

All the while Velalley felt the little fingers idly exploring the lace edging of her own nightdress; she smelled the warmth of the bed, the sweetness of the child's skin, and watched the expressive little face, saw how some strands of Suzie's hair picked up and reflected the light.

While she whispered, she tidied the bedclothes with one hand and held Suzie close with the other. She reached across for the favourite teddy bear. 'He's not frightened, see?'

At first the little body squirmed, the small feet and hands moved restlessly, but the tensions slowly began to subside.

'Everything's all right, you can go back to sleep now, ssh, I'm here,' and with more comforting talk of tucking teddy in, and what they might do tomorrow, eventually Suzie succumbed. Velalley sat for a few moments stroking her hair, watching her drift, then sink into deep sleep.

As she returned along the hall, her mother stirred.

'Jane?'

'It was only Suzie,' she called softly.

She heard Laura turn over sleepily and settle again. Only she herself was wakeful, unable now to stop the nagging fears for Angie taking hold and expanding, filling the darkness.

Angie opened her eyes. A rim of light along the floorboards beside her reminded her where she was. From beyond the cupboard door came the sound of voices, a man's, raised, and Carrie's.

'You not in bed? I've told you before about staying up all hours of the night. You've been drinking again, haven't you?'

'Sod off.'

'Why, you cheeky little cow!' The sound of a sharp slap, then a scuffle. 'Give her to me.'

'You leave her alone.'

More scuffle. There was a grunt of frustration. 'Aw, have her, if you must.' The sound of footsteps, then: 'I've bloody well worked my guts out for you and your mother.'

'In the pub, I know.'

More pacing footsteps, this time towards the cupboard.

Angie shrank away form the angry shouting, the heavy step, the shadow over the rim of light. Then the footsteps moved away again across the room.

'I gotta have some life, Carrie.'

'And leave your kid home alone all week.'

'You're safe enough here.'

'I could ring the social, say you're abusing me, lay it on thick how you hold me down and –'

'I promise you I'll take the strap to you –'

'Beat me! Yeah, why not?'

'You think you're so clever, Carrie Anderson.' The man's voice was quieter now, but barely under control. 'I should have chucked you out with your mother. You're two of a kind.'

'You! Chucked her out?' She gave a weird kind of wheezy laugh. 'She left, don't you mean? I don't blame her running off to Spain.'

'Don't forget she dumped you too.'

'That's not true,' Carried screamed. 'She said as soon as I'm old enough –'

'And how're you going to do that, eh? She's got no money and he won't want you. You bunk off school. You lie. You steal. You'll end up in jail, girl, more like.'

'Fuck off.'

'Go to bloody bed,' the voice had risen again in

frustrated fury. A door slammed. For a few moments there was silence, then the sound of Carrie coughing violently.

Angie sat up frightened out of her wits, sucking her thumb and staring into the darkness. She'd never heard people shouting like that at each other. A little warm stream of wetness left her body and soaked through the shell suit onto the rug underneath.

For a long while she sat there not daring to move, listening to Carrie's distressed coughing increasing as she moved round the room. Then a squeak of bedsprings, the rim of light vanished and the coughing slowly decreased.

Then after a very long time, there was silence.

Her raging thirst made Angie try pushing the door. Nothing. She pushed harder. The ball catch made a little ping as it gave. There was just enough light from the window to see that Carrie was asleep, but her breathing was fast and irregular, as if she was very hot, a kind of strange puffing. But she was asleep.

A little shimmer of moonlight crossed the room, bright enough to pick out the child trembling by the bedside chair and long enough for her to lift Madeline and the can of lager and begin to withdraw on tiptoe back to the darkness of the cupboard.

'Mamaa,' warned the doll in a tinny high-pitched voice.

Carrie stirred. Angie stopped, frozen to the spot, not daring to breathe. Then Carrie snorted and turned over and the wheezy breathing resumed.

Back in her hiding place, what was left of the liquid in the can was bitter tasting, but Angie drank it down eagerly. Then she turned her attention to Madeline. With the cupboard door still slightly open to allow a little light, she examined the painted eyes and the fine hair, the pretty lips. She lay down again, and moved the doll's rigid body closer, comforted by its presence.

'Mamaa,' it called, but Carrie was too far away to hear.

CHAPTER NINETEEN

SATURDAY

Very early before it was truly light, someone began moving around, but it wasn't Carrie. Through the crack Angie could see she was still asleep. She presumed it must be the shouting man getting up.

Then somewhere there was another voice... *clear skies and unseasonably cold air temperatures...* For a brief moment Angie's heart leapt... *but most of the day will be crisp and sunny. Cloud spreading in later from the west will lift temperatures slightly towards dusk and bring outbreaks of rain during the night, giving way to heavy early morning mist and fog...*

After that there was music.

Then it stopped. Footsteps, a door banged and there was silence.

The lager can contained no more liquid, not even the nasty bitter taste remained around the lid to lick, and she discarded it. It clattered over and rolled into the corner of the cupboard before she could catch it.

Carrie stirred. She opened her eyes and yawned.

Fearfully Angie peered through the crack as Carrie climbed out of bed and padded over towards her. Right beside the cupboard she picked her dressing gown up of the floor, crossed the room again and disappeared. She seemed to have forgotten Angie totally. There was the sound of violent coughing, of a toilet flushing, and running water. When she returned she pulled on jeans and a sweater.

'Madeline!'

Angie jumped. Guiltily she felt for the doll and trying not to make a sound, pushed it behind her far into the corner under the rug.

'He's taken her.' Carrie was crashing furiously round the room.

Angie wished Madeline was back out in her rightful place on the chair. She could see Carrie striding towards her again and she trembled at the thought of what the girl might do when she found the doll hidden with her.

But Carrie went on past muttering. 'I'll show him. The bastard.'

Then more noise in the other room, muffled, and then, finally, the front door banged again.

Angie stayed where she was inside the cupboard for a while, waiting, listening for any sound. Finally she scrambled out into the room, her limbs cramped from the enclosed space and from sleeping on the hard floor. She peered nervously round the bedroom door before she dared to venture out into the living room. At the wall of window she spread her fingers on the glass and watched the lines of little cars glinting in the sun as they moved along on the road below.

When eventually she turned back into the room she saw Carrie's lager can from the night before lying on the table. She took it up eagerly but it too was quite empty. Suddenly she caught sight of shadows on the wired glass panel out beside the front door. Mummy?

'Mummy?'

She heard thudding feet. Carrie? No, not just one person. More. Then someone kicked the door, people were whooping and running up and down the landing. Then there was a clatter, and something dropped through the letterbox.

Crrr-aack! Crack!

The bangs made Angie jump. Terrified she hid down behind the couch. When she dared to look, whatever it was lay smoking on the floor, smelling like spent matches. There was much loud laughter outside, then the footsteps and voices faded away. Then there was silence. It was a long time before she felt brave enough to come out from her hiding place.

She began exploring the flat. In the dingy bathroom she struggled and struggled to turn on the zinc bath tap. Her thirst seemed to give her extra strength as she tried one more time. It gave, enough for her to cup her hand under the trickle and drink. She couldn't turn it off. In the kitchen she prised the fridge door open, and recognising the yellow colour and smell of cheese in a half-eaten packet, she broke off one piece, then another, and ate it hungrily. Out in the hall again she sat on the floor with the packet in her lap and watched the door.

After a while she returned to the bedroom and rescued

the doll from the back of the cupboard. She broke off a crumb of cheese and pretended to feed it to her.

Madeline sat there, her bright eyes staring up, then she fell sideways. 'Mamaa.'

Angie rubbed her eyes. 'Mummy,' she whispered, 'Mummy.'

She took the doll onto her lap and fingered its hair, and sat humming to herself.

With the rest of the cheese in her pocket, and Madeline under her arm, Angie wandered back out into the hall. The latch on the front door was very high up and she and Madeline stood for a long time looking at it.

Eventually she put the doll down and went back to the kitchen. Carefully she began to manoeuvre a stool out into the hall. It was a struggle to get round the corner, but pushing sometimes and then dragging, she worked it slowly right the way along to the front door.

When she climbed up and stood on top of it, she could reach the latch with both hands. She twisted the knob. The door sprang open, but as she clambered down the stool pushed against it and the door clicked shut again. Frustrated, she leaned back against the wall. Then she licked her lips and frowned determinedly, and with Madeline in one hand, she climbed awkwardly back up onto the stool again. Standing unsteadily on tip-toe, she stretched up with her free hand and undid the latch a second time. Holding the door open a little way she pushed the doll into the space and let go. Madeline slid slowly and delicately to the floor, half in, half out. Triumphantly Angie climbed down, pulled the door open wide and gathering up Madeline, stepped out on the concrete landing into the brightness of the mid morning sunlight.

Chapter Twenty

Carrie Anderson made her way back along the canal. This time without the hindrance of the child she walked dangerously close to the water on the concrete ledge and now and then bounded up to balance on old railway sleepers which lay beside the path. Sometimes she paused to catch her breath and watch the sun sparkling in the water. The roar of the overhead traffic and the taint of carbon monoxide increased as she approached the motorway bridge. Just beyond it there was a dinghy on the canal and a small group of men on the other bank. For a while she observed them from the shadow of the pylon. A frogman came up beside the boat, and then dived again. She wondered what they were doing.

It was cold in the shadows without a coat and she moved out into the sunshine again. The men appeared not to notice her but she thought better of them seeing her turn into the railway cutting. Instead she followed on upwards towards the road, approaching the Eastern Shopping Mall from the ornate entrance near the car park. Inside the main hall and in no particular hurry, she loitered by the restaurants for a time listening to the footsteps echoing on the tiled tiers, the voices, the general hubbub of the crowds, watching the comings and goings with interest. She considered the thrill of a little pick pocketing, but decided against it. There seemed to be an unusually high proportion of security men on duty.

At the far end there was a disturbance, some shouting and a small crowd gathered, and she wandered along to see what it was. Several women with young children were walking around holding up placards. Some old bag was speaking to anyone who stopped to listen, droning on about safety. 'Our children need protection... law and order... What are the police doing? This government needs to...' So on and so on. Boring.

Back near the supermarket an electronics shop usually had video games on hands-on display. Today only one was 'on demo'. There was a long and rowdy queue. Plenty of local parents sent their children down to the Mall. It was considered a sensible choice. No traffic, and the kids liked going there, so Carrie knew there was nothing to make her stand out from the crowd and she moved with confidence among her peers. It was half term after all. Kids her age had every reason to be off school. Anyway, she remembered, it was Saturday.

Eventually she took a shopping basket and proceeded through into the supermarket aisles, helping herself to goods. Some went into the basket, smaller things found their way into her pockets. The money she had taken from the hiding place in her father's room wouldn't stretch to everything. Beside the sweets she bent down to do up the lace on her trainers, and slipped a bar of chocolate down into her sock. She glanced round. There was nobody to see. She took another. Something sweet might make that little kid more co-operative.

It made sense to buy a meal-for-one for her father. Why she should bother she didn't know except it was a kind of insurance. It might shut him up if he noticed the money was missing. He could hardly accuse her of stealing if she'd taken the cash to buy food for him. She headed for the freezer aisle and chose the cheapest and ugliest.

Now what she wanted was the least busy checkout, to make a quick getaway. At the far end one cashier was signing off, another was waiting to take over. Customers were avoiding it so she hovered nearby fiddling with the choice of foil wrap, her breathing quickening. The replacement girl sat down, switched on her light and removed the Sorry-Closed sign. Carrie moved in.

A queue built immediately behind her. She watched as the cashier rang up the goods one by one from the basket. The till bleeped and buzzed, the girl leaning back and forth methodically. Carrie handed her the ten-pound note, and packed the items as casually as possible into a free plastic carrier while she waited the few seconds for her change. Then she was away.

Outside in the Broadwalk she grinned, and pausing to open a packet of sweets she'd taken, popped one into her mouth to stop a sudden bout of violent coughing. Then she sauntered confidently towards the Mall's main exit. More coughing.

'Just a moment, Miss.'

The shock of the arresting hand landing squarely on her shoulder snatched all her breath away at once. She felt wildly unsteady, as if someone had just thumped her in the chest. Around her the Mall began to spin, she wanted to be sick as she gasped for air.

'Hey! What's the matter? You needn't think –'

She was vaguely aware of other people running towards her as she tried desperately to breathe. The security guard seemed to be swaying and waving his arms.

'Quick, get some help.'

Now there were more people, and less space.

'It's a fit.'

'She's going blue.'

Everything was spinning round. There was no air, no air.

'Listen. Are you asthmatic?'

She was gasping to stay alive. She couldn't move her head to answer.

CHAPTER TWENTY ONE

Sergeant Blake narrowed his gaze at the young man, sizing him up.

'Is that what she said?' Christopher Drury's pale blue eyes blazed. 'She got what she was asking for, and I never saw her again.'

'That is not the point.'

Perhaps there was little too much temper, a touch too much protest; what she was asking for was an odd way of describing a reasonable sexual encounter – and there was far too little concern for the real question.

'The issue here,' Blake reminded him, 'is the whereabouts of the child.'

'So I'm supposed to have stolen her, am I?'

'You must understand, Mr Drury, we are following up every possibility, every chance. A four year old child has been snatched –'

'How could I take her when I didn't even realise she existed?'

'But we didn't know that for certain, sir. I can assure you we have no intention of stirring up old problems. Unless it becomes necessity of course.' He paused to underline what he had just said. 'We would merely have kept you under temporary surveillance –'

'You weren't very subtle.'

'No, perhaps not.' Toms and Beatty had been far from subtle, openly showing their contempt for Drury by allowing him to sense their presence, and Blake meant to tear them apart for it. 'But now we've established you're not involved –'

'Oh, you've established that, have you? What about my reputation? That woman has made accusations.'

There was a definite likeness to the photo of Angie – the blonde hair, the wide set of the eyes. The suit he was wearing was fashionable and expensive; this art studio, furnished totally in black and white, was light and airy, apart from a strong smell of linseed oil. Instead of curtains, black fabric was draped artistically around the windows. Spread out on a shelf a magazine open at an ad for the Mediterranean, a painting, and original paintings hung round the walls. Women, mostly. A couple of nudes. Blake walked over and took a closer look at the picture still on the easel. A woman bending in over a campfire. The face was striking, and somehow almost familiar. The brush strokes were broad and confident. The man obviously had talent.

'Yours?'

Drury nodded. 'I travel,' he said defiantly. 'I like to record what I see. I spent some time in Cairo recently on an assignment.'

'Advertising pays well then?'

A bead of sweat rose on Drury's flushed temple. He had things to lose.

'So what does she want?'

'From what you say, sir, you have nothing to worry

about, have you? Though there might be a question of maintenance?'

Drury stared at him.

'There have been no official "accusations" – there was reference to the night the child was conceived, simply because we had to find the father.'

'It's her word against mine.'

'As it stands, that's exactly true, sir. The young woman was not at all keen for you to be involved and she had no idea where you might be. It took us time to trace you, and right now with the child at risk, time is what we have very little of. Speaking to you directly has, in fact, speeded things up and so far you have co-operated in a difficult situation. I would say that seems to put you,' Blake tempered his words to disguise his own contempt, 'above suspicion.

'But now,' he said, anxious to return to the search and have done with this disagreeable young man, 'there should be no reason for any further direct contact, either with us in the future I hope, or with the lady. Indeed,' he said firmly, making the warning abundantly clear, 'she is determined there should be absolutely none. Do you understand?'

'I should hope she is!' There was renewed confidence in his strident tone as Christopher Drury showed him out.

Relief probably, Blake thought, as he headed back along the motorway through the Saturday morning traffic. Many men got away with using brute sexual force, but it was a strong woman who could handle such conflict and put her life back together as creatively as Faye Simmons had done.

But Angie was her life...

The call on the radio was urgent.

'Sergeant Blake, sir? You're wanted at the hospital immediately, sir.'

He put his foot down hard on the accelerator.

CHAPTER TWENTY TWO

Angie emerged out into the light after negotiating the difficult descent of the dark concrete stairwell. Ahead of her she saw and recognised the landmark of the wrecked car lying on its side in the shadow of the building. Stripped of its wheels, windows smashed, paintwork scraped and scarred, it threatened a kind of deep despair which she did not understand, but it was typical of everything else she could see here. She hugged Madeline closer and edged past the wreck warily.

She crossed the mud and kicked-up grass of what had originally been a designated playing area. She remembered crossing the road with Carrie and she walked purposefully towards it. There were cars parked on either side.

'Mummy,' she said out loud, and stepped off the pavement. She didn't feel the cross wind of the car hurtling past, didn't hear the terrifying screech of brakes and the dull crunch of metal on metal as she ran out, only the shouts of abuse hurled at her as she reached the safety of the parked cars on the other side. It didn't occur to her to look back.

'Bloody stupid kid! Keep off the fucking roads!'

She slid away from the ugly angry voice, down the

slope and out of sight. She caught and grazed her finger on the jagged rocks at the bottom. Fighting back tears, she sucked it hard and slowly the stinging seemed to diminish.

Her finger still comfortingly in her mouth, she hesitated momentarily, unsure which direction to take. She shaded her eyes. In the very far distance she could see cars flashing along a raised motorway. It seemed familiar somehow, its brightness urgent and attractive. With Madeline tucked under her arm, she headed out into the wasteland towards it, between heaps of foul smelling refuse and rows of empty oil drums.

Beside one of those she found a clump of pretty yellow dandelions, and she stopped to pick some. The spiky yellow petals shone and she thought of making a daisy chain. She sat down and tried to put a hole in one stem like Mummy did, to thread another through. The stem bent and broke. She tried another. After a while she gave up and picked more and made a posy instead. A fat, black beetle scurried past. She sat very still, fascinated by it, watching its progress over the ground. It hesitated by a narrow crack in the hard surface, and wiggled its antennae. She wasn't sure why its legs suddenly collapsed under it and it disappeared head first down into the dark opening. Maybe it had found its way home.

She got to her feet, picked up Madeline again and clutching her posy, pressed on. At first the sun and the exercise cheered and warmed her; but after a while she felt hot and thirsty, and she discarded the flowers which were drooping now and sticky in her hand.

In a barren and unproductive landscape no one saw the tiny child tramping urgently along. Some distance ahead of her lay an abandoned and disintegrating warehouse and beyond that some allotments, and then the motorway and clusters of houses dipping down into the eastern border of the town. Further away, far off to the right and glinting in the sunlight was the canal, and then beyond that the river turning away south towards the darker depths of the sea.

CHAPTER TWENTY THREE

Velalley woke at lunchtime unrefreshed. The tiredness that weighed down on her seemed unrelieved by sleeping. She forced herself out of bed and into her dressing gown, and padded down the hall.

Suzie was lying back on her pillows, flushed and bright-eyed. Velalley sat down on the edge of her bed.

'Are you all right, sweetie?'

'Mmmn. Where's Ewik?'

'He'll be home soon.'

'Today?' asked Suzie eagerly.

She stroked Suzie's forehead, and thought of Faye, deprived of this simple pleasure, something so easy to take for granted. 'Now he knows you're ill,' she said, 'he's coming home specially fast.'

Erik arrived back half an hour later.

'Darling!' she said, but there was something different about the way Erik kissed her. He seemed to be standing back, avoiding her attention.

'Have you been terribly busy? Let me make you some coffee. Where are your things?'

'Where's Suzie?'

'In bed. She's much better.'

'I've brought her these,' he said producing a small picture book version of Cinderella and a cartoon DVD. 'I'll take them up.'

Velalley followed him up the stairs.

Suzie was thrilled. 'Read it? Read, Jane?'

'In a minute, darling.'

'Go on,' said Erik. 'I'll listen too.'

She sat down on the other side of the bed and looked across at Erik. Something was wrong.

'Go on.'

She opened the book, and turned over a few pages. 'There aren't any words!'

For a moment Erik laughed, the familiar spontaneous and deep-throated laugh, but when he saw the way she was looking at him, he looked almost as if he might cry. When he spoke his voice was serious again, self-conscious. 'It's a self expression book – you make up the words from the pictures. Don't you know the story?'

She stood up, irritated. 'You do it,' she said, 'I'll make us some sandwiches.'

Downstairs Laura said, 'I could have done this.'

'Suzie hasn't seen Erik for days,' Velalley said crossly, but her mother could very well have made the lunch, and she wished she'd stayed upstairs.

It was nearly half an hour later when Erik carried Suzie, wrapped in her duvet, down to the living room. He set her up in front of the television and put on the cartoon for her on a low volume. Suzie, with a piece of cake and a glass of squash, sat transfixed to the highly coloured antics on the screen. When he came over to the table, Velalley wondered why she should be feeling so apprehensive.

He sat down and Laura helped him to sandwiches and some of her cake.

'Have you got time to talk now, Jane?'

She watched him pick at the cake, and lick the icing nervously off his finger. 'Why?' she asked.

'What time do you have to go in?'

'Five.' Suddenly she wanted a reason to cut things short, 'or earlier if I can.'

'I imagine you're pretty busy.'

'Yes.' It was like talking to a stranger.

Over by the television Suzie was heavily engrossed in her film.

'Jane,' he began, then he looked across at Laura. 'Could you leave us on our own?'

Whatever was wrong, Laura had sensed it too. Her face had blanched.

Velalley sprang immediately to her defence. 'If it wasn't for her these last two days –'

'I'm sure that's not what Erik means, dear,' her mother's voice had taken on a forced cheerfulness.

'Keep out of this, Mum.'

Laura stood up, said she wanted more hot water in her tea and left the room. She was visibly upset and Velalley bit her lip, desperately wishing she hadn't snapped at her.

Erik leaned his elbows on the table and stared down at his cake. 'Jane, I –'

'What?' she asked.

'Look,' he kept his voice low, 'this is awful. I hardly know how to... Jane, but if I don't tell you –'

'Tell me what?'

He put his head in his hands. 'She wasn't even attractive.'

'Sorry?' she asked abstractedly. Then it hit her like a bullet, shattering her senses. 'Who wasn't?'

'It wasn't like us, not important I mean, and I realise it was just stupid, but...'

She closed her eyes.

'Jane?'

She prayed she hadn't understood him properly. 'What do you mean?'

'I gave her a lift across town and... and –'

She opened her eyes. He averted his.

'We....'

'Who? Someone at work?'

'No. She's a friend of Peter's – that photographer I know. I never meant it to happen, Jane...'

He was talking but he sounded a million miles away. The details were floating past her. She began to push her own cake around on the plate. The icing fell off it, the slice began to crumble.

'What about me?' She could feel her lips trembling, her mouth going dry.

'I've been trying to talk to you for ages now. You always seem to be at work.'

'It's my fault, is it?'

'No, of course not, no.'

'But we could go out. As soon as this case is over.'

'But now there's Suzie –'

'Suzie?'

'No, I didn't mean that.' He covered his face with his hands. 'I don't know what I mean.'

She picked up the teaspoon and held it very tight.

'Jane –'

'Is it..? Her. Is it over?'

'Yes.'

'Then' she said furiously, 'for God's sake, why are you telling me?'

He looked up nonplussed.

'Oh, I see. She was going to tell me?'

'No! No. But I've hated myself for being dishonest with you. I've spent the last two nights trying to think what to do. In the end I knew I should tell you the truth.'

She turned away. 'And now you feel better?'

'No! Jane?'

He tried to take her hand but she pulled it away sharply. 'Pete's suggested I stay with him for a couple of nights.'

'So you can see her?'

'No! That's not possible. I wouldn't! No. But I don't know how things will work out. I'm scared for us.'

She dared to look at his face but her tears were beginning to blur the images. 'I thought you loved me. I trusted you.'

'The last thing I wanted to do was hurt you. I'm trying to be honest with you now because I didn't want you to hear it from anyone else.'

'You'd rather tell me to my face. Thanks.'

'I know it's awful, Jane.'

'You're doing to me exactly what my father did to my mother.'

'I know.'

'And he never came back.'

'But it's over. It was nothing. You have to believe me.'

'So, what's she like?'

'I... um...'

'Tell me!'

'Homely, I suppose, even though she's a model.'

'God!'

'She liked talking to me.'

'And I don't, you mean.'

'You have your career, Jane.'

'You'd better go to her then.' Velalley smeared the tears away with the back of her hand. 'Oh, Christ.'

'Ssh!' He glanced over at Suzie: 'We shouldn't be talking in front of her.'

'Why not? You obviously don't care about her!'

'Ssh! She'll hear you.' He lowered his voice. 'I can't bear the thought that I've let you down, Jane. Now, I mean, just when Suzie needs us.'

'You should have thought of that.'

'Maybe she could come and visit me?'

'What?'

Suzie looked up but a sudden shriek of laughter from the film captured her attention again.

'When you're working?' Erik whispered. 'It might help.'

'It's certainly out of the question! No, no!'

'When she's better.'

'You are leaving then!'

'No, but –'

'If you think I'll ever let you have that child.'

'Listen,' said Erik quietly, with his eyes firmly fixed on Suzie, 'I have no intention of making any trouble for her. She's just a little girl. We're all she's got now, and I want us all to be together but... Oh God, this is so difficult... if we're not – I'm trying to make things right.'

'Right?'

'Jane, listen to us now. If we can't work things out better than this, what kind of a life would that be for Suzie?'

'Did you take her to the beach?'

'Sorry?'

'Your "friend". Did you take her to the beach?'

'Yes, for a walk. How do you know?'

'The sand.'

He looked bewildered.

'Sand in your shoe.' She put her head in her hands and the two of them sat for a while in silence, the mad noises and laughter of the cartoon filling in the background.

'I feel so angry,' she said. 'So hurt. How can you expect me to forgive you?'

'I thought if I told you.'

'If we break up, Erik, what am I going to do?'

'Get yourself a decent babysitter, one that doesn't get spots,' he said almost flippantly, turning angrily away.

'For Christ's sake, be serious. What would happen to the house?'

'Look, Jane, you're jumping to conclusions. I don't think we're sure of anything right now, are we?'

'You were sure enough to go off with another woman when it suited you.'

'It was a mistake, Jane, something I'll regret for the rest of my life.'

'Maybe a fatal error.'

'If you say so.'

'I don't say so,' she said angrily. 'It's not me.'

'You're so damn determined to be superwoman though. When have we spent any time together lately? Can you remember?'

'No,' he said when she didn't reply. 'Nor can I.'

'What about your work?'

'Want me to take some time off?'

'I want –' she faltered, searching for some direction. 'I don't know what I want.'

'You always want everything. How come I ever married you?'

'Why did you then?' she said ferociously.

'You've got dark lines under your eyes,' he observed.

'Thanks a million.'

'You're working too hard. Too many hours.'

'Don't start, just don't start.'

He held up his hands in angry submission. 'Far be it for me to criticise your career.'

'I don't want to discuss it.'

He stood up. 'I'd better go then.'

'Back to your friend?'

'To Pete's, damn it. He just thought it was a good idea for the moment. Give us some breathing space. And I knew you'd –'

'I'd what?'

'I just thought it'd be better if I stayed away for a few nights.'

'Maybe it is.'

'But look, tomorrow's Sunday. I could spend the afternoon here with Suzie. If you're working it would give Laura a chance to go home and get a few things.'

'I don't think –' It infuriated her to think he had time when she didn't. She wanted to deprive him.

'Laura told me about the abduction case.'

She tried to pour herself another cup of tea. 'I'm

detailed to the mother.' Her hand was shaking, and he took the teapot and finished pouring it for her.

'I expect she's in a terrible state.'

A sob caught in her throat. 'Dreadful.'

Erik pushed the cup towards her. 'Jane, please, please, go on loving me. I need you more than you know.'

She turned away, not wanting to listen to another word.

CHAPTER TWENTY FOUR

Carrrie Anderson lay back and looked at the doctor over the clear plastic mask which covered her nose and mouth.

'How do you feel now?' he asked.

She took a breath to speak. 'Okay, I guess.' Her voice sounded muffled and computerised, far away, as if her ears were blocked with cotton wool.

'This mask and equipment we've been using is called a nebuliser, Carrie,' he said, sitting down on the edge of the bed. 'It was the best way of treating you when you were brought in. What we need to do though, is to get your asthma under control for every day. Have you had acute attacks like this before?'

Carrie shook her head. She felt physically very tired and this time it had really frightened her not being able to breathe, the awful clawing for oxygen. The more she'd fought for air, the worse it was – but she wasn't going to tell him.

'Have you had difficulty sleeping lately?' He was making notes on a clipboard as they talked. She shrugged flippantly. 'What about breathlessness after exercise? When you're walking?'

'Maybe.'

The doctor smiled, rewarding her for answering him. 'I'm sorry you're in the adult ward, but it was the only bed we had. This morning wasn't your sort of weather, was it? Those cold air temperatures?'

She looked away, ignoring his irritating professional camaraderie, and heard a pleasing annoyance in his voice when he said, 'Do you understand what happens, Carrie? You should, because it's possible to control asthma. I see you GP has you on Intal, but have you been taking it properly?'

'I take it when I think of it.'

'Your mother could remind you.'

'Yeah. She could ring me from Spain.'

'She's away at the moment then?'

'Pissed off, hasn't she, with her toy boy.'

He glanced up from his notes.

She didn't need his sympathy. 'Who cares about her?'

'So you live with your father? Don't worry, someone will already be informing him you're here.'

'He won't be bothered.'

'Won't he?' More notes. 'Well, Carrie, you should learn how to look after yourself. Asthma affects the airways to the lungs. If you can imagine a tree,' now his voice had gone all professional, 'how its branches divide into smaller and smaller stems. The windpipe is the tree trunk and the airways spread out like branches. With asthma, the patient's airways have a tendency to narrow. There may be an increase in the secretions – the mucus. Then the muscles in the wall of the airway go into spasm, and the walls themselves may swell. It all makes less room for air to get through.'

'I've heard it all before.'

'So you know there are things which might trigger an attack?'

'Yeah, yeah.'

'What do you think caused it today then?'

'How do I know?'

'Well, you need to get to know, Carrie, because it could make a huge difference to your day to day health. Does your father smoke?'

'Sometimes.'

'Do you?'

She didn't bother to answer. What if she did pinch her father's fags? It made her feel better sometimes, more confident.

'It certainly wouldn't be a good idea. Are you eating properly?'

Carrie cast her eyes up to heaven to show him what she thought of that question.

'We'll make sure you take home a list of what to avoid eating and drinking.' He looked at her sideways. 'No alcohol for instance.'

She wondered if he knew about the lager or if he was just guessing.

'Any pets?'

'No chance!'

'That's just as well. Sometimes animal fur can set off an attack. I see you live on the Quale estate.' He made more notes. 'And of course there's the weather. You can't avoid that. What is very bad for you is putting yourself in a stressful situation like today. I hear there's some question about not paying for goods from the supermarket?'

'Fuck off.'

Either he hadn't heard or he didn't take any notice. Perhaps he was just diverted. His bleeper had begun to sound and he stood up.

'If you want to keep well, learn to stay calm, Carrie. Danger may seem like fun, but for someone like you, it could actually be fatal.'

'So what?'

He put the clipboard under his arm. 'I want to keep you in for observation for the moment. Later I'll be giving you a peak flow meter and a chart so that you can monitor your health day to day at home, and a rotahaler for taking medication. From then on your own GP will be keeping a careful eye on you. But basically, Carrie, it's going to be up to you.'

She scowled at him.

He pulled back the orange curtains which had surrounded the bed and supposedly given them privacy. 'I'll see you later then.'

She lifted the mask to make sure he would hear her this time.

'Bugger off.'

He left her to the disapproving eyes of the women on the ward.

'What'ya looking at then, you old bags?'

She smiled to herself suddenly. None of them knew what she had at home in the cupboard.

Chapter Twenty Five

Erik had gone.

Suzie wanted to see her DVD again. It was almost impossible re-programming the player through stifled tears.

When eventually Velalley went out into the kitchen, Laura said: 'Are you all right, Jane?'

She wanted to say, No. No I'm not! I'll never be all right again. She swallowed. 'Fine.'

Laura reached into the refrigerator for some milk for another cup of tea. 'Erik told me at the door what's happened, dear, and I know how difficult all this must be for you but –'

'Not now, Mum, I have to go to work.'

'Jane?' Laura followed her up the stairs. 'We did cope, didn't we, you and Beth and me, together? But it would be too sad to see you try to manage on your own with Suzie.'

'I have to get dressed,' she said, taking her skirt out of the wardrobe and pulling it off its hanger.

'Perhaps I made you too independent.'

'You're saying it's me, aren't you!' Indignation surged up inside her. 'He finds some new woman and it's my fault!'

'Don't cut yourself off, Jane.'

'What?'

'You were just like this when your father left.'

Velalley tried to ignore her and dress.

'Making out you didn't care. You wouldn't write to him – I had hoped he would write to you, but he didn't. You worked so hard at school and I was proud of the way that you particularly took on responsibilities. I loved the way you organised things for me and Beth, but you never mentioned him, never asked about him, or let me talk to you about it. While Beth needed me, you drew away.'

Velalley searched frantically through her underwear drawer for a particular pair of tights. 'He left you when you needed him most, Mum.'

'I had you two.'

'He went off with some other woman as if we were nothing.'

'You weren't old enough to understand.'

'I was eight!' she said, doing up her blouse. 'Anyway, you didn't talk to me about it.'

'I told you what was happening.'

She caught the edge of the dressing table. She felt shaky... Daddy's going... he wants to live with someone else... 'Mum, I'm trying to get ready for work.'

'I tried to explain. It was difficult to know what to say. You wouldn't listen. You shouted at me. You did!' Laura repeated. 'And you shut yourself in your room.'

A fierce sense of guilt engulfed Velalley... stifling, like her mother's embrace that day... her own words rang in her ears, remembered clearly: her fury that her parents would not do what she wanted them to. She shouted she didn't want to hear... she told them she wanted things to go on as they were. They were happy, weren't they?

She'd felt the confusion physically, not wanting to be touched, hugged. And hadn't the same sensation come over her today when Erik told her..? Just the same, as if the remembered hurt was somehow programmed into her?

She sat down at the dressing table and stared at herself in the mirror. Back then, she had wanted to break out, away... After all, wasn't it mummy's fault? Mummy's fault Daddy was going? She wanted to hug her mother, wanted to console her, but more importantly, not to hug her too, to punish her, because wasn't she to blame, driving him away with her constant arguing? Depriving her, her of her father. But then later, in the silence of her bedroom, that wasn't true. It was her own fault, something she had done – not little Beth, she was sweet and loving. No, it was some awful mistake of hers. She was the reason he had stopped loving them and found someone else. And now she saw herself, the little girl sitting alone on the bed playing idly with her doll, and recognised an unconscious decision had been made that day that she would always have to prove her worth.

Now Erik, Erik, was undermining all her built up adult confidence and strength, because now he was doing it too.

'I'll tell you something, Jane – your Erik's ten times nicer than you father. Don't turn away from him now. He's been foolish but he really loves you.'

She couldn't make her hair go into the clips properly. 'Mum, he's leaving me for another woman.'

'No. Marilyn means nothing.'

'Oh, so you know her name then. God, my mother knows more than I do about my life.'

'I can see you'll break your heart, Jane. And Erik's.'

'I'm not to blame!'

'No, but be gentle with him, forgive him. And perhaps you should review things a little. You've made the decision to take on Suzie. That doesn't mean you can't do your job, but let Erik know how much you care about him. When you are home, be interested in him too.'

Velalley turned away miserably. 'It's all too late,' she said. 'And I have to go to work.'

It seemed so petty, she thought, to take this particular short cut and drive down this particular road to work, just to glance up at the windows of the terraced house where she and Erik had first lived.

Not petty – demeaning. It was as if by doing it, she was preparing to admit that the original warmth of their relationship had begun to slip away like the retreating tide, that she might no longer matter enough, that another woman could steal Erik from her.

She waited for the red light to change.

So what's she like, she'd demanded. 'Homely,' he'd said, and that had really hurt. 'She talked to me.' 'And I don't, you mean?' 'You have your career, Jane.'

Velalley smeared the tears away with the back of her hand, and wound down the car window for some air. 'Your energy is what I adore about you,' he always said, and everything had been fine before. The future had been mapped out so carefully – but how could anyone have anticipated Suzie's arrival? And Suzie couldn't have been sweeter. It wasn't anything to do with her.

She put her foot down on the accelerator and turned onto the West Side Road crying as she'd cried when the front door banged behind him and she'd heard awful unmistakable finality in it, defeat. She had lost him, hadn't she? And – strangely, it was something she knew now she had always feared. Like history repeating itself.

She pulled into the Station yard and parked. There was more than an hour before she was actually due back at Faye's flat but she knew she needed to work, to concentrate very hard. Besides there was an urgent investigation in progress involving an innocent little child. She must keep a clear head, and try to hold back on her emotions, or she might miss something vitally important. Wiping away her tears she turned the car mirror to check if her eyes were too red. Bad. To cheer up her appearance, shakily she applied a bit of lipstick. As she climbed out of the car and locked it, even the wind scraping the leaves across the car park seemed to be whispering… he's going… you're losing him…

She walked in crumpling the tissue around in her pocket, hoping no one would notice the red rims round her eyes.

'It's his wife and kid I feel sorry for.'

'How did it happen?' Velalley asked, feeling quite unstable. She was in the incident room, talking to PCs Gibbeson and Radcliffe, and surrounded by computers bleeping, faxes coming through.

'He and Johnson. Last night. Emergency call-out, up on the North West Road.'

Radcliffe nodded. 'Near the estate.'

'Quale?'

'Where else! A bunch of drunks in the alley beside the pub.'

'Kids really,' Radcliffe chipped in again.

'While Dougie Phillips went to see what the hell was happening, more of them started on the vehicle. You know what they're like up there.'

'There's Johnson calling us, and trying to stop them. Phillips rushes back and one of the bastards pulls a knife on him. One inch to the left and he'd be in the mortuary instead of Intensive.'

'Jesus!'

'And the Sarge had just told Barry to tell 'em to stick together. The DI's gone up to see Dougie's Mrs.'

'They've got a baby, a few weeks old.'

'I didn't know.'

'You off back to Simmon's flat?'

'Shortly.'

'That's a cushy little number,' Radcliffe suggested. 'All cups of tea and easy chairs.'

She stared at him. 'You should try it.'

'I'd rather be out on the streets, darling, doing some real work, facing the enemy.'

'Don't you speak to me like that!'

'Hey, Velalley, this is not like you,' Gibbeson intervened tactfully.

Radcliffe strolled off grinning.

'He's just winding you up,' Gibbeson said.

She took out the tissue and blew her nose. 'I'm not in the mood.'

'Forget it. Sergeant Blake's interviewed that Chris Drury, by the way, and apparently he isn't anything to do with it. Oh and Blake wants to see you. He's in his office.'

On the Sergeant's desk was Angie's file, open at her photo.

Blake looked up as Velalley came in. 'Good,' he said, 'you're here. Heard about Phillips?'

She nodded.

He reached across the desk, 'I've got your next case waiting already.'

The folder had her name on it, and was marked 'Carrie Anderson'.

'Take it, but look at it later. She's thirteen. Caught shoplifting this morning in that same supermarket in the Mall. She's in hospital.'

'Are we beating them up now?'

'Christ, it's no joke, Velalley. She had an asthma attack.'

'Sorry, sir.' How could she be so stupid to make such a tasteless remark.

'I'll put that down to tension,' he said curtly.

Velalley took a tighter grip on herself. 'Asthma, you said, sir?'

'The security guard had never seen anything like it. Blue in the face she was, apparently. Could hardly breathe. The hospital said they needed to know what relief drugs she was on and as I was nearby, and they were trying to trace the parents, I went to the address. Guess where?'

'Don't tell me.'

'It gets worse up there every day.'

Velalley nodded.

'What a bloody dump Quale Estate is. Only a few residents now mind, and that makes it worse. Everything kicked in, vandalised, no lifts. The graffiti on the stairs – the language is blinding. The flat's fifth floor.' He puffed at the thought of it, and she noticed suddenly how tired he looked. 'So when I get there, the door's open, there's no sign of life. And the state of the place! Smells to high heaven. Maybe they piss in the cupboards. It turns out mother's done a bunk to Malagar with boyfriend, and father's more out than in.'

Velalley flicked through the few notes in the file.

'When this other thing's through, I want you to do a CYP on her.'

'Yes, sir.'

'She could do a whole lot better and she needs some official help the hospital say. They're already making a report to Social Services themselves. Although she's had some medication in the past from her GP, apparently she doesn't bother to use it. Then there's the shoplifting. So when you're ready –'

'Tomorrow?'

'Hell, no! We've got enough to be going on with. They're keeping her in until Monday anyway, and monitoring her closely via her GP after that. Get onto it as soon as this is over.'

'Yes, sir.'

'You've got problems at home, I believe?'

She blanched. What did he know? Had Erik talked to him? Or her mother? She'd kill them if they had. It was hard enough to cope. 'Nothing I can't handle,' she said, hearing the tension in her voice.

He was looking at her quizzically. 'Sure? Anything you want to discuss?'

'No sir! And I'd prefer it if you didn't speak to members of my family. My private life is my own.'

'Right,' he said rather abruptly, and looked back at Angie's photo. 'This little kiddie's our big worry.'

Velalley left his office smarting with rage. Her home life was certainly not going to be a topic for the gossips here. She glanced down at her watch. Still too much time. It would help to get out of here and concentrate. She'd go via the estate and have a preparatory look at Carrie Anderson's situation.

Close in, the condition of the main building on the housing estate shocked her even though she had seen it before. Litter like confetti. Unimaginative and vicious graffiti. The lift wrecked, slaughtered long ago by vandals. All that was left for the smattering of residents still stranded here was an exhausting and humiliating climb up the concrete stairwell to reach what could hardly be called a home. Most of the flats were boarded up, hated and rejected by even the most desperate families. It was partly to do with design – long dark passages, row above row of flats, approved by planners who couldn't see that there could be no pride in what were just doors opening off grey ramps into box-like compartments. And no privacy, no getting away from rowdy neighbours, no escape from the gangs who roamed around the estate unchallenged. Fear and decay had been allowed to creep in and once established had taken over. There seemed no way forward except the proposed demolition which was long overdue. A pall of depression hung over the place like a nuclear cloud. And it was where this kid lived day after day.

Velalley reached the fifth floor and followed the numbers along, hearing her shoes clicking on the unyielding cement surface and beginning to sense danger all around her. She was grateful not to have to be in uniform. That would be like a red rag to a bull. A short way ahead of her two boys of about seven or eight appeared, and stood leaning back against the wall, their eyes wide and watchful. They could tell she was a stranger. She half-smiled at them. They grinned, friendly, butter-wouldn't-melt grins.

'Hi,' one of them said, as she passed.

'Hello.'

When they suddenly jumped her and made a grab for her bag, it was the last thing she expected. She held on to it and managed to cuff one before he shouted 'Bitch!' and pushed her back hard against the wall our of his way.

The collision of her ribs against concrete hurt, and she leaned back heavily for a moment catching her breath. She heard their trainers thudding away as they disappeared back down the stairwell. As well as being winded, she was stunned. Only little kids. Little kids! But no point in pursuit. They were long gone. Worse, they might come back with other older mates. She mustn't linger. She'd been foolish to come here alone, particularly after last night's fracas. How absurdly easy it was to step into the path of danger without thinking, even with the kind of training and experience she'd had – and to let idiotic remarks like Radcliffe's 'facing the enemy' get to her.

She hurried to the end, number 513, and rang the bell. A curtain twitched. She knocked. 'Mr Anderson?'

The door opened a crack.

'WPC Velalley.' She held up identification. 'If you have a few minutes I want to talk to you about Carrie.'

Jack Anderson still didn't open the door.

'Why?' he demanded. 'You from the Social?'

'No, I told you, I'm a police officer, Mr Anderson. Could I have a quick word?'

'Carrie's all right now, isn't she?'

'Yes. I spoke to the hospital on the phone twenty minutes ago. She's progressing well.'

'So?' His expression darkened. 'I don't know anything about last night.'

'That isn't why I'm here.'

Jack Anderson's gaze shifted past her.

She could hear footsteps at the far end of the ramp. She thought she would cry with frustration. 'Could we possibly talk inside?'

For a moment he looked at her as if he might leave her out there, then he relented, removed the chain and let her in.

'Ours is a tight little community. They don't welcome strangers,' he said, as he shut the door smartly and she followed him into the living room.

'I can see that.'

The flat was appallingly cramped, much smaller than Faye's, which was a conversion from an old Victorian house. This one, modern and purpose built as two bedroom accommodation, was meanly proportioned and quite oppressive. Even the large feature window, fixed and facing back enviously towards the town and to the green hills beyond, was like a barrier too, offering no escape.

She tried to begin sympathetically: 'Your wife's in Spain, I believe.' It was not a good start. Now Jack Anderson was glaring at her – obviously she'd touched a very raw nerve.

She tried again. 'It must be difficult coping on your own with Carrie.'

Again he didn't answer.

'This morning, sir,' she switched to a more authoritative tone, 'your daughter was stopped in the Eastern Shopping Mall, for alleged shoplifting.'

'Caused her bloody asthma attack, it did. My kid's in hospital because of you.'

'The supermarket security apprehended Carrie,' she corrected him. 'No arrest took place, in fact, but in the circumstances I am required to make a report, Mr Anderson, a youth help report, and one of the things I have to find out is the condition in which she lives.'

'Then ask the bloody council.'

'Are you in full time employment, Mr Anderson?'

'What do you think?' he said sourly.

'I don't have a great deal of time today, Mr Anderson,' Velalley stuck with her business-like tone, and looked through one of the three doors leading off, 'but I wanted to introduce myself and have a quick look, if I may? Is this Carrie's bedroom?'

He shrugged.

She took that to be yes and stepped inside. She noted the pile of used tissues, and the grubby sheets on the unmade bed. In the cupboard a pair of jeans slung over a coat hanger, a school skirt screwed up on the shelf, a navy anorak. On the floor underneath, a blanket, and an old stained pillow which smelled distinctly of the ammonia of urine. Way back in the corner down there, something white caught her eye.

She picked it up and turned it over on her hand.

Designed to exactly resemble a child's first shoe, this miniature edition obviously belonged to a rather nicely dressed doll. She glanced round the room. No sign of toys, but then Carrie was thirteen, wasn't she, and unlikely to be still interested in such things now. Velalley placed it on the small scratched cupboard beside the bed and returned to the main room.

'Do you have a dog, Mr Anderson?'

'Here? You must be bloody joking.'

She frowned thoughtfully and moved on. 'I see you have a separate kitchen.'

The rubbish hadn't been emptied for days. Perhaps that was understandable five floors up, but nobody bothered with any kind of cleaning. Nobody bothered at all. Some mother Carrie would make one day with this kind of example. Sergeant Blake was right – the kid could do a whole lot better.

'You think it's my fault, don't you?' Jack Anderson stood leaning against the wall sullenly watching her appraise his existence. 'You don't know what it's like, you lot in your cosy jobs. My wife's run off and left me with Carrie to cope with. I've been out of work two years and there's no employment to be had round here. Even if there was, if I gave this address they'd tell me to sling my hook. See that TV? After we were burgled for the third time, I bought it cheap so maybe even the thieves'd turn it down. And then she goes and breaks it, snaps all the knobs right off. Kicks the remote to pieces. What can you do with kids now?'

'Doesn't Carrie like watching television?'

'Yes, but she did it to spite me, so I couldn't watch it. That's typical of her, cut off her own nose.'

Velalley glanced at her watch.

'Look, Mr Anderson, I can't stay now, but you do know, don't you, that the hospital will only release Carrie once they know there'll be someone here to look after her? You'll need to talk to them. And may I give you a bit of friendly advice? It would be in your interests to give the flat a really good clean up. Social Services will be in touch shortly – they'll be assessing Carrie's situation and will probably assign someone to her. And once I get all the details of the case together, and find out what the supermarket intends doing, I'll come back and see you about that. I'd like to talk to Carrie too when she's feeling better.'

'You'll be fucking lucky,' he said.

She descended the concrete stairs fearfully, knowing that any moment some kid might jump her again, and was grateful to emerge unmolested back into the late afternoon sunlight. She breathed a sigh of relief and crossed the cracked tarmac to her car.

Two fingers wide, the scratch glinted silver against the contrasting dark blue metal. She touched it angrily, knowing eyes and laughter filled the shadows behind her. The coin, or whatever they'd used, had etched a deep uneven groove into the surface running the entire length of the vehicle. 'Little bastards,' she muttered.

'What the hell are you doing here?'

She jumped.

The DI strode across the grass towards her. 'I said, what the hell are you doing here, Velalley?'

'I came up to do a preliminary check on Carrie

Anderson, sir. Sergeant Blake wants me to do a CYP on her.'

'Alone?'

'I had an hour before –'

'Didn't you hear about Phillips?'

'Yes, sir.'

'Didn't you think, Velalley? Nobody but nobody comes up to this estate alone, you hear me?'

'Yes, sir.'

'You hear me?' He wasn't expecting an answer. He was just vigorously remaking the point.

She waited.

'Leave it a few days,' he said in a more conciliatory tone. 'And for Christ's sake, bring someone with you next time.'

'Yes, sir.'

'Aren't you due back with Simmons?'

'In a few minutes, sir.'

'Then take one thing at a time, will you, Velalley?'

'Yes, sir,' she said, smarting at the unjustified rebuke. It was her time she was putting in here.

'We have the area down there near the pub cordoned off. There's a diversion. Take the Canal Road instead.'

As she opened the car door, he saw the scratch and understood immediately what had happened. 'Is this your husband's car?'

'No, mine.'

'Erik's his name, isn't it?'

She was furious. Had he heard about the affair too? 'Yes. Why?' she said indignantly. But he just smiled and ran his eyes down her figure. She glared back at him with contempt.

He nodded at the scratch. 'That'll cost,' he said.

She climbed in but he caught the car door. 'PC Phillips died half an hour ago,' he said, before he closed it.

For a moment she sat staring numbly ahead of her. Then she turned the ignition key and drove away from the Quale Estate and down towards the town.

CHAPTER TWENTY SIX

'Want to come to the Ship?'

Erik shook his head. 'No thanks, Pete. But you go,' he added, trying not to seem like a complete burden.

Pete was already putting on a black suede jacket and looking down into the street. Then he ran his hand back thought his hair to tidy it and smiled at Erik.

'Scotch there and TV controls somewhere under that lot,' he said, pointing to a corner cabinet and then to a pile of photographs on the coffee table. 'Those are those ones I took in the mist. You'll be all right?'

'I'm fine. Look, it's kind of you.'

Pete waved a hand bountifully in the air. 'Think nothing of it. Why not make yourself at home?' He cantered down the stairs and opened the door. 'Hey,' he called up. 'Your car's half over the double yellow. Chuck me your keys. I'll move it for you. Don't want a ticket on top of everything else.'

Erik dug in his pocket. He threw the keys and Pete caught them deftly. 'Thanks.'

The door downstairs banged.

For a while Erik sat in silence. Then from the corner cabinet he poured himself a polite amount of scotch and returned with it to the rather splendid isolation of the leather sofa.

Using the remote control he flicked round the TV channels. Saturday afternoon sport. And more sport. An old thirties film. He switched the television off. Instead he thumbed through the prints on the coffee table – and began to marvel. Each photograph was brilliant, a masterpiece in composition. Throughout, the fog had blurred the stark edge of the black and white, making the trees seem soft and pliable and three dimensional. Real, almost breathing against the insubstantial landscape. A line of lights stretched away like stars into the distance. Shadow added a richness to the Afghan's fur. Without recognisable boundaries it could be anywhere, anywhere in the world. Britain, Russia, the moon...

Somewhere a phone began to ring. It rang and rang and eventually Erik got to his feet and followed the sound to the landing downstairs to a door marked Studio. It must be pretty important to have continued for so long. He opened the door. Darkness, and a sour smell. Chemicals or something. Peter still developed photos from film, as well as working digitally. He flipped the light switch back and forth. The bulb must be out. He felt his way across the room towards the sound and felt around. He picked up the phone.

'Hello?'

Silence.

'Hello? Pete Miles Studio? Look I'm sorry he isn't here. Can I take a message?'

There was a click and the line went dead.

He replaced the receiver. A girlfriend maybe. And the wrong voice answering.

Back upstairs he sat down again, took another sip of his drink and looked around him. He had been here twice before, not with the lights on, and not with Pete. With some shame he recognised the Persian rug on the floor. Now he could see that the rest of the flat was everything he had imagined then it might be: typically dark and eccentric like Pete himself. There was antique furniture everywhere. Heavy brass candlesticks in this room, and a tropical palm in one corner, and on the walls, dominating the space, marvellously atmospheric enlargements, black and white photographs of the faces and bodies of women. Not all of them were beautiful. Obviously Pete was not afraid to use shock tactics to achieve extraordinary photographic effects and Erik sat staring at them, filled with admiration at the man's temerity and talent.

After a while though, surrounded by so much bare flesh, be began to feel uncomfortable. Why had he chosen to come here? Here, of all places? It was terrifically lonely somehow too, sort of cloud nine-ish, as if the world in the street below didn't exist. Even the window was small. And the women in the photographs seemed unreal, and unhappy, ugly and pornographic – and there were some pretty specific positions. Erik thought back. He had hardly ever seen Pete with a woman except for that one occasion with Marilyn. He wondered why that was. Perhaps though, Pete was just secretive – there was evidence of women in the bathroom, perfume, a packet of tampons, a discarded lipstick. Pete was an attractive guy after all. And women always looked at Pete first – always, before almost coquettishly they cast their eyes further on to look at less interesting men, men like him. Then there was a kind of sexual envy in their expressions, he thought, that there he was, talking to Pete instead of them. Marilyn had said women could see right through to a man's soul... and Pete's soul was surely sexy. Look at the kind of photography he did. Erik remembered Pete saying photographs gave him a kind of control, a way of seizing the person and the moment. And with a wry smile he'd added: 'Just like a perpetual orgasm!'

'No wonder you're successful then.'

Pete had laughed. 'It gets ever more difficult.'

Erik leaned back further into the soft leather. He sipped his drink letting the flavour of the scotch lie for a moment on his tongue and imagining a life like Pete's. The travel, the money, the women, the sex. Then he swallowed hard and looked down at the Persian carpet at his feet.

'Jane,' he whispered, closing his eyes, 'Jane...'

He was surprised to find an hour had passed when he opened his eyes again. He had not realised how exhausted he was. He blinked and picked up his glass again.

No. Not more scotch. Coffee. He needed coffee.

There was another picture on the wall behind the sofa, and as he got to his feet he was shocked to come face to face with a huge portrait of Marilyn. Suddenly all his guilt rose up again within him. Jesus. How had he not seen this photo immediately?

He twisted painfully away and stared hard into his empty glass, trying to will the picture to disappear. Through the bottom of the glass the pattern of the Persian carpet glowed. He was probably standing on the very spot where... He felt the hairs on the back of his neck rising as if Marilyn's eyes were beginning to pierce through him, drawing him round again. He turned slowly, fearfully. He remembered the magnetism of her weird sexuality, a kind of hypnotic fervour that within minutes that night had robbed him of self control and filled him with desire, making him forget everything, who he was, where he was… and go on and on to the darkest edges of his being, making him want to feel his whole body dissolving into hers.

He drew back. He could almost smell the scent of her on the air.

And yet…

He took a deep breath and made himself stare straight at the picture. The effect of it was startling – her face in focus up very close to the lens and the body in that huge black hooded cloak, open, revealing her breasts, and tapering away from the camera, tapering in triangular form down the centre of her body, past her own dark triangle, on down to two pointed feet, all on a pure white background, surreal, like some Salvatore Dali painting…

Suddenly he shivered and stepped back, utterly repelled by an ugliness about her that seemed now to scream across the room at him. She was so thin the skin on her face hardly disguised the bones of the skull beneath. There was such a far away look in the enlarged pupils of her eyes, such a frighteningly deadpan expression around the mouth. How could he ever have seen her as beautiful?

It had been an illusion, just an illusion born out of his own frustration, his own self-pity. He had seen only what he had wanted to see.

He poured himself another stiff drink and gulped it down.

It took a mere five minutes to gather his few belongings together. He scribbled an apologetic note about having to be in the office at the crack of dawn, left it on the table with Pete's spare keys and not daring to look back, went downstairs and let himself out into the street.

He felt in his pockets. 'Damn.'

But Pete was just coming out of the pub followed by another of his friends. He blanched as he saw Erik and then clutched his arm dramatically.

'Erik, I was just coming back to warn you.'

'Warn me?'

The man behind Pete peered around him and stared at Erik.

'Obviously you haven't seen the front page of the evening paper, have you?' Pete said.

'Why?'

'That woman found murdered by the motorway. They've revealed her identity – it was Marilyn, Erik, your Marilyn!'

CHAPTER TWENTY SEVEN

Faye Simmons faced Velalley accusingly. 'You think she's dead, Jane, don't you?'

'No, Faye, *no*! There's no reason to think that.'

'Then why have you stopped coming?'

'I haven't! I needed to have a little time off, a few hours, to eat, to sleep.'

'Why should you sleep? Why should any of you sleep when my child's out there. Lost...'

Nervously Judith Colston pulled on her coat and signalled Velalley to follow her out to the door. 'She's been tidying the rooms obsessively. Her parents came in for a few hours but that didn't stop her. She's made and re-made the child's bed at least eight times. I don't think she's sat down once since I got here. It's exhausting.'

'Has she eaten anything?'

'I made her tea several times. She doesn't take more than a sip. I asked for some sandwiches to be sent in at lunchtime but she wouldn't touch them.'

'Okay.' Velalley smiled encouragingly. 'Thanks, Judith. Watch out downstairs. PC Warren's on the door but there are still plenty of reporters hanging round.'

'I'll go round the back. Oh, and there's still nothing

from the search. I spoke to Sergeant Blake about quarter of an hour ago – nothing at all.'

'I know.'

Colston opened the door to let herself out. 'Hey, did you hear about poor Dougie Phillips?'

'Yes.'

'God, I can't believe it.' Her eyes were wide. 'He was only out on an ordinary emergency call.'

'Don't be frightened, Judith. It's pretty rare, an attack like that.'

Colston hesitated in the doorway. 'I'm shit scared actually,' she confided. 'Aren't you?'

'Yes.'

Her eyes filled with relief. 'It makes me feel better to know I'm not the only one.'

'As far as possible, stick with your colleagues,' Velalley said, then not to sound so clever, she added guiltily, 'that's what the DI said anyway.'

'That makes good sense,' Colston said nervously.

'You look positively whacked, Judith. Better go home and get some sleep.'

Faye was moving round the room, dusting anything, rubbing at every surface. Velalley stood watching her, unable in the face of all this activity to sit down herself. Faye disappeared into the kitchen, returned with another cloth and started on the paintwork.

'Stop it, Faye, for God's sake.'

'I have to do something.'

'Let me get you something to eat?'

Faye shook her head. Her eyes were red rimmed with

tiredness, her face pale and drawn.

'For Angie's sake. You must keep up your strength for her.'

Faye paused, then rubbed more slowly at the doorframe.

'Please,' Velalley coaxed.

Her arm fell to her side and the cloth slipped out of her hand. She swayed a little. Velalley guided her to a chair. 'You need some tea,' she said firmly. In the kitchen she phoned through on the mobile. 'Something real, Barry, like stew or broth. No plastic take-aways. And more sugar, milk and tea bags.'

It was barely ten minutes later when the doorbell rang.

'Food,' announced the young man on the doorstep. He stepped in.

Velalley looked at the large flat box in his hand and smelled the spicy aroma of pizza.

'I told Barry no take-away,' she said irritably. 'Is that the best he could do?'

'I don't know anything about that,' he said, kicking the door shut and striding past her. 'Where d'ya want it?'

'Give it here,' Velalley said, but he was already through into the living room.

'So you're the mother,' he said tactlessly. He abandoned the box and reached into his pocket.

'Who are you?' asked Velalley urgently.

A flash lit up Faye's terrified face.

The suddenness of it shocked Velalley for a second before she realised what it was. There were two more in quick succession before she could grab him.

'Hey! Who said you could come in here?' She snatched

his left arm and wound it round behind his back. 'You're under arrest, laddie.'

'Quite the little firecracker,' he said, struggling to re-pocket the camera with his free hand.

'Hand it over,' she aid, tightening her grip. 'Come on.'

'Look,' he argued, 'the name's Hughes. I'm just doing my job. Our readers want to help.'

'Oh yes?'

'People are doing everything they can to find that kid. The mother's distress is important. It's the emotional angle. They see her, they start to think what if it was their kid? They begin to wonder if they know anything. Little events come back to them. They start to care.'

'They care already without your interference. And it's the child's photo that counts. You've had plenty of opportunity to use that.'

He wrestled in her grasp. She wished she was within reach of her radio, or the mobile.

'My paper's opened up a fund. She'll be pleased when this is all over,' he said, eyeing Faye and using the promise of money like a weapon.

'Get out!' Up to this moment Faye had been too shocked to speak. Now she was advancing on them, her eyes blazing. 'Give me the camera,' she demanded. 'Give it to me.'

'Careful, Faye.' Velalley swung the man round until she stood between them. 'Don't over-react here.'

Hughes held up his free hand to defend himself. 'Hey, hey – if it's that important! You'd think she'd welcome our help.'

'She might have,' Velalley said, trying to calm things down, 'if you hadn't burst in like this.'

The doorbell rang. Velalley thought quickly. What if it was another one? She couldn't take the chance of Faye answering the door.

'Now,' she said, 'that's my Sergeant. I'm expecting him.'

'Better still,' Hughes said. 'He'll see reason.'

'Don't count on it, sunshine.' She loosened her grip, and set him free. 'No more photos, you hear me, or I promise I'll do you for trespassing. And hand over the camera.'

He though he was going to refuse, but surprisingly he didn't. He produced it from his pocket and she took it with her to the door.

'Who is it?' she called.

'PC Warren, Jane. You in trouble?'

She let him in thankfully. 'He's taken pictures,' she whispered. 'It's the last thing the mother wants.'

Back in the room Warren eyed Hughes and took the camera from Velalley.

'Nice,' he said, examining it. 'I'm into photography myself. What's this do?' There was a click, the back opened, and the card fell out. Warren stepped sideways, as he leaned down to rescue it, crushing it under his shoe. 'Oh dear,' he said examining it ruefully, 'I hope I haven't ruined anything important?' He put it in his pocket.

Velalley stared at Warren, stunned by his audacity. He was really pushing his luck, but Hughes didn't look particularly dismayed.

'You win some, you lose some,' he said. 'I would have got paid well for an exclusive like that. Anyway, what's she got to hide? She's a pretty girl.'

'May I see your press identification, sir?' Warren wrote

down the name and address. 'This is private property, Mr Hughes. The lady could have you for trespassing.'

Faye shook her head miserably. 'Just get him out.'

'Hear that? Now, hop it, and be thankful you're not under arrest.'

'Yes sir,' Hughes mocked him, 'it'll make a good story though, even without the shots.' He turned to Velalley and grinned cheekily. 'Mind if I ring you sometime? I could do a great piece on your kind of woman.'

Velalley showed him the door.

'I saw Colston driving away just now. Maybe she didn't quite secure the back door,' PC Warren said glumly. The two of them were in the kitchen now.

'Someone like Hughes wouldn't hesitate to shimmy up a drain pipe.'

'I thought something might be up. One minute they're all standing around bored out of their trees, next minute they're in a huddle and I can't see one of 'em.'

'I'd just ordered some food. I fell for it because he had pizza with him.'

He nodded. 'Good trick, that.'

'Want some more tea?'

'Better not. The DI will be here in a minute. Don't forget Hughes got past me. If I'm seen drinking tea.'

He looked back through the kitchen door at Faye who was seated now, wrapped up protectively in the duvet again. 'She all right?'

'Like a rubber band,' Velalley whispered. 'I don't know how much more she can take.'

'Looks bad for the little kid, this long,' he said, keeping

his voice low. 'It's been so cold the last day or so, and it won't be long before it gets dark...'

CHAPTER TWENTY EIGHT

The sky was clouding over and the roar of the motorway was still some little distance away. The isolated warehouse cast languid purple shadows over her as Angie looked up at its high prefabricated sides. She longed for somewhere to curl up and sleep, not out here in the open, but in some dark and concealing shelter. Carrie must know by now it was not her father who had taken her precious Madeline.

Clutching the doll, Angie forced her aching little legs forward, following the dirt path beside the wall to find a way in, some small access. The wide door was barricaded and padlocked, but further along was a low air vent with loose wood around it.

It had been kicked in by vandals, barred with planks, and attacked again, so she was able to push one wide plank completely out of the way. Madeline, eyes bright and staring, went through first and Angie clambered in after her, catching her clothing on a sliver of glass. As she pulled away it ripped her sleeve before it released her.

Inside, as her eyes adjusted to the diminished light, she could see metal shelves along the walls, and a vast pile of rubbish in the centre. Nothing else. She retrieved Madeline and held her very close in the half darkness.

A noise behind her made her jump. She turned in time to watch the planks over the vent shift again, and then slither back over the hole. Then a piece of wood above, loosened by the disturbance, slipped down with a sudden definite thud pinning the planks firmly back in position.

'Mamaa,' the doll moaned as Angie hugged her tightly. 'Mamaa.'

With no way out behind her, Angie stepped gingerly forward to explore her surroundings. Apart from the rubbish, the centre area of the warehouse was bare, with great dust marks on the floor where there had once been vast machinery. Unnerving scuttling noises came from the middle of the refuse. She backed further away from that and followed the shelving along the wall to the far end. In the corner was an old zinc basin with a dripping tap which she couldn't turn on, even by abandoning Madeline and using both hands. She cupped her hands under the slow leak and licked each drop eagerly as it fell onto her fingers. Though it tasted funny, stale somehow, it was a little liquid and her thirst was very great.

After a while she picked up Madeline and held her lips to the tap too. 'Nice water,' she told her. She thought she saw the doll smile at her.

She yawned. A little further along was a wooden chair and she used it to climb up onto the first level of the high shelving and she sat there with Madeline on her knee, swinging her legs and chanting softly, 'Bysie-bysie, bysie-bysie.'

Down on the floor under the sink in a sudden little gleam of light, she noticed there were some blue crumbs. She stared at them hungrily. She had never seen blue biscuits or bread, and she wondered what the taste would be like. But she was too tired to climb down to find out.

'In the morning,' she said to herself. 'Biscuit in the morning.' She looked into Madeline's wide-awake eyes. 'Bysie-bysie, bysie-bysie,' she said, and laid the doll out carefully to rest. She lifted her feet up onto the shelf and lay down next to her. She stared across at the crumbs again as she pulled the doll in close to her.

'Mamaa,' Madeline cried, as Angie shut her eyes.

CHAPTER TWENTY NINE

Sergeant Blake stared numbly out of his office window for a moment, the idea of attending a memorial service for Phillips severely depressing him. Rain clouds were closing in and the few people in the street were hugging their coats close, while everything around them was brilliantly outlined by a sudden gleam from the setting sun. Below the two squad cars involved in the search, and temporarily parked on clearly marked double yellow lines, glinted red. Out on the motorway the never ending traffic rushed furiously by, mirroring the sun's temporary radiance in a kind of repeating strobe pattern.

A man turned into the High Street and Blake recognised him as Velalley's husband. He watched with interest as Erik Velalley crossed the road and walked towards the Station entrance.

He was directed up and Blake met him at the head of the stairs. 'Mr Velalley. Erik, isn't it?'

Erik looked up apprehensively. His brown hair was ruffled; his hands were pressed deep into the pockets of the long black coat and his shoulders were tense.

Blake offered his hand.

'Good of you to help us with our enquiries,' he said.

Erik tried to smile but his mouth quivered at the unfortunate choice of words. 'I believe I have to see Detective Inspector Kendrick?'

The convector heater in Kendrick's office fumed and creaked. Behind his desk the Detective Inspector leaned back in his chair. He was smiling, but Blake knew that expression well. It was Kendrick's cobra smile. He was noticing everything, every little shift Erik made in his chair. The DI's real detection talents however lay in collating information, and piecing the clues together like an intricate jigsaw – and very definitely not in his blunt dealings with people.

'So, Mr Velalley, what else do you want to tell me about Marilyn Farr?'

Erik Velalley, sitting very upright in his chair, suddenly looked genuinely afraid of him. He stared down at the floor. 'I knew her, that's all.'

'Meeting her about a month ago in the Ship Inn down on the waterfront hardly constitutes information. You had an affair with her, did you?'

Blake was stunned. He glanced across at Kendrick. The DI's face was hard and bland.

'I – er...'

'That's why you're here, isn't it?'

Erik sat motionless in his chair. 'It was hardly that,' he said after a moment. 'We -'

'How often did you see her?'

'Can I just ask,' Blake interrupted carefully, 'if you've told Jane about this?'

Erik nodded uncomfortably.

Somehow Blake was relieved by that.

'It was only once –'

'It would be better,' Kendrick said, 'if you spoke the truth, Erik. May I call you Erik?'

Erik ran a hand through his hair. 'You can call me whatever you like, for Christ's sake. I saw her once.'

'I could call you a cheat, Erik.'

Erik's eyes glinted with anger. 'I have been very foolish, Inspector Kendrick, and I have cheated on my wife, but I have also confessed to her –'

Kendrick's eyes narrowed. 'Confessed?'

'Look, I saw Marilyn in the street one evening about three weeks ago when I was on my way home from work. She was waiting for a bus. I offered her a lift.'

'And the other occasion?'

'We…' He hesitated, realising his error. 'Okay,' he said, 'I did see her again another night. We went for a walk and –'

'What time?'

'About six, I think.'

'What evening was this?'

'A Monday.'

'The twenty-fifth. Last Monday?'

'Yes.'

'Go on.'

Erik undid the buttons of his coat. Blake watched the edges of it dragging on the floor as Erik began to shift around uneasily in his chair. 'We went back to the friend's flat again and –'

'The friend was there?'

'No, but Marilyn had keys, and we – had sex. There was no more to it than that.'

'For the second time.'

Erik nodded miserably.

'And afterwards?' said Kendrick.

'I left. I went home.'

'To your wife.'

Erik looked ashamed. 'Yes.'

'And what time did you leave?'

'About ten, I think.'

'Six until ten.' Kendrick raised his eyebrows. 'And where did you tell your wife you'd been?'

'Jane wasn't home. She was doing an extra shift here.'

Blake thought about it, then he nodded. 'That is right,' he confirmed. 'She was on duty.'

Kendrick leaned forward over the desk. 'I have to tell you, Erik,' he said, 'the twenty-fifth is a difficult date for us. A very difficult date. It is almost certainly the night Marilyn Farr died.'

Erik turned pale. 'Jesus, you don't seriously think I killed her, do you? As if I'd want to come and talk to you.'

'Guilty people do strange things. No-one saw you come home?'

'Marrietta left as soon as I arrived – she's the girl who minds Suzie.'

'Oh yes, your sister-in-law's child. Is this Marrietta attractive too, Erik?'

Erik jumped to his feet angrily. 'Now you're just being obtuse. This is very difficult for me. I came to you in good faith because I know how much every little piece of information helps build up the complete picture. And in spite of how this looks I love my wife.'

'That's a very expensive coat you're wearing, Mr Velalley.'

'What? Um...' Erik looked down at it in surprise, 'a friend lent it to me. I'm not at home right now... and.. um.. I'm staying –'

'With a Peter Miles?' Kendrick smiled. 'He rang me earlier. He's very concerned about you. He's anxious for you to know you can go back there tonight.'

Erik stepped defensively behind his chair. 'I'll probably stay at my office.'

'Did you come here by car?'

'Yes.'

'And you drove home on the twenty-fifth?'

'Of course I did.'

'Did you give Marilyn a lift home that night?'

'No. She said she'd take a taxi.'

'Your wife has her own car?'

'Yes.'

'Does she ever use yours?'

'No, never. I need mine, she drives hers. Unless she uses one of the cars here.'

'May we look at yours?'

'Of course.' Then a look of fresh apprehension swept over his face. 'You're hoping to find Marilyn's fingerprints, aren't you? And my God, they'll be there.' He was beginning to panic.

'Would you bring it into our car park, please?'

'You really think I killed her, don't you?'

The DI didn't answer. He stood up.

Blake rose too.

'Look, if it's at all possible,' Erik said quietly, 'I'd rather neither of you mentioned this visit to my wife.'

'It would appear you like to keep a great deal from her,' Kendrick observed.

'That's not true. But I don't think I mentioned Marilyn's name, and with this abduction case… well, she's just so keyed up at the moment. It's been a bad week.'

He appealed to Blake instead. 'If it's possible? I don't want her to worry.'

A few minutes later when Erik Velalley had gone, Blake asked: 'The car?'

'Cars have boots,' said Kendrick. 'I want a SOCO on it immediately.'

'Mmm.' Blake paused at the door. 'Is that Peter Miles, the photographer?'

'Influential friends, eh?'

'Look, sir, it is true Velalley is heavily involved in the Angie case right now. Can't we leave this until we get a result? Only a couple of the lads will have seen Erik here. They could keep it to themselves.'

'I want to know what he told her.'

'Enough, if he's spending the night away from home.'

Kendrick continued making notes. 'I'll see,' he said.

'Give me a few hours. Just until we find the kid?'

Velalley had a right to know what Kendrick was thinking, but this could stop her in her tracks. She might end up killing him for not telling her, but hell, what choice had he got? Finding Angie was absolute priority.

CHAPTER THIRTY

Although George Longman was shifting agitatedly from one foot to the other, and there were tears in Ida Longman's eyes, Sergeant Blake could see why Velalley had found them unsympathetic. He could understand their grief and anger. It was their grandchild, although according to Faye they hardly knew Angie, but he wished they would stop shouting and go away, and let him get on with the business of finding the child.

'So when all's said and done,' Ida Longman's voice was so shrill, 'what? What have you achieved? Nothing! It's time the police were made accountable. All the resources, all the taxpayers' money, and our grandchild's still out there, stolen! And you can't find her.'

The trouble is what the woman is saying is true, Blake thought, for all our strenuous searching. But without witnesses, without leads, where the hell do you start?

'You're all bloody incapable.' George Longman echoed his wife's anger. 'When we were burgled last year. The police made a report but never even bothered to follow it up. When I asked them why, not worth it, they said. Not worth it? And when Angie was abducted, where were the police then? How can a child just disappear in a huge supermarket like that?'

'Angie's disappearance is particularly frustrating,' Blake said quietly, 'because there were so many people there and apparently no-one saw anything.'

'So now it's Saturday evening. She disappeared on Thursday. What's happening? What's being done?'

'There are search parties out locally and house to house enquiries. We're using the national computer link-up. We're following every possible lead, Mrs Longman, every possible lead, I assure you.'

'Oh, it all sounds so pat. I suppose the person, whoever it is, will eventually be let off with the customary caution you read about nowadays?'

'That decision will be for the courts. Our concern is to find the child without delay.'

'Our daughter,' said George Longman, 'went to a good school, you know. We gave her everything, and we sent her to that college. She won all sorts of prizes for her art. Mind you I could never see why, myself. But look where that got her! She'd have been better off getting herself a proper job. There's no reason not to make a respectable go of life, however high-flying your ideas may be.'

Ida Longman applied a handkerchief to her eyes. 'So she'll get some sort of compensation now?'

'Compensation?'

Yesterday Ida Longman had suggested selling an account of Faye's heartbreak to the highest bidder and now here she was again, anxious to see what future money could be made. Blake was finding the whole conversation utterly distasteful. 'The Criminal Injury Board is an independent body, Mrs Longman,' he said coldly. 'I suggest when the time comes your solicitor helps you on that one.'

He opened the office door. 'Now it's late, you'll have to excuse me.'

'Don't think you've heard the last of this. The sheer incompetence and lack of effort with which this case is being handled...'

When, a full five minutes later, they eventually left, Blake sank gratefully into his chair. Everybody dealt with disaster in their own way, mostly with anger. He leaned on his desk, his head in his hands and thought of Faye, her silence, the proud way she held her head, and her dignity in the face of almost total despair.

Gibbeson appeared at the door.

'Sir, I think you'd better come out to the desk.'

Blake listened carefully to a man in a dripping anorak and grubby jeans who stood steaming under the bright fluorescent light.

'As that newspaper's offering a reward I reckon it might be worth a mention. Lucky I didn't kill her, running out like that in front of me.'

'Where was this?'

The man brushed the rainwater off his forehead. 'Up on the Northwest Road, near where that copper was topped. This morning.'

'What time?'

'Orh, nearly lunchtime. I was going down to the pub.'

Could be a try-on, but –'Can you describe her, sir?'

'Little kid, about the right age. Light blue outfit.'

'Outfit?'

'Shiny, a bit like a track suit, you know the sort. And blonde hair. I did see that.'

'Just a minute.' Blake leaned round into the control room. 'Barry, get the DI down here urgently, will you?'

'He's gone home ages ago, sir.'

'Get him on the phone then,' he snapped, and turned back to the man. 'Now, sir, you're quite sure it was this morning?'

'Yeah.'

'Why didn't you report this sooner, Mr - ?'

'Hannan, Geoff Hannan. Er... well, a bit awkward, you see. I.. er...'

'Get on with it!'

'I hit a parked car. I had to swerve, and... I wasn't too keen to stop, you see...'

Blake saw. Probably no insurance. No tax disc. He ignored the implications of that and went on. 'Which way did she run across?'

'Eh?'

'Which direction? Think!'

'Er... from the estate, yeah. Away from Quale.'

Quale. Always Quale. 'Did you see anyone else? On the pavement? On the other side? Anywhere?'

'No.'

'No-one?' Could she have been abandoned? Escaped? What the hell was happening?

Hannan nodded. 'I know that for sure. I remember thinking, at least there's no real witnesses. If I just drive away...' his voice trailed off.

'Look, that's another matter,' Blake said. 'I'm more interested in the child. So if she ran that way it would take her –'

'Down onto the wasteland!' Hannan concluded.

Blake looked anxiously at his watch. Worth a start tonight, even though it would be pitch dark for hours yet. But those hours might make all the difference. It was presently raining and the air temperature was cold and the child might still be out in the open. She wouldn't survive very long without some sort of shelter. A proper orderly search could begin in the morning with the extra men they'd drafted in, but right now –

'Barry,' he called urgently, 'I want to know every available car's position, and line me up anyone who's on offer here.'

'Yes, sir. Got the DI on the line for you, sir.'

The steep bank would have been slippery even without the rain. Blake negotiated its darkness as best he could, hearing in the grunts of his colleagues in similar physical difficulties. The six separate flashlight beams darted in all directions until eventually they formed a common pool of light on the stones of the level ground below.

'Bloody weather.' Blake shook himself, expelling a layer of wetness from his Mac. Considering the reputation of this district and the fate of PC Phillips, and looking out into the blinding mist ahead, he wondered if he might be going mad starting immediately, flying in the face of the DI's more reasonable orders. Mightn't it indeed have been wiser to wait until first light? The gooseflesh on the exposed wet skin above his collar gave him his answer. If the penetrating cold and the fear of dark isolation here unnerved him, a grown man, and one trained to deal professionally with it, what effect it might have on a child of four he could hardly begin to imagine.

'We'll stick together in three groups of two, lads, with radio contact between us. Sort yourselves out. And be careful. Any one of us could come a cropper out here in this. The two cars are following us over on the perimeter. It'll take longer on foot, but a kid that size, it'd be easy to miss her.'

'Are you sure she's here somewhere, sir?'

Blake shook his head. 'But if that sighting is correct and she is out here alone, she won't survive long in these conditions.'

In the moment of silence that followed his words the five ghostly faces illuminated by the flashlights around him were not the young disciplined faces of his constables, but fathers or older brothers. To a man they grasped immediately the fearful gravity of the child's situation.

'Where's that bloody map?'

'Here, sir.'

The flashlights trained in on it, dripping onto the already buckling paper.

'It's not shown here but there's a dump just out there ahead of us, empty oil drums, all sorts. There,' he slid his finger across directionally to the west, 'is the canal, and a couple of the old original warehouses. Across to the east there, is another one.'

'Why haven't we done this already, sir?'

'We have, Gibbes-sy, yesterday, only maybe a day too soon if our witness is correct. Right, you might as well come with me as anyone. We can all start with the dump.'

They headed out into the gloom, their stout shoes crunching into the stony ground, the light of their torches diffused by the rain. They divided the dump into three areas; Blake could see the others' flashlights appear and disappear, and hear the hollow ring of the metal oil drums as Radcliffe and his partner Ward searched them, while over on the other side, Toms and Carpenter took on the wrecked cars.

'Angie? Angie!' they called.

Below him with gentle thuds Gibbeson threw aside piles of cardboard and moved boxes, while he himself climbed on top of a mountain of trash and peered out into the darkness, calculating the odds against the child's survival.

The rain had given way to mist as Blake and Gibbeson trudged east towards the warehouse. It was hard to say if the dawn was coming up or if it was just the headlights on the raised motorway beyond that pierced the gloom.

Blake checked his watch. Nearly five. His limbs ached with the damp and the exertion and the lack of sleep; he longed to call the squad car cruising out on the roadway nearby to take him home, to see his wife to rise up sleepily from her bed to make him something hot to drink and then lie down beside him, comforting him with the warmth of her body. He shivered. It was a dream, no more, for in reality he knew she would not stir. Her nights, heavy with the inertia of sleeping pills were no longer for him, but forever frozen into a darkness eighteen years before when he had climbed in under the bedclothes, wanting to lay his own head against the new tenderness in her breasts, worshipping her in wonder and bewilderment, this lovely woman who was his wife, and who to his joy, was soon to be the mother of his child. In the quiet hours that followed their love-making, he lay unable to sleep himself for the pleasure of watching her, listening to her breathing, understanding some real purpose and pattern at last in his existence. Eventually with satisfaction he had closed his eyes, knowing that life had reached a turning point.

And his life was altered, altered inexorably, as with rain and then dense fog much like this, the new day dawned and he woke to witness the twisting and writhing of her late miscarriage. Other than to summon medical assistance, how helpless he had been, how totally useless, unable to stop her pain or his own tears. After the initial grief, and the patronising it-wasn't-meant-to-be sympathy from friends and relatives, nature had not offered a second chance. Perhaps eventually he had been almost grateful, for he could not bear to have her endure the experience over again. But now, years later, all that seemed to survive between them was the blame; he was convinced he could still see accusation in her eyes, as though in some way he in his loving enthusiasm had been responsible for dislodging the foetus. When occasionally just for old times' sake, she would delay the sleeping draught and allow him to touch her, he found no enjoyment in it, only sadness and anxiety. Unresponsive and brittle, worn too thin and fragile, she herself was truly breakable now, and he worried he might crush her with a single kiss.

A short burst of voice interrupted his thoughts. He lifted his radio to his lips.

'Yes? Found anything, Radcliffe?'

'No joy so far, sir. Nothing in the first building, no sign.'

'Keep going.'

Ahead of him the dilapidated and boarded up warehouse was almost obscured by the mist. Gibbeson had reached it and was working his way along to find some way in. Bankruptcy and abandoned buildings, Blake noted wearily. Where once the hum of manufacturing had made this little area a thriving work place, now it was a no-man's land of cracked-up concrete surfaces, deep potholes and rampant weeds. With the old disused rail depot to the east, and the other warehouse over near the canal, this land and the motorway divided the poorer housing estates right off, as though the edges of the town couldn't be supported. Investment had retreated away south, towards the better streets, to make sure the haves were protected from the have-nots.

He shone his torch up the wall at a scrawl of white spray paint: Fuk of yo shit heds. Education was even failing to teach the young how to spell the four letter words they used with such alacrity. Casual crime, misplaced persons, vandalism, he saw it all, not from the streets where he might do something about it, but from under a mountain of bureaucratic and protectionist paperwork.

'Here, over here, sir...'

Gibbeson was crouching down signalling with his flashlight.

But his call was suddenly overshadowed by a more urgent voice, bursting out of Blake's radio...

'Sir? Sir, there's something funny going on here...'

Raised voices then a sharp ear splitting crack... an unintelligible shout...

'Radcliffe?' Blake depressed the switch. On, off, on. 'Radcliffe?' On again, to a continuous empty buzzing.

Gibbeson stood up.

'Control?' Blake yelled into the radio. 'All units, all units to the canal warehousing. Car Two, pick me up, now!'

'Sir?'

'Leave that, Gibbeson!' He plunged into the gloom in the direction of the perimeter road and Gibbeson followed. In the distance a set of headlights dulled by the fog turned urgently towards them.

CHAPTER THIRTY ONE

SUNDAY

Jane, Jane, Jane. An insistent little voice, calling out, commanding attention, somewhere in the aisles, somewhere among the rows of freezer cabinets, someone is taking her hand, somewhere someone is leading her away...

'Jane?'

Velalley opened her eyes. The child was silhouetted by the minimal light from the sash window, the outline of her head blurred by wisps of hair, the face dark, shaded, indistinct. A little hand was stretching out... If she could catch hold of it, if she could just move fast enough. She lifted her arm. 'Angie...'

'Jane?'

Velalley, fully conscious now, focussed properly on Suzie's astonished stare. 'Hello.'

'Were you dweaming?'

'Mmmn.' She smiled reassuringly and patted the bed, 'Want to hop in?'

Suzie wriggled in under the bedclothes, her little body

surging with energy. The flushed cheeks and dullness in her eyes had almost disappeared.

'Oooh, your feet are frozen. Owch! Don't you dare!' She pulled away, laughing, from the rampaging toes. Suzie yelped with excitement as inevitably the game increased into a chase, under the bedclothes, over them.

'Got you!' But Suzie darted away again, squealing with delight. 'Shh! We'll wake Granny.' Eventually Velalley lay back, breathless, too exhausted to move. 'No more,' she pleaded.

Suzie's mind wandered. 'Where's Teddy?'

'Maybe he fell off?'

Suzie disappeared headfirst over the side. After much scuffling beneath the bed, she emerged, dragging him up by the ear. 'Teddy's very hungry.'

'Doesn't he mind being carried that way?'

She climbed back up and sat swinging her legs. 'No, he likes it.'

'Oh.' Velalley languished on the pillows, unwilling to take on the world too soon.

Suzie snuffled her face into the bear's fur, then she looked up eagerly. 'Where's Ewik?'

Velalley glanced resentfully at the other side of the bed and sat up.

'Let's have some breakfast,' she said, reaching for her dressing gown.

The kitchen cupboards contained more than usual, a new brand of muesli, fresh crusty bread, some deliciously fruity jam. She sighed with relief at her mother's thoughtfulness, her knowing what she most needed was a little comforting, some ordinary homeliness.

Suzie sat up at the breakfast table cosily wrapped now in her pink dressing gown, and her feet in Kermit-frog slippers, a treasured reminder of her old life, swinging back and forth against her chair and wriggling in understandable frustration at the constant urge to scratch. The spots were not quite so red, but they were still there.

Velalley put the kettle on to boil, and made some toast while Suzie chattered on, partly to the bear, partly to her. 'And wear a rain hat. You have to hold my hand, or Granny'll be cwoss. Teddy says he wants some milk.'

It was still barely light. Water trickled down the leaves of the ivy outside the window and dripped rhythmically onto the sill. Through the mist, the small wrought iron bench in the garden that Erik had bought when they'd moved in was only just visible. How they had laughed together at his fantasy of 'his red-haired beauty sitting there, captured inside the ivy clad walls, with a basket of roses on her lap'. His red-haired beauty… did that… did that… Marilyn – she could hardly contemplate the name. Did she have red hair? Velalley viewed the garden suddenly with a new eye. Tiny, private, and very personal. A dark garden with high walls. For one.

Laura had come downstairs and taken a cup of tea through to sit on the couch.

Suzie was only picking at her toast, converting most of it into crumbs which she pressed into the woolly smile of her scuffed teddy bear, abstractly encouraging him to eat with a little song which had no clear melody or direction. 'This the blue bear… sat on a wall… blue bear… twinkle, twinkle…'

Velalley herself felt as unconnected as the song. She took a nervous sip of tea, then put down the cup and played with her own toast, thinking hard – about Dougie Phillips first, then inevitably of the phone call of a couple of moments before.

Blake had sounded distraught. 'How early can you get here, Velalley?'...'Is something wrong – what's wrong, sir?'... 'PC Radcliffe is dead.'... 'Radcliffe? ... Radcliffe is?'

It was hard to take in, harder still to face her own mortality, for that was what it proved. Both Phillips and Radcliffe were only doing what any of them at the Station did. And in the ordinary pursuit of her duties, any night, any day, she too might meet a madman with a knife or a gun, and die. She wondered briefly what it would be like, whether you would actually feel the flesh fracture as the knife went in, or the velocity of the bullet tearing through, or whether there would be a time delay, a brief second between the lightning strike and the onset of the pain, and like watching Suzie falling over, or simply dropping a dish, it would have that strange helpless, slow motion quality, a sensation of time standing still, as if you could stop it happening if only you could move fast enough...

To stop herself thinking, she switched on the radio, agitatedly flicking away from the Sunday Sunrise Service. *Early morning fog will clear by lunchtime to leave a cold bright afternoon, with a light westerly breeze....*

She snapped the weather forecast off and stood up, but in place of that radio voice, a worse thought came to her, unbearable, infinitely more shocking than her fear of dying. What would happen to Erik? And to Suzie? And what if she hadn't kissed Suzie that day? What if Suzie didn't have anyone? Erik would certainly remarry, Velalley thought wryly. But would he take Suzie? And if he did, the child would end up living with another woman, a new Mrs Velalley. A stranger. A wave of unbearable grief swept over her at the thought of her life being cut short, and losing her time as Suzie's protector, as - As her new mother.

But Erik? What about him. With this new wife? This other woman.

'Blue bear... blue...' Suzie was smiling, enjoying herself in some private fantasy world. The bear's face was messy, his old gold fur sharpened into spikes by butter and the morning light. Suzie's hair was shining, red-gold and un-brushed from bed. A tiny red eruption temporarily flaming on one cheek was all that marred her perfect little face.

A kind of violent panic made Velalley's words rush up from deep inside. 'Mum? If –'

Laura looked up. 'What did you say?'

Velalley hurried over to the doorway. 'If anything happened to me –'

'Don't talk rubbish! How can something happen to you?'

'Promise, Mum, promise me you'll make sure Suzie is...'

'There's no promising about it, Jane. You ought to know that. She is my grand daughter. Who was that on the phone before?'

'No-one,' Velalley said quickly. Then, 'Sergeant Blake. He wants me in early.'

'Then leave those plates, dear. I'll wash up. Erik rang last night – I'm sorry I should have told you already. I'm no good in the mornings – he said he'll be back to mind

Suzie this afternoon while I pop home. It'll be nice for them to spend some time together.'

Velalley picked up some of the breakfast plates and smacked them onto the work surface. 'No!'

There were crumbs on the teddy bear's muzzle. Suzie, her fingers sticky with jam, was busy breaking off more toast and grinding it up. 'Don't, Suzie!'

'But Teddy's hungry.'

'Don't, I said!'

Suzie drew back into her chair submissively, her eyes wide with resentment.

'Oh, darling! Sorry! I'm just - ' Pricked by her own stupidity, Velalley strode out to the front hall and bent down to collect the newspaper. From the front page in undeniable and shocking black and white, the child's little face looked out from under the headlines.

Little Angie Where is she?

Eight a.m. Sunday morning and the station was in a state of shock. There was an eerie and unnatural hush and alarm on every face, as Velalley walked quickly through the corridors in search of Sergeant Blake. She found him talking on one of the land lines in Records. She waited for him to finish, disturbed by the exhaustion in his voice, the puffiness under his eyes.

He caught sight of her. 'No...' The tone of his voice altered. 'No, this is not a good moment...'

Normally he was a common sense cop, a father figure, reliable and friendly, someone she could turn to for advice and assistance. She liked his dry sense of humour, and the deep sort of good-heartedness which almost always showed through the rather tough exterior. Right now though, according to the others, he was in deep trouble. His personal initiating of the fruitless search for Angie last night, in advance of the support group, had turned with the dawn into disaster. Now he was carrying the can, and his temper was on short fuse. No matter that a hidden cache of hard drugs at the warehouse had been seized. It was Drug Squad territory, and Radcliffe and Ward had inadvertently waltzed in on some long and secret surveillance job.

'No!' Abruptly he ended the call, replaced the receiver and turned to her.

'You wanted me in early, sir?'

He hesitated before he said: 'You're back with the mother in a couple of hours?'

'Yes. But last night, sir – I heard there was a witness. Didn't you find anything?'

'Look, just before all this drugs business –'

'Let me go back there, sir.'

'No, Velalley, I don't think –'

'Blake?' The DI's voice thundered down the hall.

He covered his forehead with his hands and pressed with frustration.

'Blake!'

'See Gibbeson,' he said, authoritative again. He picked up a file. 'Do what you need to, Velalley.'

PC Gibbeson was drinking a machine coffee at his desk. He was short by station standards, and little overweight, with a buzz of black hair. He'd only been at West Side a year and this morning he seemed unusually wary, probably spooked by being involved in the night's events.

'Blake says I should speak to you.'

'Why?' he asked sharply.

'I think we should go back to the warehouses.'

'I – I just finished my shift.'

'And I'm on duty at ten.'

He stood up and stared at her. Then he nodded. 'Right.'

'Do you know where he means?' Velalley asked as they drove east.

'When the emergency call came through, he and I had just reached that warehouse at the eastern corner and I'd found what could have been a way in, and, well, in that light, I can't be sure –'

'What?'

'Threads from material. But it was only a glance, and Radcliffe's message...'

'Okay, let's get there.'

There were two threads, pale blue ones. Velalley bent low to examine them, marvelling for a second at Gibbeson's powers of observation, all the more astonishing in the reported mist and darkness of the hour. The point of entry however was less remarkable, indeed highly improbable; a hole or vent, kicked in by vandals at some time, but boarded up since. She pushed hard against the wood, then tried again, harder. It did not give.

'Surely not here. How could she?'

But he was already further along searching for some other way in. She followed him anxiously. There was a window high above them, open but impossible.

'I'll go round the other side,' she said, and set off, but a shout from him had her running back almost immediately.

She found him kicking in what was left of some rotten wood at the end of the building. He crawled through the ridiculously small opening and she followed him with difficulty.

They emerged into an office, empty of all furnishing except a couple of fusty filing cabinets. The door out of it was locked.

'Got any skeleton keys?'

'I think so. Back in the car.'

'Break it down then.'

'It's private property, Velalley.'

'Break it down! No, Hold on!' She leaned up close to the door, and spoke firmly and clearly. 'Angie? Angie, are you in there?' She waited, straining to tune in to some responsive movement or spoken reply. She turned to Gibbeson.

He shook his head. He hadn't heard anything either.

'Angie, can you hear me? We're going to break down the door. Don't be frightened, Angie. We're here to help you.' She stood back. 'Okay.'

It was particularly difficult. The door opened inwards, he was working against the rim lock and the frame. He tried kicking. It was a fire door, stout and well made. It did not respond.

'What about that?' She pointed to a large air vent high up on the wall. Together they heaved a filing cabinet over and he climbed up.

'I've got an army knife,' he said, fishing in his pocket.

'With a screw driver?'

He held it up.

'Then take the rim lock off the door, for God's sake.'

'Right.' He leapt down and began to undo the screws.

They were tight, he was panting with the effort. 'Sorry, should have thought of this first.'

A cold fear had gripped her. 'Just hurry,' she said.

The last screw gave. Gibbeson ripped the lock off and the door opened at the touch of his fingertip.

She steeled herself and stepped through. Gibbeson followed. Just a warehouse, a large open area, shelves along the sides, light falling from high windows onto a grey concrete floor, a large pile of rubbish heaped up in the centre. Velalley lifted her head catching the whiff of a sour and recognisable smell she could not quite place.

'Angie?' No sound. 'You take that side.'

They searched systematically, circling the rubbish heap. They returned to the sides, met at the end, and turned.

'Nothing,' said Gibbeson. 'Look!' He pointed. 'There's another room near where we came in. Toilets or something.'

He saw it at the same time she did, lying on the floor at the far end. They broke into a run. He reached it first, leaned down.

'It's a doll. Erh! Its face is covered in crumbs.'

Velalley stared at it. The crumbs seemed to hover in mid-air as Gibbeson brushed them away. Blue. Bright insidious blue. Then she caught the smell again. She leapt past him into the toilets.

She would always remember it, the strange slow motion quality, a sensation of time standing still as she dropped down beside the child. Angie, with her knees drawn in tight to her chest in the foetal position, the blonde hair pasted with sick across the pale unblemished cheeks, the blue tint around the mouth, the fingers of the hands pressing inwards towards the palms, the acid small.

'Get an ambulance,' she screamed, 'quick!' But she knew even as Gibbeson streaked away that no one could help Angie now. Her skin was as cold as it was soft, downy like a cool peach. Ignoring the rules, she lifted the limp little body and rocked it gently back and forth, back and forth in her arms, tears streaming down her cheeks, mourning the child as a mother would, mourning the child for Faye.

CHAPTER THIRTY TWO

They hurried up the stairs but Velalley balked at the door, fiddling nervously, first with her coat's collar, then with its buttons, seeking to delay revealing the brutal truth a little longer, letting Faye have one more minute's peace. But it wasn't peace, was it, this waiting, this clinging to pathetic hope?

'Come on,' Gibbeson whispered, 'she has to be told.'

She had no stomach for the pressure required to ring the bell. Gibbeson leaned across. Colston answering the door read disaster in their eyes and backed away.

'Make some tea, Judith,' Velalley said quietly, fighting to regain her control. 'Stay here,' she said to Gibbeson. If Faye's soul was to be laid bare then it was she and she alone who must do it. At the sight of the thin hunched shoulders, the dark un-brushed hair, the words she had so carefully prepared dried on her lips. But when Faye's eyes turned to meet her own, there was nothing to be said. She crossed the room to take her hand. The woman knew, knew already, by some telepathic means. Death had cast dark shadows across her face and her future hung over her like the sword of Damocles. She pulled the white duvet close around her like a protective shroud.

'She is dead, I know she is. You've found her, haven't you?'

'Yes.'

'Where have they taken her?'

'To the mortuary at the hospital.'

'Were you there? Had she been... harmed? You know...?'

'No. I'm sure not, Faye. But no. We think she escaped from her abductor. She seems to have taken shelter in the warehouse where she was found.'

'Who found her? Was it you?'

Velalley nodded, wishing it had been someone else.

'Isn't she beautiful?'

She thought of the pathetic little figure curled up in her arms, the blonde hair, the acid smell, the fingernails digging deep into the palms. 'I've never seen a more beautiful child.'

'H-how did she die?'

'There'll have to be a post mortem but...' It was too cruel. But Faye would find out soon enough. Perhaps it was best for it all to come at once. 'We think she may have eaten poison.'

There were no tears in Faye's eyes to blur the vision of her child's final moments. After a pause she said, 'C-can I see her?'

'Are you sure you want to?'

'Yes.'

'We can go just as soon as –'

'Now.'

Gibbeson appeared silently at the door, and held out the doll. Velalley reached for it and passed it on to Faye.

'What's this?'

'It was there. We think she had it with her. Do you recognise it?'

'I've never seen it before.' She abandoned it and stood up. 'Will you come, Jane, and see Angie with me?'

They waited, side by side, surrounded by the hygiene and white walls, a purity that seemed to Velalley to transform the mortuary into a place of incubation, a higher level, halfway between life and death. Nevertheless she found it threatening somehow, the silence; then a tapping on the highly polished floor, as footsteps came towards them, and then the rolling of wheels. She wanted to turn away, knowing what was coming, not wanting it to arrive, wishing it could be otherwise.

Faye was in a state that could only be described as a kind of elation, her eyes glistening and wide at the thought of seeing Angie. It was essential the child should be officially identified, but Velalley sensed it would be equally important for Faye to touch her, to re-establish some bond before the child vanished forever, some tangible experience on which to centre her grief.

Once the identification was done Velalley touched the pathologist's sleeve and drew him away.

'Have you established a time of death?' she whispered.

Taking her lead he spoke softly. 'Not definitely yet, but the early hours, five, six a.m. Maybe even as late as seven.'

'Mum?… I was just checking how Suzie - … Yes, I know she's all right with you… I'm not fussing… Yes.'

'Erik rang again. He wants to come over later to see her.'

'No! No! I'll be home later this afternoon myself!'

There was a moment of silence at the other end of the line. 'Has something happened, Jane?'

Through the door she could see Faye clinging onto her dead child's hand. A blurred image of Suzie had somehow laid itself over Angie. Her stomach contracted. 'Mum, I've got to go. I'll talk to you later,' she said, and hung up.

The pathologist was restraining Faye, covering the child up. Faye was in tears.

'Let me take her home,' she sobbed, 'tell him to let me take her home.'

'You can't,' she said gently. 'There has to be a post mortem,' but now Faye was hysterical, hitting out at him, at her.

'Why? Why didn't you find her in time? Why was it my child, my Angie? Why wasn't it your child?'

Velalley fought her way through the blows and held Faye close, felt the sobbing diminish slowly, and the abject grief weigh her down again into a solemn and terrible calm.

Outside the day was brilliant with sunlight. It outlined the litter on the hospital lawns, and glared off the sash windows. Velalley opened the car door for her.

Faye paused, lifting her tear-stained face. 'Listen.'

She heard it then too, a silver-tongued litany on the clear cold air, the peal of bells from the church tower.

'What will you do now?' Faye asked vaguely, as they drove back through the deserted Sunday streets.

Velalley had no answer. The question had taken her breath away. What could she say? When I leave you I shall go home to my child, a child who has been given to me? Nor could she ask in return: what will you do, Faye, what will you do, now?

'There is nothing that can happen to me now,' Faye said as if she'd read Velalley's thoughts. 'I don't care if anyone sees me. In the past few days I feel as if I've grown old while time's stood still. I feel as if my life is over.'

'A counsellor will come, tomorrow, probably.' And how inconsequential it will all seem to her. What is there to say when your child dies? What words are adequate? 'There's your family. And I'll come anytime you need me, anytime.'

'You'll have new problems, other women, other...'

'I'll leave you my phone number,' Velalley said quickly, but she knew that Faye was right. She thought of her narrow little office, the dull green curtains, the files full to bursting with personal sadness, various levels of anger and despair. Of sitting there working meticulously through the paperwork, as if by reading it, understanding it enough, caring enough, she might miraculously solve some of it. Right now it all seemed insurmountable, hopeless.

She radioed ahead to have the officers at Faye's flat hold back the reporters. The original few who were still staked out in the street had been joined by several more, jostling for position.

As Velalley helped Faye through to the door, somebody said: 'All right, Jane?' She turned and there was a flash, then several more. The first camera lowered and it was Hughes again, smiling broadly. She scowled back at him.

Faye seemed hardly to have noticed the crush as she allowed herself to be ferried through but Velalley was relieved to be inside.

'That wretched photographer is amongst them,' she said to PC Warren, and he went to look, but Hughes had disappeared.

Velalley was due to stay with Faye until Colston came with the Longman's, but it seemed unnecessary. Faye was totally immersed in a private grief, sitting perfectly still and staring into space, and the silence stretched between them. Their common bond had been the waiting. Now Colston seemed more suited to the silent task of minding the bereaved.

Velalley sat fingering the doll, idly playing with its blue dress, examining its one white shoe, stroking its short, shiny, unreal hair. Its eyes followed her, painted bright eyes, with curling painted lashes. She must take it back to the station. Even if Faye didn't recognise it, it was probably the last thing Angie had touched before she died.

CHAPTER THIRTY THREE

Velalley was angry to find Erik with Suzie, and her mother gone.

'Laura wants to check things out at home. You're off duty tonight. She thought it would be good for you to be alone.'

'It would have been.'

In her sombre mood his presence was intrusive. She wanted to have Suzie to herself, to hold her tight, to mother her. But Suzie was buzzing round Erik's legs, eager for his attention. She begged to be picked up. His hand rested briefly on her head and he ruffled her hair. She clung to his thigh. He let her stand on his toes and swing back from his hands squealing, as foot by foot he walked her along.

'I'll make some coffee before you go.'

He looked upset. 'All right, if that's what you want. But I thought it might help if I was here to mind Suzie for you for a few hours. Give you some time to rest.'

'Don't get her too excited, Erik.'

'No.' He leaned down. 'Where's your Cinderella book, sweetheart?' Suzie went immediately to find it for him.

'I… er…'

'Look, Erik, I'm not really in a mood for conversation.'

'No,' he said sadly. 'Did Blake talk to you?'

'I've hardly seen him. Please –'

'Is it that kid's disappearance?'

She turned away from him to fill the kettle.

'What's happened, Jane?'

The water splashed over her hand.

Gently Erik took it from her, finished filling it and plugged it in. 'Tell me what's wrong.'

'Everything's wrong,' she said miserably.

'Yes, I know.'

'I found the missing child this morning.'

'Isn't that good?'

'She was dead, Erik. I found her dead.'

'You found her?'

'The search last night was called off temporarily. There was a shooting. Radcliffe was shot.'

'I've met him, haven't I? He's a nice guy. Is he okay?'

'No. He died instantly.'

'God Almighty. That drug thing on the news?'

'Yes. The Sergeant sent two of us back later to go on looking for the child.'

'Sent you? How dare he –'

'It wasn't the same place. And I'm perfectly capable. Don't panic.'

'Had she been murdered then?'

'No. I don't think so. Everything points to her getting away from whoever it was. She was alone and hiding in a warehouse. They're pretty sure it was rat poison.'

'Jesus! What? You mean she ate it?'

'It looks like it. There was no sign of anyone else there.'
She gripped the side of the sink suddenly feeling sick.

'Hey, hey.' He pulled her round to face him, and she clung to him and buried her face gratefully in the mass of his shoulder.

'She'd only been dead a couple of hours.'

'Ewik, Ewik!' Suzie was calling. 'Weach it down, Ewik, weach it down.'

'In a minute, sweetie, in a minute.'

Velalley was appalled to see herself on the evening news, arriving back at the flat and bundling Faye through the photographers.

'You looked furious!' Erik said. He was more cheerful than he'd been for days. 'I wouldn't like to be a criminal meeting you on a dark night. Oh, I don't know, though.'

'It was awful.'

'It's fame. The WPC who shared the mother's agony.'

'Even you don't realise how sad it is.'

'No,' he said, suddenly serious again. 'No, I don't. It must be awful.'

'That woman has nothing left, nothing, except a few little mementoes of her child.'

'Come on, you did what you could.'

She put her head in her hands. 'But what did I do? I couldn't help her, we couldn't find Angie for her, and now I can't make her grief any less. What if that had been Suzie?'

He took her in his arms. 'Come on, why don't we make some dinner?' he said.

With Suzie bathed and hugged and tucked up in bed,

Velalley went back downstairs to the kitchen. Erik was washing up.

She had not intended to kiss him, but she felt safe again with him suddenly. His arms were gentle, protective, and she huddled against him, comforted by the warmth of his body through his shirt. His wet hand stroked her hair, caressed her cheek, tilted her chin upwards, and his lips covered hers.

'Come to bed,' he whispered.

'No.' She twisted away.

He caught her shoulder urgently and turned her back to face him. 'Please, Jane, I love you. I love you. Please. What happened… that was so foolish – to chance everything for what was only sex.'

'Maybe this is only sex.'

He shook his head.

'But you did chance it.'

'I know, and I have to live with that. Even if you forgive me, I can never forgive myself for hurting you. You, and Suzie now, are the most precious things I have.'

He pulled her close again, and held her tight.

In the dark her fingertips explored the familiar contours of his body, the soft hair on his chest, the strength of his shoulders, the hardness in his erection. There was the familiar scent of coal tar soap on his skin, and the ambrosia of his desire, the sweetness of fresh linen on the bed. His kisses on her breast stirred a deep physical rapture of feeling really alive. She arched her back, his hand moved further down. When he entered her, she welcomed the comfortable weight of him, the power, the anticipation of his pleasure, her own lack of control, the brushing sound of his hair against her cheek, and the inevitable sense of release.

For a while they lay together in the dark, him drowsily content, his arm across her protectively. Eventually she moved a little. The tension was returning. He opened his eyes, watched her.

She did not mean to ask but somehow it was a question that she couldn't escape. 'What was she like?' The words stung the air. As soon as she said them she wished she could take them back, wished his eyes were closed, that he would pretend to be asleep.

He moved his arm a little, did not answer her, stared at her silently and fearfully in the dark.

She went on now, on, unable to drop it. 'Is she pretty?'

Somehow his silence confirmed his faithlessness and this other woman he could not mention reared up between them, stealing him away again after all to live with her – happily ever after. Happily ever after.

Suddenly she pushed his arm off, and sat bolt upright, thinking hard. 'Cinderella!'

'What?'

'Cinderella. Why not?'

'Are you mad?'

'What time is it?'

He leaned across, switched on the lamp, and stared at her. 'It's ten.'

'Stay with Suzie until I get back,' she ordered, leaping out of bed.

CHAPTER THIRTY FOUR

Velalley looked determined, Blake thought. He watched her through the glass partition urgently tapping out her entry code and then pushing through the swing door. Did she know?

'Where's Sergeant Blake,' he heard her asking.

'In his office, I think. What's up?'

He signalled to her. 'Over here.'

She hurried past the computers towards him. She was not her usual tidy self, no make-up either.

'You're supposed to be off duty.'

'It's important, sir. Can I have a word?'

She walked in long purposeful strides ahead of him to his office, her back very straight. Strands of auburn hair had missed the clasp that held the rest together, softening the harsh neckline of the dark jacket. She had dressed fast. As well as everything else her child was ill, he remembered. He took a deep breath, preparing himself for her anger. Hell, maybe she was even going to ask for leave. He closed the office door behind him.

'Velalley, I –'

'Sir, I think I know where Angie was held.'

Not about Erik then. He walked round to sit down at his desk and nodded for her to elaborate.

'The doll we found at the warehouse –'

'Wasn't hers though, was it? You said the mother didn't recognise it.'

'No, but I think Angie took it there, all the same. There seemed to be traces of rat poison on its face, when Gibbeson picked it up. I'm sure she was pretending to feed it, like children do with a favourite toy. Like my Suzie... um... Like Suzie does with her teddy.'

'Have the Lab boys had a look for that?'

'Gibbeson brushed most of it off, I think. There's one print on it of Angie's apparently, and –' She bit her lip. 'A couple of his and mine.'

'Hell, Velalley! Between you, you did a bloody good job, him tampering with evidence and you moving the body!'

He saw a flash of defiance glisten in her eyes, and thinking what she might yet have to face from Kendrick with Erik, relented immediately. Anyway she'd cradled the child out of compassion – she had a youngster herself now to care for, and it was her case. And if he himself had been appalled at not reaching the child in time, what must she be feeling being so much closer in to the mother's grief?

He said in all sincerity: 'You did the natural thing. Actually you've coped with it all very well.'

'Thank you, sir.' Her eyes held a moment of grief in them, then she was spirited again. 'But more important, that doll only had one shoe. And I'm sure I've seen another just like it.'

'Where?'

'On the Quale estate. In Carrie Anderson's bedroom.'

Blake frowned.

'It was at the back of the wardrobe. It caught my eye and I picked it up. I'll swear it was a match.'

'I imagine all doll shoes are much the same.'

'But there was no doll anywhere in that flat, sir. No toys. And the bedroom cupboard – there was something funny about it. I thought maybe it was the dog's bed – there was an old pillow and a crumpled rug on the floor in there. Smelt of urine too.'

'I remember thinking that myself. But then the whole place was pretty bad.'

'They don't have a dog. No pets allowed, Anderson said.'

'Maybe they do have one. He wouldn't want anyone to find out if it's against the rules.'

'It's Quale we're talking about, sir. Who pays any attention to rules in a place like that? But there would have been some other evidence of it, a water bowl, dog food. You would have noticed something, surely, sir. And Anderson wasn't expecting my visit, and he didn't have time to hide a dog. Or a cat.'

Blake narrowed his eyes, scanning the scene again in his memory. She was probably correct. 'Okay. So let's kick the idea around. What are you saying?'

'Well, maybe Carrie snatches the child from the supermarket on Thursday afternoon and takes her home.'

'What's her motive?'

'I don't know, sir.'

'No motive.' He stood up and studied the map on the wall tracing a route with his finger. 'If they went via the old railway cutting and up there… past the canal… and across the wasteland… It would explain why nobody saw anything.'

'And the father's out, more often than not you said.'

Blake nodded. 'How much is he out? Have we checked his movements?'

'I don't think so. So far we've only been concerned about Carrie's welfare when she comes out of hospital. There's been no reason to consider Jack Anderson's activities over the past few days.'

'Okay. Say he's away. Can Carrie keep Angie in the cupboard for all that time? Wouldn't the child cry?'

'Maybe not, maybe she's too scared. And who is there to hear? Most of the flats are empty now.'

'And on Saturday morning?'

'Carrie goes back to the supermarket for food.'

'And gets arrested for shoplifting!'

'Only she has an asthma attack and ends up in hospital.'

'And Saturday lunchtime's when the witness sees Angie run across the Northwest Road, alone. It's possible.' He pulled abstractedly at the lobe of his ear, thinking. 'The door was open when I got there in the early afternoon.'

'She could have made it as far as the warehouse by nightfall. Gibbeson's theory about where her point of entry is very likely. A plank had fallen down on the inside over the hole. She would have been trapped.'

'And eventually very hungry.'

'Very hungry,' she repeated softly.

Blake sat down at his desk again and leaned back in his chair considering. Velalley was poised on the balls of her feet, ready to go if he would say the word.

'Find out if Carrie's still in hospital,' he said, 'and organise a search warrant – I'll pick it up on the way. And see if Gibbeson's available to go with me to Quale.'

'Let me come with you sir? I know what I'm looking for.'

'You're off duty, Velalley.'

Her eyes stung him. 'But it's my case, sir.'

Her skin was smooth, the pale luminous skin of red heads, the lips full and prettily drawn, even without lipstick. Velalley was an attractive young woman, but for all her determination and enthusiastic commitment to what always seemed to him to be such a masculine world, she had a fragile quality about her that made him feel protective, particularly now. He should be sending her home to her husband. Hell, he should be telling her about that. He heard himself answering: 'It's Quale. I don't want a woman along.'

She kept her cool, even though her neck flared crimson. 'I can take care of myself, sir. I've been there before, if you remember, and alone. And I'm more experienced than Gibbeson.'

He lifted the phone as soon as she was out of the room. 'Tell Gibbeson he's needed. And I want someone to re-check the statement from that witness on the Angie Simmons case again,' he said. 'Find out if she was carrying anything. Hannan, that's him. Go back and talk to him. Yes, you heard. Tonight. I know it's Sunday and it's late. Tonight, damn it.'

No moon, a black hole of a night, and no working lighting on the concrete stairs, just their flashlights and their footsteps, and their eyes scanning the darkness as they climbed to the fifth floor landing. Blake was already regretting Velalley's presence. It made him uneasy, partly because of the atmosphere of danger, the feeling of suspicious and resentful eyes all around him, but more importantly because against his better judgement and because he felt guilty, he had given in to her.

There was a light under Anderson's door. Gibbeson knocked politely.

'For Christ's sake,' Blake did it himself, much louder. This was Quale after all.

The door opened. Anderson, holding a can of lager and swaying on his doorstep with the false confidence of alcohol, noted their uniforms, and was immediately abusive. 'Bloody rozzers. Round here all the fucking time. What is it now? You've put my daughter in hospital. Come to arrest me, have you? Bugger off.'

'We'd just like a quick word, sir,' Gibbeson said. Too politely Blake thought. Anderson was clearly drunk. A heavier hand would be much more appropriate. Besides they had the search warrant.

'It's about Carrie,' Velalley said quickly. 'Can we come in?'

Anderson squinted into the darkness at her. 'You were here before.'

'Yes, sir. So may we come in? It's extremely important.'

Perhaps it was the firmness in her voice, or the feminine touch, and her confident smile. Whatever it was, it did the trick, more easily that the threat of the warrant in his pocket. Let her have her head, then.

'What's so important?' Anderson demanded when they were all in the living room. Behind him through the window the lights of the town twinkled like so many fallen stars. 'Carrie's all right, isn't she?'

'Is there any other medication in her bedroom?'

Blake liked Velalley's inventiveness. He continued the theme. 'The doctors are anxious to know if she was using any tablets or inhalers, other than those we found already.'

'You saying my daughter's a junkie?'

'Oh no, sir,' Velalley sounded so innocent, 'but would you mind if I checked her bedroom in case there's something we missed? It might make all the difference to the speed of her recovery.'

Anderson looked nonplussed, then he shrugged.

Velalley looked for approval and then disappeared into the bedroom.

'The stuff she had comes from the doctor,' he said. 'Little cow is more likely not to take it.'

'Sergeant?'

Anderson staggered back slightly to allow Blake past.

Velalley was standing looking into the cupboard. She'd already found the doll shoe, but she pointed to something hanging over the rail inside. She said quietly: 'Wasn't the abductor wearing a navy anorak, sir?'

Blake looked at it, then down at the pillow and the rug – it was tenuous but if forensic could prove a link...

'Anderson,' he said, leaning round the door into the other room, 'were you here with Carrie last Thursday?'

'I – um. Course I was.'

'All day?'

'Yeah.'

'What about Friday?'

'Sure. What's she been saying?'

Velalley appeared beside him. 'Nothing, sir, but the doctors are trying to find out if there was a build up to

Carrie's attack. Did you notice anything unusual about her on either night?'

'No. She was up late Friday. When I got back...'

'So you were out on Friday?'

Anderson collapsed down into the couch and took a swig from the can. It was late, and he was obviously well past caring.

Blake held out the warrant. 'Mr Anderson, we have reason to believe Carrie may have been involved in an incident last Thursday and –'

'Supermarket going to prosecute, eh? I warned the stupid little bitch...' In spite of the language there was an emotive catch in his voice. He raised the can of lager before drinking again, as if he was drinking a triumphant toast. 'I told her not to go shoplifting.'

Blake kept his voice down. 'I want a Scenes of Crime officer here as soon as possible, Velalley, but I'm not inclined to leave these.'

'Okay.' She produced rubber gloves and two evidence sacks from her shoulder bag and placed the pillow and rug into one, and the anorak into the other.

'Careful – I don't want to lose anything.'

'Mr Anderson,' she said, as they emerged back into the living room and she passed the sacks to Gibbeson, 'I'm hoping to go to the hospital to Carrie tomorrow. I wonder, has she got a special toy, something I could take her that might cheer her up?'

He didn't answer. He sat there staring out at the distant lights in the town.

'Gibbeson,' Blake said, 'make a note that we've taken a pillow and a rug all with Mr Anderson's full co-operation. Oh, and an anorak.'

'Only that bloody doll.'

Blake spun round. 'Sir?'

'You could take that doll of hers, if you want to.'

'What's it like?' asked Velalley carefully.

'How do I know? In her bedroom somewhere, I expect.'

Blake looked across at Velalley. She shook her head at him.

'Is this one of its shoes?' she asked.

Anderson looked at it and nodded. 'White shoes and a blue dress. Only thing she bloody cares about. Treats it like a child.'

Too late Blake realised that Velalley, walking triumphantly ahead of them along the dark ramp, was vulnerable. The violent blow she sustained across the shoulders before either Gibbeson or he could react made her stagger. Two dark shapes whacked viciously at her again. She fell back as they sprinted away and Blake could hear them whooping provocatively as they escaped down the stairs.

'Bloody hell!'

Gibbeson dropped the sacks and was already summoning assistance on his radio.

Blake bent over Velalley. 'You all right?'

She moved her arm with difficulty. 'I – I think so.'

He breathed a heavy sigh of relief. 'Jesus.'

'Just when we're getting somewhere! That'll teach me!'

'Did you get a look at them?'

'No.'

Gibbeson leaned down. 'Sir, hadn't we better see if we can get downstairs?' he whispered. 'After the last few days this could be a set-up.'

Blake held out his hand. 'Think you can make it, Jane?'

Velalley pulled herself painfully up onto her elbow and forced an apologetic grin as he helped her to her feet. 'Bastards got my handbag, sir,' she said.

'Didn't I say you should have gone home?'

In the distance sirens began closing in, screaming northwards across the town towards them.

CHAPTER THIRTY FIVE

Rest and warm baths, Mrs Velalley, they'd said, it will help the bruising to come to the surface. Outside the window the sky was glistening with the first light of dawn. The hot water was soothing and restorative, and beginning to relieve the pain that spanned her shoulder blades and bit into her neck. But for the ache deep inside her there was no cure.

Not even time would heal it.

For time itself was the culprit. Angie's time of death had been definitely established to be just short of 7 a.m. She and Gibbeson had found her at 8.25 a.m. If in the small hours the search had been started, not at the northern end but on the eastern side of the wasteland, if there had been no drugs surveillance and Radcliffe had not been killed, if Blake and Gibbeson hadn't rushed urgently away to his assistance. No, she would never have denied him that – but they were so close. If she'd gone into work earlier, if she and Gibbeson had gone back to the warehouse sooner, if the witness had come forward more quickly. If, if, if. One small alteration in any of it, and they would have been bearing Angie back to her mother's arms alive. She would have seen the relief on Faye's face, witnessed the joy of the mother hugging her rescued child. And instead of dying, Angie would have grown up. That downy peach skin would have bloomed into the warm flesh of womanhood. Her hair might have grown darker with the years. Maybe she would have had her mother's love of art and gone on to college. Probably she would have married and had children of her own. But time and circumstance had dictated her dramatic little ending and frozen her into a picture that Velalley knew would haunt her always, the beautiful blonde four year old child lying limp in her arms, too long dead and far beyond her reach.

There was the other picture too, that glossy little photograph Faye had lent them to use for the search. In it the short blonde hair, the heart shaped face, the appealing eyes which would stare out again from the front page of every newspaper in the morning, a child whose sad little fate would draw sympathy from the whole nation for a few brief hours, but who, because time inevitably hurried on, would soon be buried and forgotten. Except by Faye.

And her too, for nobody else, not even Faye, had seen the fine strands of gold hair catching the early morning light, the delicate fingernails pushed into the palms on the tiny undeveloped hands, the pale skin, bluish round the pursed up lips; or sensed her distress, or smelled that hideous acrid scent, the burning acid that had poisoned and destroyed Angie's little life.

Velalley felt sick with anger at the waste.

There was a knock at the bathroom door and Erik was calling softly.

'Jane?'

She didn't answer.

'I did hear you come in but you might have let me know you were back.'

Velalley sank lower under the water. It lapped gently around her shoulders and steam rose up.

'Jane?'

'Sorry,' she said.

'You're not in the bath? It's still practically the middle of the night, for God's sake.'

The water splashed as she rose up. 'Is Suzie all right?'

'Ssh! Of course she is, no thanks to you. What kind of real mother runs off in the night on some case or other? It's just as well I was here.'

'It was vitally important, Erik.'

'But it's always vitally important. Why did you go out?'

She didn't answer.

'Darling, seriously, you can't save every child.'

She sank down again, deep into the warm water, not wanting to listen.

'You want to get your life in perspective, Jane.' He sounded really frustrated. 'And look around you, for God's sake, closer to home.'

'What!'

'I –' There was a moment's silence, then: 'Suzie's ill and you're chasing off after some other child who means nothing to you.'

She was out of the bath and wrapping herself in a towel now. 'Sod you, you don't know anything about it.'

'Well, now you are home, Suzie's your responsibility.'

'You'll be sorry when you see –' she shouted, angrily wrapping a towel round her hair and grabbing another, then flinging open the door to show him her bruises.

But the hall was empty and downstairs the front doorbell had rung and voices were floating up the stairs towards her.

'Mr Erik Velalley?'

'Yes.'

'Detective Inspector Kendrick wants you down at the Station again, sir, in connection with the murder of Marilyn Farr.'

'Would you keep your voice down please.'

She leaned urgently over the banister, steadying herself against it. Marilyn? Marilyn Farr? 'What? What are you talking about?' But awful recognition of the situation had gripped her like a vice.

Erik looked up. It was too dark to see his face.

She ran down the stairs, clutching the towel around her, water dripping off her feet.

'What are they talking about? Erik?'

It was PCs Johnson and Toms at the door.

'Look, Velalley,' Toms said, looking down at the towel, red faced, 'it's just enquiries.'

'What enquiries?'

'Kendrick,' said Johnson.

She tried to take Erik's hand. 'Wait, I'm coming with him.'

'No,' Erik said, resisting her touch. 'I'd rather go alone. You stay with Suzie, Jane.'

She stared down at his hand and then up again at his face. His eyes gave nothing away. 'I'll... I'll put on some clothes. We'll bring Suzie. Wait for me!'

'No, Jane.' Erik took his jacket and stepped outside and closed the door behind him.

'Wait,' she whispered.

★

Suzie was fast asleep, her room comfortingly lit by the soft night-light. For a while Velalley stood still as still by her bed listening to her funny little breathing sounds, watching her, the fuzzy red-gold curls, the tilt of her little nose, the mouth, pursing occasionally as she dreamed. Her small arms were flung out wide across the pillow.

She crept out and went downstairs. The house was silent. She wandered vacantly along the hall and fingered the long black cashmere coat on the hook by the front door. On into the dining room – a pretty room, with bay windows, but one they never seemed to have time to use now. Practically every waking moment was spent at the back of the house, in the kitchen, and the comfortable living room which opened off it. For a time she stood looking out through the gauze curtains. Outside the wind was lifting the scattered autumn leaves, whirling them, dropping them, blowing them along again. The white gauze and the lamp's orange glow in the early morning light gave the street a ghostly, abandoned appearance.

'Enquiries', at this sort of time?

She could not control the trembling increasing inside her, not by breathing faster, not by breathing deeply, nor even by leaning back close to the wall supporting herself against its strength. Marilyn… Marilyn Farr was dead, and murdered brutally. Just enquiries… it's just enquiries, Velalley.

Out in the kitchen she put on the kettle. Maybe a hot drink would help her calm down. She carried the hot weak tea back to the bedroom but at the sight of the double bed she began to cry. Sitting among the crumpled bedclothes she allowed herself to let go, to be frightened, to doubt Erik and then to weep that she could, and then to regret all the recent arguments with him, the mistakes, and the wasted opportunities for intimacy. She lay down quietly and closed her eyes and tried to calm herself. She longed to be beside him, to listen to him, and to hear what he was saying.

Kendrick wouldn't be questioning him without some sort of evidence – would he? He would be following proper police procedures.

'I'd rather go alone. You stay with Suzie, Jane.'

She sat up, suddenly filled with the most awful fear.

CHAPTER THIRTY SIX

MONDAY

Carrie Anderson pressed her face close against the glass partition hardly able to believe the evidence of her eyes. Madeline was on the telly! She couldn't hear the sound but she watched spell bound as the doll was held up in several poses, and then the camera zoomed in to her face for the close-up. Somehow her being on television made her seem so real, so alive. Carrie smiled proudly to herself. Confident as ever, Madeline, eyes bright, and her beautiful short blonde hair shining, appeared relaxed and fully in control, despite this sudden and quite unexpected early morning fame. Back again to the head-to-toe. But the blue dress looked grubby and creased, and she was missing a shoe. What had she been up to?

Now the subject seemed to have changed and there was a picture of a factory or something. All the occupants of the television lounge were facing away from the door absorbed in the programme, whatever it was. Carrie wasn't surprised. Anything with Madeline in it would be compulsive viewing.

She opened the door.

Instantly some interfering old woman in a paisley dressing gown turned round. 'It's her!'

All the heads turned.

'Don't let her in. Out, you!' The paisley gown pointed a bony finger accusingly. 'You've been banned.'

Somebody else joined in. 'Ring for the nurse, Doris.'

Now another woman was leaning across to a bell on the wall, and there was general mindless clamour. You couldn't hear the television for all the racket.

So? Let them try to throw her out. Ring the rotten bell, why not? She stepped inside. She was just as entitled as they were to watch the telly.

They spread out, magically using up all the chair space.

'Go on, get out!'

'You should be in the children's ward, you.'

'Doris' pressed the bell.

Carrie stood for a moment debating her position. Breaking the remote control on Saturday night because nobody would let her watch a particular programme hadn't been a popular move, and the nurses would certainly remember and throw her out. She glanced back at the screen wishing Madeline would re-appear.

'Press the bell again, Doris!' screamed the one in the paisley gown.

Carrie pulled a face. Old slags. 'Who'd want to sit here anyway?' She pinched her nose, 'Phew! What'ya in for? Incontinence?'

There was deep satisfaction in seeing the shock register on their faces. The paisley gown's mouth opened and closed like a stupid half-baked goldfish. Carrie slammed the door behind her triumphantly for extra insult, and stomped along the corridor to the water cooler.

She took a cup and filled it, then alternately sipped the liquid and chewed on the white waxiness of the lip of the container while she considered how Madeline had come to be featured. And in what programme? It might have been the news. But why would Madeline be on the news? Was she lost? Had her father lost her doll? Were they trying to find the owner? Anyway, stuff them, she would soon be out of here. She poured what was left of the water over the electric plug at the back of the machine. There was a pleasing phfft. She screwed up the paper cup and shoved it back up the dispenser.

Madeline was her doll. She had every right to know where she was and what was happening to her.

CHAPTER THIRTY SEVEN

Velalley left her bed and paced the house. When the newspaper arrived there was a small photograph of her on the front page and a fabricated item headed: 'How I waited with tragic mother – See page 3'. It was the last straw. She rang Blake.

He sounded thoroughly stressed out. 'I've just spoken to Carrie Anderson on the phone a few minutes ago and she swears she knows nothing.'

'Come on, Sergeant, you know why I'm ringing.'

'Erik's still down with Kendrick, Velalley, that's all I know. I'd tell you, for God's sake, wouldn't I?'

'But you must have known?'

'Hardly anything. You know what Kendrick's like.'

But she was sure he was hedging. 'So find out what's happening now!'

'No! Look, just as soon as... trust me, Jane.'

'Mmmn.'

'Trust me!'

She didn't want him to know she was crying. She didn't answer.

'Everyone expects miracles. The SOCO's been at Anderson's flat an hour but he hasn't come up with anything yet,' he snapped, changing the subject abruptly.

She fished in her dressing gown pocket for a tissue and blotted her eyes. 'But it is Carrie's doll?'

'Yes. She'll be out of the hospital this afternoon and they can't wait to be rid of her. Mind, the poor kid is stuck in the adult surgical ward. But you won't believe this – she rang me demanding the doll back! Says she lost it in the supermarket when she went shopping for her father on Thursday morning.'

'What?'

'Indeed! And I've had a call from the duty social worker at the hospital too. She thinks Carrie's telling the truth.'

'Do you, sir?'

Suzie, emerging sleepily from her bedroom tugged at the sleeve of Velalley's dressing gown. She bent down to her, hand cupped over the receiver. 'Ssh. In a minute, sweetie. I'm on the 'phone.'

'Are you cwying?'

Velalley swallowed hard. 'No, darling. Wait for me in the kitchen?' She straightened up and tried to concentrate again.

'Perhaps she did lose it?' she said vacantly.

'Can you see a kid Carrie's age taking a doll to the supermarket? She's thirteen, Velalley.'

'She must be lonely. Her father said she treats the doll like a child. Maybe she does take it shopping. Her mother's run off. It might be a sort of comforter.'

'A bit far fetched though, wouldn't you say? Angie happens to pick up the doll, then is stolen herself?'

'But if Carrie has anything to hide, why get in touch with us?'

'God knows. How does the female mind work?'

'How does the guilty mind work, male *or* female?' she snapped. Oh God, Erik, how does it work?

'Shoulder any better?' His tone was placatory.

'Yes thank you.'

But in the mirror on the wall beside her she could see how dark the lines were under her eyes. She pushed her hair back from the bruise on her shoulder and winced at the effort. She tried massaging her neck gently; it gave some temporary relief.

'I suppose you've seen the paper?' Blake said.

'Yes, but –' She had hoped he hadn't, fearful he might think she'd courted the publicity. 'I never said anything to them, sir, apart from that statement I was asked to make. It had to be that photographer Hughes, the one Warren and I threw out of Faye's flat.'

'The TV cameras were always going to be there, but the piece in the paper today was the DI's idea,' Blake said.

'What?'

'He went to see the editor personally. He fed him a bit of information about you to take the heat off, he told me. Off Simmons herself.'

'How dare he? Everyone's going behind my back.'

'Relax, Jane, don't give me grief on this one. It doesn't hurt for the public to see us in a kinder light. And surely it's worth it for Faye's sake? Since the press boys had that to print, most of them have moved on. And we have more important things to think about now.'

Velalley took a sharp breath.

Blake heard it. There was a pause before he said: 'Look, you're due a break. Take today off while your luck's in.'

'But I can't just stay here, can I, sir? Not now. Besides, there's... there's Faye.' She'd nearly said Erik.

'Kendrick won't let you get involved in the Marilyn Farr thing, if that's what you're hoping. I know you want to help Erik but don't worry, I'll find out what's happening. And as for Simmons, she's getting proper counselling.' He was trying valiantly to change the subject again. 'Did you hear that bastard we arrested for murdering Phillips got bail this morning?'

'No.' The words resounded in her head. Murder, bail, murder, murder.

Suzie wandered back and settled onto the floor at her feet, waiting patiently now and humming softly to herself.

Blake sounded so tired. 'Well, you can come in if you're sure you're okay? We do need some results soon or the press could start to crucify us. They won't be co-operative for long. And things are tight without Radcliffe and ...' his voice trailed off.

Then he said angrily: 'Jesus!'

'I'll only be a little bit late, sir.'

'No, Velalley. Look, forget I said any of that. Stay home, for Christ's sake, you've been injured. I know you haven't had any time off, and no chance with your family lately. We'll manage.'

'But I want to know what's going on. I only have to wait for my mother to get here, sir.'

But Blake had already hung up.

CHAPTER THIRTY EIGHT

Judith Colston, framed in the doorway of Velalley's tiny office, looked at her accusingly.

'I can't understand your attitude. Why?'

'Because,' Velalley said tetchily, reaching for a file, 'he's too chilly and idealistic, the kind of person you'd shrink away from, not open up to, and in Faye's state –'

'You're the one in a state! Anyway,' Colston looked almost offended on Denholm's account, 'he's the sort of person I'd open up to. He spent absolutely hours with her yesterday afternoon.'

Highly trained to comfort and console, to counsel victims of violent crime and bereavement, James Denholm proffered his most sincere sympathy and understanding while his subjects talked through the worst possible of circumstances. He had several letters after his name to prove his credentials and he was deeply respected by the Constabulary hierarchy.

'I don't doubt he's conscientious, but I think she'd be better off talking to a woman. For one thing, what could he know about losing a child? He's not even married.'

'No, but he's very experienced. He deals with huge numbers of cases.' Colston stalked off.

Denholm might be experienced and have seen no end of other people's sorrow, but Velalley disliked him intensely. To her he was too textbook, and Faye was her case, not his. She began trying to catch up on the mountain of paperwork. The wintry sun was shining in onto her desk. She leaned over and pulled the curtain across but after a few minutes, unable to concentrate, she abandoned the files back to the in-tray.

'Before you ask, Velalley, Erik's gone back to Peter Miles's flat and Kendrick's out and I know nothing more. And you're probably better keeping busy – so no, you can't go home.' Blake flipped over the pages of an interim report from Forensic irritably. 'Let's get on with this.'

She nodded.

'We'll be bloody lucky if we can find a link, you know. Angie's fingerprints are on the doll all right, and Carrie's too, but if we can't disprove Carrie's story about losing the doll in the supermarket, we've had that one.'

'What about the doll shoe we found at Anderson's flat?'

'Doesn't prove anything, anyway it's clear, except for your prints.'

She winced. 'When I found it at the back of the cupboard. What about the flat itself?'

'Anderson got a friend to help him clean it from top to bottom!'

'He what?'

'He said he was worried they wouldn't let Carrie come back there.'

Velalley sank into a chair. 'Oh God, I told him to.'

Blake stared at her.

'When I went there on Saturday, I suggested that if he wanted Carrie home, it would be sensible to clean it up.'

Blake swung round furiously in his chair and sat gazing out of the window.

'Did they find anything with the blanket or the pillow?' she asked hopefully.

'They're still looking at those. They're snowed under with work, so right now all we've got is a theory.'

'Yes, sir.'

'You better make a start on the CYP as soon as possible. And have another word with the supermarket. They've said they don't want to press charges because the kid's asthmatic. They didn't like all that business of the ambulance at the time, right after the furore of Angie's disappearance, but it won't hurt to talk to them again. Hey,' he said, as she turned for the door. 'I didn't mean that about not going home. If you want to –'

'We're still short staffed, sir. And I do need to be doing something. Besides this case is important to me.'

'I know,' he said. 'To us both, Velalley, to us both.'

There was an air of false calm in the supermarket, breezy echoing music, tills efficiently bleeping and buzzing, people packing their shopping and leaving, more customers entering the store. Through the plate glass windows, Velalley could see cars pulling out of spaces and being replaced almost immediately by others.

'My company does not intend,' the manager was saying nervously as she followed him towards his office, 'to proceed with a prosecution. The girl was arrested by our security people, and subsequently had a sever asthma attack. It might not be in our best interests.'

'I can see that,' she said, as they reached his office and he held the door open for her. 'Was she a regular customer?'

'I'm afraid I have absolutely no idea. At the time the staff were interviewed. No one recalled her particularly. We have so many people through our doors.'

'So no previous suspicion of her shoplifting.'

'The security man had never noticed her before. Do you want to talk to him?'

'Not now. The day the child was taken –'

'Thursday, yes, very sad, very sad. A very difficult situation for us as you can understand. We're most concerned that it doesn't put people off.'

'The cashier who thought she saw the child with someone? Is she on duty now?'

'I believe so. Do you want to speak to her again? Shall I call her?'

'If you wouldn't mind.'

He lifted the phone and spoke a few words.

'Carrie Anderson says,' Velalley said, as he hung up, 'she says she dropped her doll when she was in the store late on Thursday morning.'

'I'm sure we can replace it for her,' he said nervously.

'That certainly won't be necessary!'

'Lost property would be handed in at the desk. What did it look like?'

'It was found in fact, but can we ask your other staff again if anyone remembered Carrie here on Thursday? A girl of that age carrying a doll might be noticeable.'

There was a tentative knock at the door and a young cashier entered.

'Miss Cotten, this is WPC Velalley. Could you tell her again exactly what you saw last Thursday afternoon?'

'I said everything.'

'You can imagine, Miss Cotten, how essential it is for us to be as helpful as we can to the police.' But there was nothing new to be gleaned. Just the possible sighting of what might have been Angie's abduction: a young woman, perhaps a girl, in a navy anorak and a child in a pale blue outfit walking out of the store hand in hand.

'Was the child carrying anything?'

'I couldn't see.'

'And there was nothing on the security cameras?'

'Most unfortunate that.' The manager shifted his feet. 'As I explained to your colleagues the whole system was being updated. We were off the air for Wednesday, Thursday, and Friday. The whole Mall.'

Velalley sighed. 'And had you ever seen the young woman in the anorak before, Miss Cotten?'

'No,' she looked at her manager. 'It's so busy. You don't have time. And I wouldn't have seen the two of them then, except that I glanced up at the clock to see if...' She blushed. 'To see if it was time for my tea break.'

None of the other staff could recall seeing a girl answering Carrie's description on the Thursday either, with or without a doll.

As Velalley left, the manager said: 'We're installing a safety play area next month. Head Office have given me a budget.'

'Will there be a member of staff responsible?'

He nodded unhappily. 'Oh yes, I can't afford anymore bad publicity. If anything else were to happen here, my job would be on the line...'

Back in her office Velalley rang home.

'No, Erik isn't back. Yes, Suzie's fine. We're making paper flowers. Stop fussing, Jane, and don't work too hard. You tell that Sergeant you should be having your proper time off.'

But now Blake wanted her to go to Faye's flat. She was apprehensive; this time it was all so official. There she would be collecting the formal information she needed to complete her report for the inquest on Angie's death, which would probably end up now with a dissatisfying verdict of Accidental Death. She was also required to make some recommendations for Faye, for what care she might need, and to advise Victim Support and Social Services. And there might be things which Faye could remember, a whole lot more information to be had on the abduction. But from now on it would be much more difficult, raking over the mistakes and the despair. They had been to the limits together. Now the emotional bond, their common goal to rescue the child, and the hope, no longer existed.

And now, of course, there was Carrie.

Two black plastic sacks were stacked just inside the front door. Faye seemed uncertain about letting her in and the whole atmosphere in the flat had changed. The gas fire was on but it was cold even so.

They sat formally over a pot of tea, Velalley being carefully polite. It was hard to get through to Faye for

242

she seemed intent on solitude, making sense of her grief by withdrawing into herself. Here again was the young woman as Velalley had first seen her, knees clenched, shoulders hunched, leaning defensively forward, pressing her palms together displaying that awful sense of disbelief.

Velalley glanced towards the bedroom and frowned. 'Have you changed the furniture around?'

'Mr Denholm thought it might help.'

'May I see?'

Faye shrugged.

Velalley was shocked to find the bedroom completely altered. Angie's bed had been pushed to the wall, covered to make it look like a sort of couch, and the other bed had been centred. The toys were gone, all the clothes from the cupboard, and the wall, from where Angie's paintings had so recently illuminated the room, was clinically bare, uninspiring and colourless.

How could Faye do that? It was the last thing she herself would want if, God forbid, it had been Suzie. She'd want to keep and touch every little thing, the teddy, and the paintings – she'd want to lie for hours staring at those, absorbing their bright energy, following their abstract lines and ideas. She'd need to hold up the little clothes, bury her face in them to try to catch some elusive scent that might still linger in the folds, explore every possible memory and define it exactly, and store it all carefully in her heart.

Back in the living room too there were other things gone as if the flat had been stripped of the past. 'I'm trying to look forward,' Faye said.

Velalley attempted to look encouraging to hide her alarm. 'That's understandable,' she said, wondering whether she should proceed. Once she started asking the necessary questions for her forms, Faye would have to think back.

'Why are you here?' Faye asked, as if to provoke her.

'There's some information I need, but if you like we can leave it a few days.'

'No, I'd rather get it over with.'

Velalley reached into her pocket for a pen and her micro recorder. 'Do you mind if I use this? It's easier, in case I miss something, so I won't have to ask you again.'

At first the questions were simple, Angie's date of birth, place, checking the formal information that required not too much emotional confrontation with the past. And yet, Velalley thought as she filled in the answers, surely date of birth would remind any mother of the first astonishing sight of her child, a new baby's halo of soft hair, little pursed lips, curling perfectly formed fingers, the miracle of birth itself. Even the simplest question must bring back memories. She hurried on, as if speed might stem the flow of feelings.

'That's all the forms.' She shuffled the papers into line. 'Faye –' She glanced up. The grey eyes were fixed on her. 'Faye, in the supermarket when Angie disappeared – I know we've been through all this before,' she said guiltily, 'but can you think of anything else, anything at all, maybe an impression of someone close by, or anything that struck you as unusual?'

'No.'

'Was Angie good that day?'

'Yes. N-no. She wanted sweeties. I couldn't afford them. She was cross with me.'

'I remember you saying.'

'She was hanging back.'

'Yes.'

'I turned the corner, into the f-freezer section.' Faye's face was growing paler, and the words tripped over each other. Velalley wished she could let her stop, but not yet, not just yet...

'Angie was following. There might have been some... someone on that corner, I don't know... it was half term. I did notice there were more kids about. I remember the sound of the freezers... humming, and the air in that aisle was cool. I picked up a packet of peas, further along the beans were cheaper, so I discarded the peas and went for the beans and then back to the trolley and... and... Angie wasn't there. For a moment I thought she was hiding...'

Velalley waited, but she knew somehow Faye would not continue beyond that moment. Afterwards there was only the frightening panic, and the shock of losing her child, the waiting, the mounting terror, and the final awful outcome.

'While she was in the store, did Angie find anything, or pick any object up?'

'No.'

'Are you certain about that?'

'Yes, I'm quite sure. She was upset she'd forgotten to bring her teddy.'

But that, Velalley thought to herself afterwards, as she switched off the tape recorder, might make it all the more likely she might pick up a doll if she found one. Had there been time when Faye looked away, a moment in between, just before the child's disappearance?

At the front door Faye said: 'Do you have any idea yet who took her?'

'Maybe. We're working on a lead.'

Faye bit her lip. 'I want some sort of justice.'

Velalley looked down at the black plastic rubbish bags beside her. 'What will you do with those?'

'That one's clothes and things to give away. The other's to throw out. Could you...?'

Velalley frowned. 'Are you really sure you want to do that?'

'Yes.' Faye's expression was glazed.

'Isn't it a bit soon?'

'Please?'

'Will you be all right?'

'Mr Denholm said he'd look in late this afternoon. My parents are nearby if I need them, but really I'm best on my own.'

'Ring me, Faye, if you want to talk. I left my home number too in the kitchen for you.'

Down in the sunlight at street level Velalley stashed the plastic bags into the boot of her car. Then she radioed in to Blake.

He listened carefully.

'Do you think the child might have picked up the doll without Simmons seeing?'

'No, sir. Angie might have been hanging back, but I'm sure Faye was aware of what she was up to.'

'Except for those few seconds.'

'But would that have been long enough?'

'Maybe not. Okay, Velalley. Bring the tape in. I want to listen to it. And the bags too. We should look, there might be some clue in there. After that, go home. You've done enough today.'

It was about time Velalley thought, Blake told her what Kendrick was up to. She was about to leave her office to see him when Denholm rang.

'I've just been in to check on Mrs Simmons, WPC Velalley. Could you please tell me why you removed the child's things?'

'Hey, don't talk to me, Mr Denholm. You told Simmons to get rid of them, which I think was a pretty stupid idea. Look to the future you said.'

'Simmons has misunderstood me. She's still in shock, and very capable of misinterpreting what is said to her. It's a classic case of denial.'

'What do you mean?'

'You better read up some more, WPC Velalley,' his voice was so quiet, so controlled, 'if you're going to handle this sort of case. It's all part of the process of grieving.'

'Even suggesting parting with anything of Angie's?'

'Were you there?'

'No.'

'Did you hear what was said?'

'No, but –'

'Exactly.'

'Simmons is my case.'

'Do you operate some single handed crusade, Velalley, or are you part of a proper co-operative team? Finding Angie was you case. Now she's dead, Simmons needs proper sympathetic counselling. I want those things returned to Faye Simmons by the morning. And kindly leave it to the professionals.' He hung up on her.

The stinging rose up her neck, and burned across her cheeks. Some counsellor. Rude, ignorant bastard. Whatever he'd said to Faye had made her think she had to get rid of Angie's belongings. Supercilious bloody creep.

She marched out to the incident desk. 'Where's Sergeant Blake, Barry?'

'Won't it keep? Give him a break, Velalley. It's the first early night he's had in weeks.'

CHAPTER THIRTY NINE

Erik was home, alternatively hovering around her silently, then pacing the floor, unable to settle. Eventually he resorted to drinking a very large glass of brandy to calm down. Velalley was desperate to know what Kendrick had asked him, and she knew she should be comforting him, but she was too frightened of what he might tell her. She said nothing.

'As soon a Suzie's had this, she and I are both going to hop into our beds,' said Laura, fussing round the kitchen table, with milk and digestive biscuits, and pots of tea. 'Aren't we, darling?'

Suzie shook her head, the usual reaction to thinking what she might be going to miss. She got down from her chair and ran to Erik. He gathered her up eagerly, but when Velalley looked at him, he hurriedly put her down again, as if he was nervous to be seen touching her.

The phone rang. It was Kendrick. He launched straight in, giving Velalley no chance to ask questions.

'If Carrie is involved, we don't want her thinking she's got away scot-free. She can be officially cautioned about the shoplifting. You and Gibbeson go up there first thing in the morning, just to remind her we've got our sights on her. You can do that, can't you? Anderson's to bring her to see me – my office, Friday morning, 11 a.m. Sharp!' He was about to hang up.

She took a quick deep breath. 'May I know what's happening on the murder case, sir?'

'No.'

'But why won't you tell me? It's not fair.'

'Our job never is, Velalley,' he said, and deftly changed the subject. 'I hear you've taken on your sister's child. That's a big responsibility. How old is she?'

'Three. Please!' Suddenly it was worse not knowing what he was thinking.

'Very noble of you.' He wouldn't be drawn.

'Well, thank you, Detective Inspector,' she said, seething, when she'd hung up.

Erik was sitting alone in the dark in the living room staring out into the street. For a moment Velalley stood behind the chair, then she put her hands on his shoulders. She could feel him trembling.

'Suzie's in bed,' she said. 'Why don't you read her a story? She'd like that.' She knew he had begun to cry, though he made no sound, and she leaned down, extending her arms round his neck, pressing her cheek against his. 'It'll be all right,' she whispered. 'Nobody thinks you're involved.'

Please God, don't let it have been him. She hated Kendrick's suspicion. And then herself too for even contemplating such a fearful thought.

Erik's shaking hands explored her fingers intensely as if he might find some consolation there. 'Jane… Jane, hold me,' he sobbed. 'If only I hadn't….'

'Ssh… darling… ssh.'

Her nervousness made it like their first ever night together. She made an elaborate exercise of taking off her make-up and cleansing her skin, putting off the moment of getting into bed. He sat on the other side of it, wide eyed, watching her every move.

'Don't keep looking at me,' she said, embarrassed. She pulled the clips from her hair.

'My lovely redhead,' he said softly.

She stood up in confusion, not wanting him to see tonight how easily he could make her blush. She reached for her nightgown. Best to take herself into the bathroom to undress.

'God, Jane, if you hadn't married me, you'd be happy.'

'I am happy,' she said determinedly.

He moved in close and stood behind her. He ran his finger up her back and settled his hand on her shoulder. 'You asked me the other day, Jane, why I married you. I loved you then, I love you now. My life wouldn't be any good without you.'

She unfolded the nightgown, and stared down at it, fiddling with its lace edging. His hand on her shoulder was heavy, full of the strength she had always been able to rely on.

'Without you to believe in me, I don't think I could cope right now. You do, don't you?'

She hesitated a second too long and felt his confidence diminishing even further. 'Yes. Yes, I do. Of course I do,' she said unconvincingly, and felt compelled to turn around to look into his eyes and say it again. 'I do.'

He began fiddling with the collar of her blouse, hopefully fingering the first button.

'I'm exhausted,' she protested softly, but she couldn't stop the old excitement flaring up inside her as the heat from his fingers caressed her. Her body, where it was brushing against his, was beginning to catch fire.

'Can you forgive me? Could we try again?' he whispered.

He leaned down and when his lips touched her breast, she knew she might forgive him anything.

Then for some odd reason she remembered the long black coat hanging in the hall below. 'Let's wait,' she said gently, pulling away. His eyes were wide with disappointment. 'Just not tonight,' she said.

CHAPTER FORTY

TUESDAY

It was obvious Jack Anderson had warned Carrie to expect the visit, but she was alone in the flat when Velalley and Gibbeson knocked.

The door opened a chink.

'Carrie?' It was the first time she'd seen her and Velalley was pleased to see the girl had enough sense to be careful. 'I'm WPC Velalley. This is my colleague, Constable Gibbeson. Your father's expecting us. May we come in?'

The door opened. 'You're fucking going to anyway. Why ask me?'

'Cut the language, Carrie,' Gibbeson said. 'Is your father home?'

'What do you fucking think?'

'I told him what time,' Velalley said irritably, looking at the hand pointing to exactly nine on her watch.

The flat was miraculously a whole lot cleaner. Velalley eyed it guiltily – Jack Anderson and his friend had done far too good a job. But with Carrie home, standards were already sinking fast. There were cups and plates left around, a couple of sweet papers on the floor. It was also a pity the Andersons seemed to dislike fresh air, Velalley thought, as she walked through to the living room. Perhaps it was inevitable. The main window was thick safety glass and fixed, due to the long drop down – and anything left open on the ramp side would be an open invitation to trouble. It wasn't much of a home for an adolescent girl. Then Velalley thought of the rug and the pillow found in the bottom of the claustrophobic bedroom cupboard. She tried to suppress a mental picture of how frightened a little child would be sitting in there in the dark.

Carrie sprawled out on the couch insolently taking up all the space. Gibbeson stayed standing. Velalley sat down in the only other chair and concentrated.

'I presume you know why we're here, Carrie?'

'Gimme a clue,' the girl said sarcastically, playing with the frayed threads around a hole on the inside leg of her jeans.

Bravado, Velalley thought, surprised, in spite of the insolence and anger Carrie was displaying, to find she could still feel real sympathy for her. She was only thirteen, just a kid, and in potential looks and figure, she'd not got much going for her. Her skin was pallid – too much time spent indoors probably, and she could do with losing a little weight, for the sake of her health if not for her self esteem. Her nose was flat and wide, maybe because she rubbed it so often. Her eyes shifted about, making their colour was impossible to see. She'd obviously tried bleaching her hair – rather unsuccessfully. Whatever, it could do with a good wash. She was badly in need of attention, some kindness, some mothering. She smiled a little at her.

Carrie pulled a face.

Gibbeson looked at his watch. 'Do we wait for her father?'

'We can have a chat in the meantime,' Velalley said, making a start. 'What about the medication, Carrie? Are you doing what the hospital doctors said?'

Carrie shrugged. 'Who cares?'

'Your Dad will, if you get sick.'

That made her laugh. 'It wouldn't worry him.'

Velalley frowned. 'Have you heard anything from your Mum?'

Carrie tossed her head. 'No. Why would she bother?' Her face took on an even uglier expression. 'I'm every mother's nightmare.'

'Does she write to you?'

'Na. Anyway who wants rubbishy old postcards from that cow saying 'wish you were here'?'

'Do you write to her?'

'No,' she said defiantly.

'Was it your mother who gave you the beautiful doll?'

Carrie leaned forward. 'When can I have her back?'

'I think it might be some time before –'

'You've got no right to keep her,' she said angrily. 'That's stealing, that is.'

'But you said you lost her.'

'I did!'

'Last Thursday morning.'

'Yeah,' said Carrie confidently.

'I'm surprised you didn't ask at the information desk that day if anyone had found a doll.'

'I didn't think of it,' the girl's eyes shifted across to Gibbeson, then back to Velalley. 'Not until the Saturday.'

'Is that why you went back?' asked Gibbeson.

'Yeah.'

Carrie seemed to be staying perfectly calm, and apparently breathing normally, not at all phased by their visit. Over confident, if anything.

'Although the supermarket has decided not to prosecute you, Carrie, at the hospital you admitted taking goods that didn't belong to you. We're here to inform your father officially that you are required to come to the Station on Monday to see Detective Inspector Kendrick.'

'Oh yeah?'

'A record will be kept on our files, you know,' Velalley continued, ignoring Carrie's impudence. 'If you were found guilty of any offence by a court, this occasion would be referred to. It would count against you, Carrie. And you do realise, don't you, that because of it, we have to make a report to Social Services?'

'So?'

A picture of Angie's limp little body flashed across Velalley's mind. She swallowed hard and tempered her words. Carrie was her case too, just as Angie had been. And there could be so much more to find out about her. And her family. It was essential to maintain some kind of trust between them.

'Your welfare is very important, Carrie. Now that your mother is no longer living here.'

'She'll be back.'

'Well, while she isn't here, we must make sure that you, and your father too, get all the advice and any assistance you need, and that you stay healthy and go to school regularly.'

'It's fucking holidays!'

'And that you don't get into any more trouble.'

There was the sound of a key turning in the front door. Velalley turned to see Jack Anderson striding angrily towards them. She stood up to face him.

'How did you get in?' he shouted at Gibbeson.

'Fucking forced their way in, they did!'

'What rubbish, Carrie!' Velalley turned back to Jack Anderson. 'Your daughter kindly let us in. If you remember, I did telephone you to say we were coming.' Jack Anderson was pacing the floor. She wished he would stand still. 'We made an appointment. You said you would be here.' Carrie's bedroom door was open. The sound of a child sobbing began to ring in Velalley's ears. 'Detective Inspector Kendrick wants to see Carrie at the station on Friday morning, and as her parent, you are required to be present.'

'What's she been saying?' he thundered. 'That bloody supermarket!'

Carrie started to cough alarmingly. 'My doll – they won't ever give it back!'

Back in the squad car Gibbeson said: 'Little bitch began coughing on purpose. That wasn't real.'

Velalley sighed. 'How could we take that chance? It might have been. And besides, we want her to stay in one piece,' she said grimly, 'for the courts.'

CHAPTER FORTY ONE

...brighter weather will continue to spread from the west. Later this afternoon the wind will veer northwest and increase, locally fresh to strong...

Velalley looked down at the sturdy little case by the filing cabinet with some surprise. Blake switched off the little radio on his desk and leaned over to pick it up. He lifted the lid. Inside were Angie's belongings, each item delicately wrapped now in tissue. On the top was one of her little drawings, carefully framed.

'My wife's idea,' he explained. 'It upset her, the little girl dying. She wanted to do something.'

'I think that's nice,' Velalley said.

'I hear Denholm had a go?'

She nodded angrily. 'And Kendrick won't tell me anything –'

But Blake had already interrupted. 'Simmons rang up for you earlier. Deliver this back to her and see how she's making out.'

When Velalley arrived at Faye's flat, the huge pile of letters and soft toys on what had been Angie's bed somehow shocked her. Faye herself was numbed by it. The delivery had come earlier in the morning from the local Postal sorting office, a media inspired sackful of concern for the grieving mother.

'I-I didn't know what to do so I rang you. All those letters.'

'Perhaps we could go through them together?'

Some things, cheerful toys, the bright cards which seemed to underline the child's tragedy with messages of hope, recovery and God's reliable grace, had been dispatched before the grim discovery of Angie's body. Velalley, opening each envelope or wrapping before passing the contents on to Faye, quietly separated out, as far as possible, those that were too joyous.

The gifts, the toys, were hard to bear: a woolly donkey with cobbled seams, obviously hand-knitted. Bright yellow teddies – updated versions of Angie's own careworn one. Fluffy rabbits. Numerous dolls. A postal order from an elderly pensioner. Some beautiful dark green hair ribbons. Angie would have been thrilled. How excited Suzie would be to see this abundance of playthings. But after a while as the pile grew, the quantity was somehow pathetic in the absence of the child to whom they had been sent.

The notes of sympathy were difficult to censor. What appeared to Velalley to be sentimental and gushing might very well prove comforting. She passed most of them over. But there were a few which were openly hostile, blaming Faye, accusing her of insufficient care and attention, and some which talked of punishment for sins and the Will of God. Velalley slipped that sort into her pocket, wondering what gave people the right to make such judgements.

'I was thinking before,' Faye said softly, looking up when they were about halfway through, 'these toys should go to children who need them. Is there some charity? Could you organise for them to be collected?'

'I'll take care of it.'

'And all these people –'

'A newspaper could print a few lines for you. Nobody expects a personal reply.'

Suddenly Faye stood up, her concentration drained. Velalley followed her out to the kitchen.

'Why don't I feel anything, Jane? Is there something wrong with me? All those letters, so full of emotion – everyone is grieving for my child, and I don't feel capable of it. It all seems like a series of pictures around me, without any meaning.' She turned to stare out of the window at the white clouds scudding across the bright lunchtime sky. 'Tell me, can you see your Suzie in your mind's eye, grown up? An adult women, I mean, leaving school, or on her wedding day?'

Velalley tried to think. It wasn't something she'd never even considered, but perhaps Beth had... 'Yes, maybe I can, but Faye –'

'I could never imagine Angie like that. Every day she astonished me, she changed a little, I discovered something new about her. But I could never seem to see her in the future. Prophetic, eh? It's as if she was never meant to be there.'

'I don't think that's true for a minute. You only imagine that now, Faye, because you've lost her.'

'Should I ever have had her?'

'You said to me she made everything right, she was something beautiful and pure.'

Faye was quiet.

Velalley let the silence lengthen, wondering if that had been the thing to say, if anything she'd been saying was right.

'It's only two days ago, you know?' Faye rubbed vigorously at a mark on the sink. 'My mother rings and I can't talk to her. There's nothing to say. I can hear the concern in her voice and I don't want it. I can't bear the thought of her feeling for me. I want to feel for myself, and I can't.'

'You mean there's some special way you're meant to feel? A secret pattern, and if you don't behave like that –'

'Is there?'

'Do you think there should be?'

'I seem to be failing at it if there is.'

'I don't seem to recall there's a test,' Velalley said quietly. 'Grief is individual. I can't imagine there's a particular formula.'

'But I don't feel anything. I can't even cry. Why is that?'

Velalley filled the kettle. 'I don't know, Faye. Maybe it's not the right time. Maybe you're not strong enough yet to cry. Maybe you're expecting too much of yourself.' She wondered briefly what Faye's face looked like when she smiled. 'Eventually you'll feel a little better.'

'I don't think I want to. Or even if I know how to.'

'That's okay too.'

'Would you – would you take one of those toys for Suzie? A teddy or something?'

'I don't think I can, Faye. It wouldn't be right. Let the charity have them.'

'Those hair ribbons then,' Faye said, watching the

clouds outside again. 'Take them. That green satin would suit Suzie's hair.'

The steam from the kettle rose up between them.

The case containing Angie's things lay on the kitchen table. Faye opened the lid, and touched the tissue thoughtfully. Then she lifted out the framed drawing. 'Who did this?'

'My Sergeant's wife.'

Faye ran her finger slowly over the glass, and around the wooden frame, then pressed the picture against her as if she was holding the child herself.

'Jane,' she said sadly, 'what if I never feel strong enough to cry?'

Blake was pulling on his coat, and looking excited.

'Come on, Velalley, we've got her!'

'What, Carrie?'

'Yep! Forensic have just called. They've found traces on Angie's saliva and urine on the pillow and two strands of her hair on the rug. Better still, the SOCO found another matching one in the cupboard, and some blanket fibres on the shell suit.

'Now I want to bring her in, but with kid gloves. No asthma attacks. We'll have a medic with us, and as it's Quale, Gibbeson and a few others for back-up. But I want you to go in and get her quietly. On your own.'

'Yes, sir.'

'We'll meet the others there. First though, her mother's on her way back from Spain. We're collecting her at the airport.'

Velalley left him and hurried back to the incident room.

'We're going up to Quale, Barry. Can I take this?'

'What do you want it for?'

'I don't know, but I've a feeling I might need it.'

'Feminine intuition?' he asked sarcastically.

She scowled at him.

'Okay. Don't lose it for Christ's sake. It's evidence.'

CHAPTER FORTY TWO

Deborah Anderson's length of skirt showed a bit too much tanned thigh. Her jewellery was very shiny, and dark roots showed through in her styled blonde hair. She was very anxious to be far more attractive than her daughter.

'It's harassment bringing me in here,' she said indignantly, as Blake introduced himself. 'Fetching me back from Spain, delaying me now. My Carrie never stole a thing in her life.'

He indicated a chair and sat down himself. Velalley sat down too. The customs interview room was small and unfriendly, but at least it was private.

'Who's she?'

'I'm sorry. This is WPC Velalley. She's been involved in your daughter's case.'

'What case? The supermarket have no intention of proceeding. Jack said so on the phone. So why was I asked to come back? What's going on?'

'We wanted to talk to you, Mrs Anderson,' Blake said gravely. 'I'm sure you're aware Carrie ended up in hospital last Saturday?'

'And who's fault was that?'

'She was found to have items in her possession which the supermarket's security believed to be stolen.'

264

Mrs Anderson shrugged. 'But they can't prove it.'

'In view of your daughter's asthmatic attack when she was apprehended, they have decided not to proceed with any charges.'

'In other words they were too heavy handed.'

'There is no indication of that whatsoever. However, we are getting away from the point.'

'What point?'

'I asked you to come home, Mrs Anderson, because we have reason to believe that the previous Thursday afternoon, at that same supermarket, your daughter was involved in the abduction of a four year old child, Angela Simmons.'

The colour drained out of Deborah Anderson's face. 'What?' she whispered.

'There is evidence to show that the little girl was kept for a period of days in the cupboard in Carrie's bedroom.'

Deborah Anderson leapt to her feet. 'I've never heard such rubbish!' she shouted accusingly. 'What evidence?'

'Traces of saliva and hair. Urine. From what we can piece together, it appears that while Carrie went off to the supermarket last Saturday morning, the child escaped.'

'What does Jack say? Where was he?'

'He was working part of the time –'

'Jack? Working?'

'In the course of our enquiries we've established that he drove a delivery van to Bristol last Thursday and did not return until late on the Friday evening. He arranged to return the van on Saturday morning, which he did.'

'What kind of job was this?' Deborah Anderson narrowed her eyes.

'That,' said Blake, 'is also being investigated. However it does leave Carrie in the flat on her own for the period of time in question.'

'But if she went to the supermarket, surely –'

'We have a witness who saw the little girl leaving the area of the Quale estate alone on Saturday morning, after Carrie was taken from the supermarket to hospital.'

Deborah Anderson sighed heavily with relief and sat down again. 'So everything's all right.'

'Not really. I don't suppose you've seen copies of the newspapers here while you've been in Spain. The child was found dead in a warehouse about two miles away on the Sunday morning.'

'But you can't blame that on my Carrie! How dare you? You just said the child was seen alive – and even if the rest of it's true, which it can't be, Carrie was kept in the hospital, wasn't she? Ill! Anybody could have killed the child.'

'In fact the little girl appears to have died accidentally.'

'Then how can it be anything to do with Carrie?'

'She is not directly responsible for the child's death, no. But there is the abduction.'

'She's thirteen!'

'A child over the age of ten can be held criminally responsible for her actions, Mrs Anderson.'

Deborah Anderson searched desperately in her handbag for a cigarette. She held it to her lips with a shaking hand. Blake lit it for her.

'I would like you to come with us now,' he said. 'I have to bring Carrie in for questioning, and in view of her health I think it would be far better if you're there too.'

★

Blake looked over at the estate as they turned off the main road and into the dilapidated car park. On the grass verge in the shadow of the main building, two youngsters were pounding into a TV set, one kicking it, the other smashing into it with a metal bar. The approach of the squad car did not deter them.

'See that?' he said to Velalley, and to Gibbeson who was driving. 'That's what gives these kids a kick. It's a God-awful place, and this is the best side. Over on the back street is where the dealers work.'

As soon as Gibbeson pulled up, Velalley went for her door.

'No, leave them. We've got more important things to do.' He leaned over to see into the rear view mirror. 'Any sign of the other cars?'

'Not yet, sir.'

They stared over at the boys dispiritedly.

'The strategy, starting from next week,' he said, 'is to show a bit more uniform up here, let them know we control this area, not them. There'll be a couple of dog handlers on patrol after dark every night, Special Constables at the weekends. And we're going to crack down on the trivial stuff. That's the plan, anyhow. Today though, all I want is Carrie.'

'Here come Warren and Toms with Mrs Anderson.' The other car, unidentifiable as a police vehicle, turned off the North West Road and pulled up near the car part entrance.

'Go and tell her, Velalley, to stay in the car until we need her.'

'Yes, sir.'

Plainly Deborah Anderson did not like what Velalley said. There was some argument and she climbed out of the car and the two women faced each other. For a few minutes the confrontation continued, then it was obvious Velalley had won, because the other woman got back into the car, if somewhat reluctantly. Blake watched as Velalley closed the door and leaned down and talked through the window for a minute. Then she headed back towards him.

'She was absolutely determined to go straight up. I explained to her we want to keep everything as calm as possible.'

'Where the hell's that other squad car?'

'Coming now,' said Gibbeson.

'Right! We'll keep the lid on things down here. You both go up to the fifth with the medic, and you wait outside, Gibbs-ey, with him. Velalley goes in alone. No drama. Just quiet sensible conversation. Mother to daughter stuff.'

Velalley nodded.

'If all's going well, you other two keep out of it totally. Mrs Anderson stays down here. It may make Carrie want to come and see her. Or not. You can't tell with that kid. If it will help we'll send the mother up. Do what you think is right, Jane.'

'Yes, sir.'

'What I don't want is another attack.'

Velalley leaned into the car and retrieved a large shoulder bag.

'What's that for?'

'I want to look as ordinary as possible, besides –'

'Okay,' he was anxious to get on with it. 'Got your radios?'

Gibbeson nodded and Velalley patted her bag. The medic was carrying an equipment case.

Blake watched the three of them as they set off towards the building and disappeared up the concrete stairs. He shivered. The wind was rising. It began to lift the littered paper on the grass and play games with it.

From the other squad car PC Hughes was striding urgently towards him. The radio in his own car crackled into life.

'They've been waiting to talk to you, sir,' said Hughes, arriving breathlessly.

He picked it up. 'Blake here. Go ahead, Barry.'

'Has Velalley gone in?'

'Just.'

Blake listened, then he looked up anxiously. On the fifth floor the three figures were moving along towards the Anderson's flat.

CHAPTER FORTY THREE

As Velalley and Gibbeson hurried along the ramp towards the flat with the medic following them, Jack Anderson emerged. 'There's no point you coming to see Carrie,' he said, locking the door behind him. 'Little bitch has done a bunk while I've been out – she's taken money and other stuff and made off.'

'Mr Anderson, it's most important that we find her. Haven't you any idea where she might have gone?'

'Well, she's not in there.'

Velalley glanced at Gibbeson and frowned. 'What's he up to? Maybe we should take a look anyway?'

He nodded.

There were urgent footsteps on the ramp behind them.

'Hoi! Wait a moment.'

Velalley looked round. A young woman ran up. Jack Anderson began to walk off.

'There's something going on in the flat next door to mine,' the woman said breathlessly. 'Odd noises, crying.'

'Mr Anderson, wait.'

Anderson paused.

'Where?' asked Gibbeson.

'I'm 501, down there.'

'I'll be with you in a few minutes.'

'Sod you, I bother to tell you –'

'I said –'

'It's no effing wonder this place is the pits.'

Gibbeson reached for his radio. 'I'll get someone to help you.'

'You bloody come!' She hit out at him, knocking the radio right out of his hand. He tried to catch it but it fell hard onto the concrete and slithered under the barrier wall and disappeared. Gibbeson leaned angrily over the wall and watched it fall.

'That's police property, madam!'

'If that's what it takes to make you do something,' she cried. 'There smoke, I'm sure there is. I can smell it.'

'We should take a quick look,' Velalley said. 'What if there was a fire up here?' She looked round. 'Where's Anderson gone?'

'There are steps at the other end.'

'Here, take my radio,' she said, producing it from her shoulder bag. 'Tell them Anderson's on his way down and get one of the others up here. We might have to shoulder our way in to his flat. While you're doing that, I'll see what she's on about.'

The woman led her quickly back along the ramp.

'Told you,' she said, pointing to the very vaguest suggestion of smoke coming from under a door at the end.

'Does anyone live here?'

'It's been empty for ages.'

The window was covered up and the door was a patchwork of boarding. Velalley tried the handle. It spun in her hand. She pushed the door and it gave a little. If she pushed hard…

The hall in front of her was dark. There was a faint smell of burning, just a little smoke hanging on the air.

'You wait here,' she said to the woman, and stepped inside. It was an exact copy of Carrie's flat, a door to the left, a door ahead. She recognised the lay out. But she must be careful. If there was a fire, adding oxygen to it would be dangerous. And yet… She frowned. The smell was somehow attractive, not acrid like a house fire, more like the autumn wood smoke of a far off bonfire. Burning, nevertheless. Best to get assistance. She turned to leave, then hesitated. Hadn't the woman said she'd heard odd sounds?

She called back to her: 'Go and say to the other –'

But the woman had gone.

Velalley stood in the hall listening for a second, then she put down her bag and very gingerly opened the door on her left, just a crack. The light made her blink briefly but there was no sign of smoke. She pushed to the door further. The kitchen. Wrecked. Cupboards pulled off, wires exposed, no sink, just a tap on the wall, but no obvious source of the smoke.

The door being open gave more light in the hall. The living room was ahead of her. She took a deep breath and turned the door handle. White smoke sprang out at her through the thin crack, but there was no sheet of flame. She crouched down low and pushed the door further. In the corner of the room was a kind of small campfire, smouldering on the bare concrete floor. The smoke from it had already filled the upper half of the room. She remembered the tap in the kitchen, but water would only intensify the smoke problem. Besides what was there to carry it in?

The glowing wood shifted suddenly and an ember rolled out into a pile of broken up furniture nearby. The varnish on one length of that began to catch. Velalley leapt forward and kicked most of the pile of wood out of the way and trod the spark out. The small piece that had caught, she pushed into the main fire. At least that kept it all together, and it was on concrete – but directly above it, the windowsill was made of wood and it was already beginning to singe. It would easily catch if the flames leapt up, and with the extra wood... She glanced round for something to stifle the fire with. There was nothing. The room was totally bare.

She ripped off her jacket and emptied the pockets onto the floor. She hurried back to the kitchen with it. She hoped the water wasn't disconnected. She thrust the jacket under the tap. There was an initial gush, then less pressure, then a splutter and the flow halted. But it was enough to soak the jacket through. It dripped onto the concrete below. She stepped back, and stopped suddenly in fright, as one of the electricity wires looped down around her like a snake, swaying ominously, the wire damaged and exposed, and barely an inch above the puddle of water she was standing in.

One false move and it might drop.

She pivoted slowly round on her heel, not daring to breathe. If the water was off, the electricity probably was too, but it was not a chance she cared to take.

She lifted one foot slowly high up and over the wire,

transferred her weight, then balanced on that foot and carefully lifted her other foot. She took a controlled step further, then another and then dived for the door. The wire dipped, and there was a bright flash and a loud bang. She clutched the doorframe in terror at the thought of what might have happened.

'Dear God!'

The sound of her voice was oddly comforting. It gave her the confidence to breathe evenly again for a few moments. At least now the flat's entire fuse box had probably blown. She closed the door for safety, and folding the sopping jacket in half for more density, she hurried back and laid it over the fire. Deprived of oxygen, the fire went out with a fizz of steam.

With some relief, she wiped her stinging eyes. She must go back to Gibbeson. Where was he? But it would be sensible to wait a minute or two to make absolutely certain the fire was out, and to open all the windows too to disperse the smoke. With a piece of wood she punched out the boarding over the broken hall window and took a good deep breath of fresh air. She thought of opening the one in the kitchen but she didn't dare go back in there. The big living room window was fixed, wasn't it? But there would be one in the equivalent of Carrie's bedroom. She opened that door and headed for it. She had to fiddle with the catch. It was stuck.

She jumped to hear something move behind her, and swung round.

Carrie Anderson was leaning nonchalantly against the closed cupboard door. She stared at her. Carrie stared back insolently.

Velalley returned her attention to the window, thinking fast, calculating what to say, while she tried to work the catch loose. She forced it. The window opened easily. She spoke as calmly as she could. 'Didn't you smell the smoke, Carrie?'

'Yeah.'

'What are you doing in this flat? Your father is very worried about you.'

'I'll bet he is.' Carrie began to cough. The smoke was starting to blow through.

'Smoke like that will do you no good, you know. Fires need chimneys.'

'No!'

'If it's so obvious, why didn't you think of it?'

Carrie shrugged. 'Somebody had done it before,' she said, as if that justified it.

A strange sensation, like a wave of nausea, came over Velalley, some remembered sound. By some strange trick of her imagination, Angie's presence seemed to be all around her, as if the child was in the room. She took a firm grip on herself. 'Anyway,' she said, 'I'm glad to see you. I've been looking for you.'

There was a sudden violent thump as Carrie kicked her heel back hard against the cupboard door. 'Why?' she demanded, and kicked again, harder.

It made Velalley flinch.

She swallowed hard and regained her composure. 'Because we have to talk, Carrie, don't we?'

'It's not my fault, is it?'

'Isn't it? Whose is it then?'

Carrie shrugged. She coughed again, louder this time.

'Did you bring your inhaler with you?'

'Fuck off.'

Velalley moved back to the door hoping Carrie might follow her. 'We have to go down to the Station together. You know that, don't you? We have a lot of things to sort out about Angie, haven't we?'

This time Carrie's bout of coughing was tighter, more constricted.

Go carefully, Velalley thought, carefully. 'Your mother's come back from Spain to see you.'

'Liar.'

'I wouldn't tell you that unless it was true. She's down in the car park waiting to see you.'

Carrie shook her head, unconvinced.

Velalley narrowed her eyes at her, wondering what made the girl so determined not be believe her. 'That doll of yours, she's very pretty. What's her name?'

Carrie didn't answer.

'Actually I brought her with me.'

'Oh yeah,' Carrie said, still staying where she was, leaning against the cupboard, kicking against it at regular intervals.

Velalley glanced out into the living room to the fire. It was obviously safely extinguished. She walked over and began to collect up the things she had discarded from her jacket pockets. Carrie came to the bedroom door and stood watching her.

Velalley glanced up. 'So does the doll have a name?'

'Madeline.'

'Nice.' She deliberately concentrated again on the picking up. 'Do you pretend she's your baby? Perhaps you'll have a real little girl of your own one day.'

There was a thump and then a small high-pitched sound as if Carrie's shoes had squeaked on the floor. Velalley looked up. Carrie was retreating into the bedroom.

She stood up. 'I've got Madeline in my bag.' She pointed to the hall. 'Out there. Come and see.' She held out her hand.

There was that strange thumping sound again. Carrie glanced fearfully behind her, and took another step back.

'What's the matter?' Another thump, and then another. 'What's that noise, Carrie?' she demanded.

Carrie was shaking. Her breath was quickening and her eyes, still fixed on her, were wide and panicky. The colour was draining fast from her face.

Velalley took one look and ran for the door. 'Quick! Here.' She shouted along the ramp.

The medic was racing towards her, with Gibbeson following close behind, and for a split second as she grabbed the barrier wall to steady herself, out of the side of her eye she caught sight of the squad cars below, and people looking up, and she was sure she saw Erik there too.

She rushed back into the flat and grabbed up her shoulder bag.

Carrie was kneeling on the living room floor gasping for breath, and beginning to go a dreadful shade of blue.

Velalley knelt down beside her and spoke softly. 'Ssh. It's all right, it's all right.' She reached into the bag and pulled out the doll. Carrie's eyes, wide and frightened, focussed on it. Velalley pressed it into her arms. 'Hold on, Carrie, hold on.'

The medic dropped to his knees, opened his case and grabbed up equipment.

'Keep her still,' he ordered. He fitted a mask over her face. 'Breathe, Carrie, slowly, in...nnn, ou...t. In...nnn, ou...t.'

Some sound was ringing in Velalley's ears. Not Carrie's feverish breathing. Not the oxygen. Something else. Through the hallway she could see Gibbeson out by the door talking rapidly into his radio, and Warren hovering beyond him. No there was something else, something more urgent. She let go of Carrie's hand and stood up, staring around the room in confusion.

As if in a dream she was drawn back into the bedroom. She was sure she could hear Angie sobbing; the fearful image of the poor child that haunted her conscience, Angie shut in the dark cupboard, unable to escape. In a room exactly like this.

The cupboard door shouldn't be closed. The little ghost was inside waiting to be set free. She reached out. There was no handle, the hinges were broken. She wrenched at the edge, breaking her fingernails, trying to dislodge it. It began to move, inch by inch. The sobbing was louder.

Louder. And suddenly, frighteningly, real. The squad cars. All those people looking up. And Erik. Erik's there too. 'Suzie?' she screamed.

The door came away in that strange slow motion way, falling open to a precarious angle, suspended dangerously on one hinge. She fought her way around it, and pushed it safely to one side with surprising ease. Inside the child was pressed back against the wall in terror. She reached in for her and pulled her shaking little body into her arms and held her tight.

But the child sobbing and clinging to her was smaller

that Suzie and the hair on the head she was cradling and stroking was straight, and short, and shiny blonde, just like Angie's. Exactly like Carrie's doll.

CHAPTER FORTY FOUR

At the foot of the steps, Blake watched anxiously as Carrie was carried past him on a stretcher towards the waiting ambulance. In its headlights she looked ghostly pale. A stiff breeze lifted the corners of the white blanket covers.

He grabbed the medic's arm. 'Will she be okay?'

The man nodded and hurried on.

Then Gibbeson and Warren appeared, followed by Velalley, clutching the child tightly in her arms. She glanced over at him, and he could see how angry she was.

'How could you send me up there without telling me?'

'Jane, honestly I had no idea –'

'I'll get the car,' said Gibbeson, and sprinted away.

'It wasn't until you'd gone in that I found out,' he insisted, 'and then, then I kept the others back because I thought, of all of us, you'd have the best chance –'

Suddenly Deborah Anderson pushed violently past him, struggling to break free from PC Toms who was trying to restrain her. She raised her hand. Velalley screamed and swung away to protect herself and the child. Blake just had time to grab Deborah Anderson's arm before she could strike.

'What did she do to my Carrie?' The woman was obviously hysterical. 'She could have died!'

'For God's sake!' Blake shouted at her. 'Your precious Carrie, that you're never here to take care of, abducted another child.'

As Warren and Toms led the sobbing Mrs Anderson away, Velalley hugged the little girl closer. The child was wide-eyed and quiet, frightened but apparently physically unharmed.

To Blake's relief another car drew up over beside the others.

'Look, the mother's coming. The little girl's all right, isn't she?'

Velalley nodded. 'I think so.'

The woman was running towards them.

'Emma, Emma –' She seized the little girl from Velalley and clutched her tight. 'Emma, darling…' There were tears streaming down her face as she looked back at Velalley. 'Thank you, thank you.'

As PC Warren led the pair back to one of the waiting cars, Velalley was smearing away tears from her eyes too.

'I was right, of course,' Blake said, feeling a lump in his own throat. 'You did well, Velalley. That poor child's safe and there'll be no question of Carrie's guilt now. And we got Anderson on his way down.'

She shivered. 'Erik's here somewhere?'

'No.' Blake frowned. 'Are you all right, Velalley?'

She stared around. 'But I saw him.'

Blake turned to signal over to the cars. 'Time you were going, home, my girl. You can write your reports in the morning.'

Tyres rasped on the crumbling tarmac and Kendrick drew up beside them.

'Get in the car,' he said to Velalley.

'For Christ's sake!' Blake protested. 'Not now!'

'You've got your result, haven't you? And this is important.'

Velalley glanced at Blake and then climbed into the waiting car and Kendrick drove away. The red taillights disappeared along the North West Road, and then turned south into the stream of traffic on Waterson Avenue. The wind was blowing hard and cold from the sea. It was almost dark.

For a moment Blake stared up angrily at the black shape of the Quale buildings, then he walked briskly back to where the other officers were grouped around the cars. 'Get Scenes of Crime down here tonight. I want everything we can get on Carrie. History. Everything. And turn Jack Anderson's flat over,' he said.

'We'll need another search warrant, sir.'

'Well, don't stand there, man. Get one, damn it!'

CHAPTER FORTY FIVE

Kendrick drove in absolute silence and without explanation and it gave Velalley the creeps. His route took them along the curve in the river and up and over the Bridge Road and then down again towards the docks. Out ahead of them lay the dark stretch of Southampton water. On the far shore the maze of bright lights of the oil refinery twinkled, real and reflected, like masses of pulsating stars. There was a smell of stranded seaweed on the breeze, and diesel and oceans, and the hum of ships in port.

The waves pulled urgently back and forth over the shingle beach as Velalley climbed out of the car and hurried after Kendrick towards Peter Miles's flat.

'Right, Velalley, let's catch our murderer,' Kendrick said, and banged on the door.

Velalley was horrified to see Erik open it. She backed away from Kendrick. 'You bastard, bringing me here! How dare you think it's him!'

Kendrick ignored her.

'I suggest we go upstairs to talk, Erik.'

Erik nodded submissively and let him pass.

For a moment Velalley watched in confusion as Kendrick began to lead the way. 'Leave the door on the latch, Velalley.'

Erik grabbed her hand, panic-stricken. 'He told me to meet him here.'

'Is that nice friend of yours at home, Erik?' Kendrick asked over his shoulder. When they reached the top Peter Miles rose from the couch and held out his hand. 'Inspector Kendrick!' he said warmly.

'Extraordinarily sexy, Marilyn Farr was.' The room was sophisticated and dark, contrasted by small bright star spotlights along the walls.

Velalley, aware she still smelled strongly of wood smoke, sat on the edge of the leather sofa, watching Peter Miles and picking nervously at the hem of her skirt. So this was the great photographer and friend. She glanced across at Erik who was standing uncertainly near the window staring out into the darkness.

Peter Miles was watching her and smiling at the effect his words were having. He knew. He knew about Erik and Marilyn. Of course he knew. It was humiliating. What the hell did Kendrick think he was doing, sitting opposite her, drinking scotch, making her listen to this?

'The perfect model, she was. Sensational in front of a camera. Electric!'

Peter Miles reached back to a table for a couple of photographs and pushed them into Velalley's hands. She was left with no choice but to accept the pictures from the man.

'Beautiful, don't you think?'

Erik turned round.

For an awful moment she gazed at the photos, completely transfixed. Marilyn was beautiful, in the close-up, startlingly so. Those eyes. But in the second picture she was standing wrapped in the long black cloak that she's been found in. Velalley could see it now. In the end it had become her shroud. Long rows of bright motorway lights studded the background. There she was, alive in the very area where she was later found dead.

Suddenly Velalley felt sick. In her mind she could still see the silhouette of a figure against the light and the dog running down, and hear all over again the sound of the metal twisting, grinding on impact, the children screaming – and she could smell in her nostrils, over all the fumes of that petrol, the horrid scent of this woman's decaying flesh.

She shuddered and leaned forward to pass the pictures hurriedly on to Kendrick. But Kendrick was more interested in admiring the black and white enlargements on the walls.

'Such talent,' he was saying, looking up at one above her head. 'I keep seeing your work, everywhere. Magazines, papers. It must be wonderful to be able to ask any price you like.'

'Well, it's not quite like that. For an exclusive maybe.'

'What about the one of the body on the front page on Saturday?'

Peter Miles took a sip of his scotch.

'You were there,' Velalley said suddenly, 'near the motorway that day too? When the accident happened. You were, weren't you?'

'Poor Erik,' Peter Miles said, looking over at him sympathetically, 'I felt so sorry to have to show him that evening paper. But it is my living and the story was out, so it was only a matter of time. And he didn't mean to do it. I'm sure things just got out of control, Erik, didn't they?'

Erik was staring at him in horror.

'Please don't look at me like that. I know it's hard but surely you're not expecting me to stay silent now? He and Marilyn met at my flat, Inspector. Didn't you, Erik? And I came home late on that Monday night to find blood on the studio floor. I knew he'd been here and that something fearful had happened but I couldn't bring myself to tell anyone.' He swung round to Kendrick again. 'Is that such a crime? After all he is my friend. Will I be charged?'

'I saw you!' Velalley was angry now. 'You were up on the embankment, in that long black coat you lent Erik.'

'You were there!' Erik joined in. 'All those photos you took in that mist. And there was a white dog. That Afghan.'

'Which belonged to the model, Julia… something.'

'Erik,' Peter Miles said sadly, 'please don't lie.' He turned to Kendrick. 'He confided in me and pleaded with me to help him. He couldn't go on hiding the body in his car he said. He rang me last Wednesday and asked me to meet him out there. He knew where I was filming, and the weather had suddenly become ideal. Nobody could see a yard in front of them, and no one in their right mind would stop on that busy slip road. The body was unlikely to be found for months.'

Kendrick nodded. 'A bloodstained blanket was found in the boot of Erik's car.'

'What?' Erik went pale. 'How?'

Velalley leapt to her feet. 'That's circumstantial,' she cried. 'What about forensic?'

'We've had the Scenes of Crime boys down already to examine the studio, haven't we, sir?'

Peter Miles hung his head in shame. 'Erik, you have to understand.'

'I understand all right.'

'And we did find your fingerprints, Erik.'

Erik nodded. 'All over the studio. I answered the phone. In the dark. I had to feel my way round.'

'But blood, what about blood?' shrieked Velalley. 'It would have been on his clothing. I would have seen.'

Kendrick shook his head. 'But you were on duty on the night of the twenty-fifth. There would have been plenty of time for your husband to sort that out. But in fact there was no evidence of blood at all in the studio, only some minute fragments of tissue and bone.'

'I don't understand. There'd be blood everywhere in an attack like that.'

'Perhaps you didn't realise, Velalley, Marilyn was killed with a single blow to the back of the head.'

'But –'

'It was only later, the autopsy shows it was up to two, maybe three days afterwards, that there were more blows to the head, when the blood was no longer circulating. And that was probably done on something. Maybe large white sheets of background paper such as a photographer might use?'

Erik glanced up at the picture behind the sofa.

Peter Miles stood up.

'There is one thing,' Kendrick said, smiling up at him, 'how much did the editor pay for that front page photograph of the body?'

'I think that's between him and me and the tax man.'

'It was an exclusive, wasn't it? In fact so exclusive as to be priceless.'

Peter Miles frowned a little. 'I wouldn't say that.'

'The editor told me you offered him that photo at 5.30 p.m. last Wednesday. That was hours ahead of our forensic team finishing out there and reporters being allowed anywhere near the site.'

'You underestimate the power of money,' Miles said, smiling. 'Even policemen have pockets.'

'But what if I said to you our experts can prove that photograph was taken before the body was discovered by the police?'

Velalley's heart leapt. She saw Peter Miles glance nervously over at Erik.

'He was there,' he said. 'He suggested I take it. We came back to the pub afterwards. We both needed a drink. The barman will tell you.'

Erik nodded. 'I did meet him next door on Wednesday but not until 4.30. I was working till then.'

Kendrick nodded. 'Alone.'

'The secretary was off sick,' Erik said weakly.

'The body was discovered at approximately 3.45 p.m. Yes, there was still time to take the photograph and then for you both to return here to the Ship Inn.'

Velalley stared at Kendrick in panic.

'Exactly,' said Peter Miles.

'But the meteorological office records show the fog came down at midday, and while the photograph shows all the elements of the mist, when magnified up the ground around and under the body is dry and undisturbed. Because his secretary was ill, Erik Velalley's appointments were running late. He was definitely with clients right up until 2 p.m. – an hour after those same weather reports show rain fell in that area for the first time in three weeks. When exactly did Erik meet you?'

Peter Miles licked his lips nervously and edged back towards the stairs. He didn't answer.

'Marilyn was extraordinarily sexy, was she?' Kendrick's smile had taken on an eerie quality, almost evil. 'Isn't it true that you wanted her to yourself?'

'Me?'

'And when you discovered she'd brought Erik Velalley here, you were driven mad with jealousy. Marilyn was two-timing you, here in your own flat, and sleeping with your friend. And you hated her for it.'

For a moment there was dead silence.

'Just the opposite,' Peter Miles said suddenly, running his hand back ferociously through his black hair. 'But what would you know about love?' He glared over at Erik. 'What would he know? I had to stand by while she had it off with an insignificant, ordinary little accountant like him.'

Velalley saw red. 'How dare you?'

'All he really wanted was his wife.'

'And before Erik?' Kendrick goaded.

'Anyone else I introduced her to. I'm sure she did. Men like him, men who have it all.'

Erik sounded utterly astonished. 'Surely you weren't envious of me?'

'Only on film could I ever capture Marilyn, hold on to her, until that night. She used to flirt with me through the lens, tease me, lead me on. Until that one night when I took control...' His voice was barely audible. 'It's a very sexually powerful moment, death.'

'And afterwards?'

'I wanted to keep that image forever. I worked hour upon hour, photographing every angle of that beautiful face, that body. But then after a couple of days I couldn't bare to watch it beginning to decay. I had to finish it, destroy her – to retain her beauty inside my mind.' His voice was reduced to a whisper. 'Out by the motorway hidden in that ditch there would be no one to see her until... but then I couldn't bear to leave her. I went back to have one more look and that wretched dog followed me.'

'All those children,' said Velalley softly.

He smiled a little. 'Another exclusive.'

They all stared at him in horrified silence.

Suddenly he made a move.

'Look out, he's escaping,' Velalley cried, leaping forward. But she was too late. He was already halfway down the staircase. She went after him.

The door at the bottom opened and Blake and Gibbeson blocked his way.

'Off somewhere, Mr Miles?'

'You can have the pleasure, Velalley,' said Kendrick, leaning calmly over the banister. 'Aren't you glad you came?'

Velalley took a deep and vengeful breath.

'Peter Miles, I'm arresting you for the murder of Marilyn Farr. You do not have to say anything...'

CHAPTER FORTY SIX

WEDNESDAY

Blake glanced up at the clear morning sky above the steeple. The deacon came over to close the church door as soon as he entered. As one of the four official representatives of the County Constabulary, he knew his duty was to walk immediately down the aisle and take up his position next to the Chief Superintendent, but for a few moments he hung back, feeling more like an intruder. He hadn't stepped inside a church for years.

But the congregation were gathered, and the pews were satisfyingly full. Friends, personal and from the Force, family. Community leaders anxious to make a public show of their support for law and order. Phillips' widow was on the right at the front, holding their baby son, and Radcliffe's two little daughters were standing with their mother on the left.

Blake took a moment more to rehearse his words of sympathy over again, but he was still not sure what, if anything, might be appropriate to say. The thought of talking to either of the women appalled him. He had timed his arrival carefully, but he knew the ordeal had to be faced sometime, if not after this service, then at the impending individual funerals. Eventually there'd be the service for Angie too.

There was a chorus of nervous coughing while the organist turned over more sheets of his music. With the opening notes of another subdued hymn, Blake began to walk, past members of the football club Radcliffe had belonged to, and mates of Phillips's from the local pub. Judith Colston was there, and Denholm, and further forward he recognised Velalley's red hair as he went by, though she was concentrating on her hymn book and did not appear to notice him.

She'd come then. She always looked particularly smart in Number One Dress, and today was no different. Spit and polish. Well groomed. Every inch the ideal policewoman: intelligent, with plenty of energy and common sense. And she's packing it in, he thought as he nodded to the local magistrate and his wife, just when the force could do with the best young blood it could get. Maybe she was right though – that was just what Phillips and Radcliffe had given. Their young blood.

He excused his way into the official pew and sat down.

'Good morning, Blake. You managed to make it then.' Though the Chief Super nodded politely to him, he still detected disapproval in the lowered voice.

'Detective Inspector Kendrick sends his apologies, sir. Pressure of work.'

'Hmmn. Bloody sad occasion, this.'

'Sir.'

Bloody sad, Blake thought, and glanced across at the

Phillips woman. The baby was up against her shoulder, and already fidgety and unsettled, bound to cry throughout the service. The heads of the two little Radcliffe girls were bobbing about. He shifted uneasily in his seat. He had sent their father to that warehouse last Saturday night, and on his orders, the night before, Phillips had gone to deal with the disturbance at the Lamb's Head.

'We must have lunch together, Blake,' whispered the Chief Super. 'What about tomorrow? Any good?'

He nodded. 'Fine, sir.'

Well, well, lunch, he thought. Perhaps my time has finally come.

Mrs Radcliffe leaned across to her children and said something. Both children turned and Blake followed their eye line. Fluttering against the stained glass window, he saw it too. A butterfly. How strange to glimpse one so late in the year. He followed its progress up the coloured glass, red, then blue. The organist began to play the invocational hymn, and as the butterfly flew across to the choir, dipping low over the altar, and from there, up to the arched wooden rafters above him, somehow it stirred his spirit.

The service touched him too, bringing back memories of the churchy Sunday mornings of his childhood, of his father's love of the scriptures; of late roast lunch, and summer afternoons and his mother's high teas. The community of Heydon, the minister was emphasising, was well served by young policemen like John Radcliffe and Douglas Phillips, who had been prepared to give their lives to the service and safety of others. What was it, Blake wondered. Four, or was it five years ago, when

Radcliffe had joined, fresh faced and enthusiastic? Longer for Phillips – nine years, probably. The reading, the Good Samaritan, seemed quite appropriate as he listened to it. Policemen cannot pass by.

'The Lord's my shepherd, I shall not want'… A sweet melody, he thought, as the notes of the familiar psalm, and his mother's favourite, rang through the church. The congregation rose. 'He leads me beside still waters, He restores my soul…' Blake put down the hymn book. He knew the words by heart. 'Though I walk through the valley of the shadow of death…'

'All right, old man?' asked the Chief Super, as they sat down.

'Fine, sir,' he said.

Directly the service ended the Chief Super excused himself. 'Shall we say midday then? My office?' He left him and went immediately over to both widows to express the official and his own personal sympathy. He talked for a few minutes, and then departed.

Blake remained pensively in his seat.

'She managed to rescue the second child, then.'

He looked round. 'Mmm?'

James Denholm was standing in the row behind, looking over towards Velalley who was talking to Judith Colston by the door.

'Jane Velalley.'

Blake nodded. 'I didn't think she'd come today.'

'Duty.'

'I'll miss her. She's like me, puts her foot in it occasionally.'

'And she's handled things well this last week.' Denholm's eyes twinkled, 'Twenty quid says she stays.'

Blake grimaced. 'Then either way I lose.'

'I'll make it fair. If she does leave, I'll help you drown your sorrows.'

'Thanks! But I might not be around long enough myself for you to do that. The Chief Super's having me for lunch tomorrow.'

'I hope that turns out to be a slip of the tongue.'

'Maybe not.'

The Phillips baby was crying. The two wives were talking to sympathetic friends. One of the little Radcliffe girls still had her eye on the butterfly. He glanced up at it too.

'A week ago, James,' he said, 'I might have minded. Now... well, I'd like the time to take my wife out once in a while. I'm an old fashioned copper. All I seem to do lately is push a pen, and for what? A judicial system that lets the buggers straight back out. And I don't think I want restructuring.'

'Oh, I don't know!'

'Do they think we're in it for the love of it?'

Denholm smiled. 'You are. Besides you've only got three years to go. You'll be all right.'

'Let's see what the Chief Super says.'

'He's having to look to his own laurels. Actually I happen to believe the force wants modernising, but more importantly the scales of justice need to get back in balance.'

Blake sighed. 'Now don't start lecturing me. I am old, Father Time.'

Denholm smiled. 'Velalley's a smart young woman. Want my advice? If you want her to stay on, don't ask her to. Agree with her decision to give up, encourage her to leave.'

'You're a bastard, James, you know that? Anyhow she'd see through those tactics.'

'Possibly, but she won't want any old sentimentality from you.'

'Am I sentimental?'

Denholm had the cheek to laugh.

'Is that why Kendrick clammed up on me?'

'Sorry. That was me. I was convinced he had Erik Velalley in the frame. I asked him to wait.'

'Finding that kid was more important anyway. And Kendrick swore last night he knew who it was right from the start. Did you hear Peter Miles took pictures of Marilyn directly afterwards? Even put one up on the wall in his flat.'

'Gives him a kind of power beyond the grave. Love at its most possessive.'

'You've got a very peculiar view of life, Denholm.'

'Only the darker side of the mind.'

'He certainly kept the body in his studio before he put it out there. And the photograph he took then, if it hadn't rained –'

'One of your little theories: the weather affects all things!'

'The newspaper rang me only a few hours after the body was discovered, wanting to know if they could use it. I couldn't believe they had it. It looked all wrong. And when Kendrick had it enlarged up, it gave Peter Miles away.'

Denholm shook his head. 'And you with an eye for

detail better than his, eh? I've seen some of his work on exhibition. Brilliant. It's a gift, talent like that.'

'Remember Chris Drury? Who fathered the child? Another violent man with talent. You know what? All the women in his paintings are uncannily like Faye Simmons.'

Denholm smiled as if he'd seen it all before. 'That shows a kind of repentance.'

'You think so?'

'So tell me, can you convince Velalley to stay on in spite of Kendrick? From what I've heard she'd kill to work with you again.'

'She's as rude as hell to me.'

'But she respects you,' Denholm said earnestly. 'All of us do.'

CHAPTER FORTY SEVEN

Velalley looked at her in amazement.

Colston shifted on her feet. 'Why shouldn't I go out with him? James Denholm's nice, Jane, you'd be surprised.'

Velalley glanced back into the church. Denholm was standing talking to Blake. They seemed to be on friendlier terms than she would have expected.

'Who's minding Suzie?'

'Erik's taken a couple of days off.'

Outside the old Norman church door, over Judith's shoulder, the mourners were standing in sunlight talking in tight family groups, like gatherings of black crows along the gravel pathway. Behind them, gravestones crusted with yellow lichen leaned under the trees. Velalley wished there was time to wander along the old path between them. 'It's very odd being here today.'

'Why?' Colston asked.

'Because,' she said, aware of the clarity and the lack of emotion in her voice, 'I heard this morning my father has died.'

'Gosh, Jane, I'm sorry. Doesn't everything come at once! Shouldn't you be with your mother?'

'Oh, no,' she said. 'We haven't seen him for years.

Not even at my sister's funeral.' His death, announced in a simple solicitor's letter in the post to her mother. As Laura said, such a formal communication after so long. She sighed apprehensively. 'I suppose we've got to speak to the wives? Sally Radcliffe wanted me to go back with the family, but I don't think I will. Anyhow I've got loads of paperwork to finish up. I can't leave it all for somebody else.'

She spent the afternoon in her office working but there was still so much unfinished business. Down the hall she could hear the constant buzz of activity in the control room. It was hard to concentrate. She picked up her file on Carrie Anderson and went to find Blake.

'You'd better have this now, sir.'

'I would have preferred you to follow it through with Gibbeson,' he said curtly, concentrating on the documents on his desk. 'It will take more than the month to tie it all up. You'll be called as a witness, whatever. What about that gate-keeping meeting next week? You can't let that boy down.'

'I'll go, don't worry. But I told you last night, sir, I've made up my mind. I'm sorry if –'

'Denholm said to me this morning you were choosing the right course. I don't doubt that's true. You're a young woman with a child now to think of. It's tough out there on the streets, Velalley. There are nicer jobs.'

'Are you and he in collusion?'

'Why?'

'That's about word for word what he said to me too.'

'So? Does that bother you, Velalley?'

'I'm not sure.'

'We mentioned you in passing. There were more important things to discuss,' he nodded to the file in her hand, 'like Carrie Anderson's medical report which came in this morning. But since you won't be dealing with her anymore –'

'Is she all right?' She couldn't believe she hadn't asked about her sooner.

'Gibbeson and Colston will be taking her case over.'

'Tell me!'

Blake glanced up at her. 'The asthma's under control again, but the social worker think there may have been some sexual abuse. Carrie claims there has.'

'What?'

'It would explain a good deal, don't you think? The kid needed help.'

'Maybe,' she said sceptically. 'But what if she said it to get back at her father, and make her mother regret leaving?'

'You sound more like Denholm every day.'

'What will happen to her, sir?' she asked, ignoring that idea.

'There'll be psychiatric reports as well. She might get as much as two years, but she wouldn't serve all that. The youth courts will have her health to consider. A cry for attention, Velalley, that's what it all might have been, a cry for some attention.'

'Yes, I think that's true.'

He stretched out his hand for the file. 'But you're going. She won't interest you now.'

In spite of what Carrie had done, she needed as much help as she could get, and real care and attention, and she was bound to be difficult to handle. Velalley left Blake's office feeling frustrated and utterly deflated. Did he think she was leaving because she wanted to? Couldn't he see she had her own problems?

She met Denholm in the corridor.

'I thought I would go and visit Faye Simmons some time this week.'

'Is that wise, WPC Velalley? If you're resigning –'

'I haven't given Sergeant Blake my resignation yet. And I still have work to complete. Not on her,' she said quickly, in case he immediately assumed she hadn't done all the necessary reports, 'but I thought –'

'There would be a marked difference in your dealings with her now.'

'Why?'

'Because the second child's alive, and Angie is dead.'

'I would have given anything to have found Angie in time. Any of us would.'

'We know that,' Denholm continued. 'Faye knows it too, but she'll blame us anyway. You were closest to her and you discovered Angie's body. And she has to be angry – it's all part of the process, and her rage will almost certainly focus on you.'

And I bet you've focussed it, she thought angrily. 'I had hoped,' she said coldly, 'I might be of some help to her. I will go. I have more in common with her than anyone else. I know what she went through, for God's sake.'

'Do you?'

'I understood the fear.'

'But you don't know the deep despair that stops you wanting to face the world, and even stops you turning the handle of your front door. The utter desolation of actually losing a person you love dearly – or what it is to be helpless in the face of extreme danger.'

How little he knows about me, she thought. 'I could be a friend,' she said.

'Well, let me know if you're going there and don't expect miracles – of yourself either,' he said tersely. 'It's hard work being a saint.'

As he walked away, Velalley raged. God, couldn't he wind her up! And didn't she have a personal responsibility as well as a professional one, to see that Faye was coping, whatever James Denholm might say?

She phoned Erik.

He was busy shifting furniture. 'Everything's fine this end. Suzie's playing nurse with teddy. He's covered in bandages, poor thing.'

Velalley smiled at the thought. 'You're sure she's all right?'

'I – um. Mmn.'

Back off, she thought, he needs to know I trust him. 'What furniture?'

'The dining room. You know, the idea of me having my office at home. Somewhere clients can come to me.'

'Where will you put all the stuff?'

'I'm a whiz at organisation. How did the service go?'

'All right, if you like that sort of thing. I'm going to call in on Faye Simmons for a few minutes on the way home. You don't mind, do you?'

'No, you go ahead. Is it all right if I make Suzie her tea?' He sounded apprehensive.

'Suzie would love you to,' she said encouragingly.

As she passed the Crime Desk on her way out, Barry looked up. 'Hey, Velalley? Have you heard? We've had a woman in this afternoon wanting to press charges against her next-door neighbour's cat. It ate her Chihuahua.'

'Eeerh! You're kidding!'

'Nope. Fur and all.'

It was getting dark and the town was quiet as she drove though the streets. It wasn't such a bad place to live, for Suzie to grow up in. Like everywhere there were rough patches, but overall it was a comfortable, reasonable environment. If you watched the television news… but, well, there were infinitely worse places to be.

She found a parking place easily and pulled into it. The reporters and photographers had moved on, to another place, another story. To Peter Miles perhaps. Faye had been forgotten.

There was a light on in the first floor window. Velalley climbed the stairs inside and rang the bell.

There was no answer.

Maybe Faye hadn't heard. She rang it again. What was it Denholm had said? The deep despair that stops you turning the door handle…'

'Faye?'

Silence.

She called again urgently. 'Faye? Faye?'

'Who is it?'

'It's me. Jane,' she answered, relieved to hear the trembling voice. 'I just came by to see how you are.'

'I'm fine.' The door stayed closed.

'Sure?' Velalley hesitated, not certain what to do. 'Can't I come in, Faye?'

There was silence for a minute, then the sound of the key turning and Faye opened the door. She had on a dressing gown and looked half asleep, and pale, very pale.

'Sorry, were you sleeping?'

'Um… um… no, I wasn't. But I don't really feel like visitors,' she said.

'But I'm not visitors surely, and,' she thought quickly and pushed her luck a little, 'I could murder a cup of tea. Mind if I come in?'

Faye stood back reluctantly and let her pass. She looked apprehensive somehow.

Once inside Velalley looked at her suspiciously. 'Are you really all right?'

'Yes. Hurry up and make your tea.'

She went out to the kitchen. 'Want one?'

'No.'

Faye seemed strange, and withdrawn. Denholm had been right. All the same she felt there was something she should be noticing. Not just the abject grief. The kettle boiled. She made the second mug of tea anyway and took it back out with her and put it down in front of Faye.

'Shit, don't you listen?'

Velalley stepped back. 'I'm not here officially,' she said sharply. 'I care what happens to you.'

Faye said nothing, just stared ahead of her.

'It was pure chance, the second time,' Velalley continued, softly now.

'But that child's alive,' Faye hissed accusingly. She leapt

to her feet, and began to pace up and down the room wringing her hands.

Velalley stood back against the wall, keeping out of her way, trying to think of something to say that would be enough, something that would be sufficient. There was nothing.

'Do you want me to ring Denholm?' she asked eventually.

Faye paused and looked over at her.

'I'll call him, shall I?' Velalley asked, encouraged.

Faye shook her head. 'Not tonight.' As if her grief had made her blind, she felt her way unsteadily back to her chair, and sat down. 'Not tonight,' she said again softly.

'Faye?'

'What's it like, Jane, to be dead, do you think?' she asked, as if it were a normal, ordinary, everyday question.

'I don't know.'

'Do you think I would have Angie back? Could we be dead together?'

'No,' Velalley said. 'You'd just be dead too.'

'Then I wouldn't have to cry.'

'No, you wouldn't.' She tried hard to find some words of consolation, something that would be hopeful. Eventually she said: 'If Suzie died, maybe only the closest I could come to holding her again would be to imagine her with me, to keep all the little things that mattered to her, and cry. But that wouldn't stop me loving her and keeping her alive and bright in my memory.'

'But could you always? A year, ten years from now? Twenty years? When life gets on top of you? When anything goes wrong? When your husband gets ill, or the house burns down or –'

'Yes,' Velalley said, with absolute certainty.

'But –'

'Why should a thing like loving get any less? Why shouldn't you get better at it instead? Angie will always be your child. Loving her has been part of your life. Nothing will ever change that.'

Faye sank back into the chair.

'Nothing will ever change that,' Velalley repeated.

'Nothing,' Faye murmured.

Velalley stared down at her, momentarily reminded of the child, the dead blonde child, lying back lifeless in her arms, the child she had not found in time. Now Faye herself seemed to be sinking further down into the chair, giving the impression of fading too.

Fading.

She knelt down beside the chair. 'Hey?'

Faye's hands were freezing cold, her eyes were wandering uncontrollably. Velalley glanced round the room, suddenly sure there was something she hadn't seen. Something she should have seen. And then there it was, over on the shelf, the empty brown bottle, the lid beside it, the remnants of a glass of water.

'Faye!' she said loudly, sharply, 'Who will remember Angie? Who will cry for her if you're not here?'

She pulled her to her feet and supporting her precariously, grabbed her mobile, and speaking urgently and clearly, summoned help.

CHAPTER FORTY EIGHT

It was nearly midnight when Velalley pulled up in front of her house. She rehearsed again what she would say to Erik. A few minutes late she'd said she'd be, and once more a few minutes had become hours, but knowing Suzie was safe with him, there was no way she would have left Faye's side. She thought of the ambulance, and the scene at the hospital; of Faye, lying back on the pillows, grey in the face, uncomfortable and exhausted after an emergency stomach pump, but alive; of putting her arms gently round her and feeling the wetness of her tears on her cheek, her own tears. And Faye's.

At last, Faye's.

'Who would have remembered Angie?' she whispered, 'Who would have cried for her, without you?'

'You would.'

She sat with her and held her hand until eventually Faye slept. When she returned to the hospital entrance, the Longmans had arrived, and Gibbeson. Blake was there too.

'Quick thinking, Velalley,' he said briskly, as if he'd expected nothing less.

'I should have been quicker, sir. I should have seen what was going on immediately.'

James Denholm arrived too and actually congratulated her. 'Thank God, Velalley, you went over there tonight. Simmons told me her parents would be with her. If you do decide to leave, you should consider a career in counselling. You seem to have an instinct for it. I'd be glad to give you a personal recommendation.'

A personal recommendation – from the great James Denholm!

'But I earnestly hope you'll decide to stay with the force,' he'd added.

'There's a kid over on the East side I'd like you to take on, Velalley,' Blake said. 'You're off this weekend but you could go and see his family next week. He's a right little tear-away but...'

She climbed out of her car, locked it and walked wearily up the steps. While she was looking for her house key, Erik opened the door.

'Hey,' he said, and put his arms round her.

'Just hold me, Erick,' she said, needing the comfort.

He held her tight. 'You're safe and sound,' he whispered.

After a moment she said, 'I'm sorry I'm so late, I should have let you know.'

'Sergeant Blake rang me, sweetheart. Are you all right?'

'Tired,' she said, still leaning gratefully against him. 'Erik, I've decided –'

'To stay on?'

'Mmn.' She waited for him to say something, something to prove he understood.

In the silence, she could almost hear him considering what to say, thinking so hard about what would be right, what would make her happiest – this accountant, who specialized in columns of figures and tax returns and watching the cricket on television, who never thought in terms of misery or mugging or murder.

And then all of a sudden he said happily, 'We're going to manage. It'll work. My office at home will be fine. Are you hungry? I've made this strange new kind of lasagne, my own invention. Want to try it?'

She hugged him closer, so touched she couldn't speak. 'We never really discussed having Suzie,' she said. 'Not enough.'

'No.'

'I'm sorry.'

'It was the right thing to do, Jane. I would do exactly the same, if Suzie was my sister's child.'

'Thank you,' she said.

'For what?'

'For being you.'

'Dinners will be in the kitchen from now on. Ready in five minutes. And wait till you see my new office.'

He went ahead to the kitchen and she took off her coat and hung it up.

'Sweetheart,' he called back, 'Laura brought round the solicitor's letter. She thought you should see it. It's on the hall table.'

She picked it up and fingered it, then reached back into her coat pocket.

She hurried upstairs to check on Suzie, and spent a few moments gazing down at her, tucked safely into bed and sleeping soundly, her arms flung out wide on the pillows. It made her smile with relief to see such total relaxation, and she leaned down and kissed the soft red gold curls.

In her own bedroom she examined the two envelopes.

The first, the official one, was addressed to her mother. 'It is with regret that I have to inform you'… The last sentences left her stunned. 'He has made some provision in his will for you, and the balance of his estate passes to his surviving daughter, WPC Jane Velalley. The amount is not large, but I have her address and I shall be contacting her in that regard within the next few days… Again, may I offer my sincere…'

She sank down onto the bed, astonished. Though she hadn't seen her father for long, he knew where she was, her married name, where she lived, what she did…

On the other envelope was written 'For PC Jane'. 'I found it in her flat,' Gibbeson said, when he'd passed it to her at the hospital.

She opened it slowly, tentatively, wondering if it might be some sort of suicide note. She recognised immediately the bright green hair ribbons that fell out into her hand. She remembered Faye saying the colour would suit Suzie's hair. Green against the soft red gold curls. Suzie was such a gift, to be held on to, tight and safe.

'WPC Jane Velalley?'

Erik would help her, she knew it.

She went out into the hall and leaned over the banister.

Erik smiled up at her. 'The food's on the table, sweetheart, and I've opened a bottle of wine. And it isn't wise to unnerve a novice cook by keeping him waiting on his first try.'

By the same author

THE KID ON SLAPTON BEACH
War is hard when you have to leave everything you know
and love. But what if your most precious possession is
left behind?

'Superb on so many levels… a wonderful book.'
Michelle Magorian, Author of **Goodnight Mr Tom**

'This book is beautiful. A jewel!'
Actress June Brown, Dot in **East Enders**

CUTTING IN
Watching, imitating, borrowing – to stalk in pursuit of an
image. There's no threat in that, is there?

'A great gift for portraying the agonies and ecstasies of
adolescence…a rare talent…'
Novelist Frederick E Smith

'Perceptive writing… wonderfully spiked with bitchiness."
Novelist Graham Hurley

Lightning Source UK Ltd.
Milton Keynes UK
UKOW06f0124100315

247573UK00005B/53/P